Griffith Stadium

A NOVEL

By Robert Ambros

authorHOUSE®

AuthorHouse™
1663 Liberty Drive
Bloomington, IN 47403
www.authorhouse.com
Phone: 1-800-839-8640

First published by AuthorHouse 7/27/2011

ISBN: 978-1-4634-3838-8 (e)
ISBN: 978-1-4634-3839-5 (sc)

Printed in the United States of America

Any people depicted in stock imagery provided by Thinkstock are models, and such images are being used for illustrative purposes only.
Certain stock imagery © Thinkstock.

This book is printed on acid-free paper.

St. Louis, Missouri
September 1939

J ACK HAYNES SLAMMED THE PHONE DOWN IN DISGUST.
He wiped the sweat off his forehead and looked up.
"Who the hell keeps closing those damn windows?"
he yelled, glaring at the three soaring windows on the far
side of the newsroom. Someone kept closing them despite
the ninety-degree heat. He dropped his gaze and watched
Edwards, the circulation editor, cross the floor.

"Who's gonna go for hamburger sandwiches?" Edwards asked. "How 'bout you, Haynes?"

"Are you joking? Get a punk from downstairs." Although Jack was almost thirty years old and had been an
investigative reporter for the *St. Louis Herald* for nearly
three years, the others were older and still thought of him
as the new kid.

"But it's your turn," Edwards countered.

"Put it on a Victrola record," Jack snapped as he rose
from his chair. He walked up to the windows, opened
them all, and returned to his roll-up desk. He stood
there staring at a pile of papers, wondering what to do
next. Thomas Duffy, his boss, had given him forty-eight
hours to find a new angle on the Dyson kidnapping. Jack
had given it his best; he'd approached the family, the
neighbors, the father's employees—none of them were
willing to say a word. Jack was not surprised; when the

eight-year-old son of a business tycoon rumored to be involved with the Mob was kidnapped, it was in the best interest of everyone to keep their mouths closed.

Jack sat back down at his desk and sighed. He had taken off his jacket and rolled up the sleeves of his white cotton shirt, but he still found the heat oppressive. His stomach churned; he yanked open the top drawer and shoved the contents around, searching for a bottle of bicarbonate of soda. He raised his head when he glimpsed a figure approaching—Duffy.

"Well?" asked Duffy, leaning forward as he always did when he spoke. Duffy was a tall man in his late forties, so he seemed to loom above the seated Jack. He lifted bushy eyebrows. "Ya got anything?"

Jack closed his desk drawer and stared at Duffy's brown vest, wondering how someone could wear wool in this weather. "I'm working on it," he replied.

Duffy folded his arms. "What ya got so far?"

Jack shook his head. "This ain't easy, boss. I tried talking to a dozen people; they're all dumb. No one wants to talk and that tells me the Mob's involved."

Duffy scratched his forehead. "Any louse can come back empty-handed. The paper ain't paying ya for nothing. When was the last time ya got the scoop, anyway?"

"I guess when I covered the mayor," answered Jack.

Duffy lowered his arms and clenched his teeth. He looked around to make sure no one was listening. "Stop throwing that in my face," he whispered.

"Sure thing, chief," Jack quickly replied.

Duffy turned away and stalked back across the floor. Jack reopened the top drawer, still searching for the soda.

"Who opened the windows?" someone yelled. "More flies in here than fatheads."

Jack watched Ryan run into the newsroom and rush for a desk. Dropping into the chair, he threw a sheet of paper into the typewriter. "Get Duffy!" he yelled to everyone. "I got a flash!" He wiped back his slick black hair and threw his cigarette on the floor. The others slowly approached as the middle-aged newsman started typing frantically. "Get away from me, you mugs!" Ryan yelled when they peered over his shoulder. "This is my story. Someone call Duffy."

Duffy appeared and stood flat footed in front of the man's desk. "What ya got, Ryan?"

"We got an extra," Ryan replied without looking up. "Dyson's been gunned down."

"What, the kid?" asked Duffy.

"Not the kid, the old man," answered Ryan. "Gunned down right in front of his house."

Jack approached Ryan's desk himself.

"When'd this happen?" Duffy demanded.

"About half an hour ago," answered Ryan.

"Ya got this confirmed?"

Ryan continued typing. "Saw the stiff myself. Got a police description to go with it."

Duffy picked up Ryan's phone. "Duffy here," he said. "We're running an extra. Let 'em know down in the pit and get me a rewrite man."

"You don't need any damn rewrite," complained Ryan.

Duffy put the phone down. "Anyone else get the story?"

"I was the only reporter there," Ryan answered and then laughed.

Duffy rubbed his hands together. "Finally . . . just when I thought all you bums were washed up." He strode out of the office.

"Haynes, I got a dame on the blower," someone shouted from across the room. "She wants to talk to ya."

Jack stared at Ryan, still trying to absorb what he'd just heard.

"Haynes!" the man yelled again. "Phone!"

Jack looked up. "Okay," he said, wondering if the Dyson boy's aunt was on the phone. Just the other day, he'd tried to interview her; although she refused to talk, Jack had sensed conflict in her behavior and told her to contact him should she change her mind. "Throw her on my wire."

"I can't!" the man shouted back. "It's long distance, from Washington. You got to come here."

Jack squinted. "Long distance?" He walked over and took the receiver, wondering if Dyson had contacts in Washington. "Hello, Haynes here."

"Mr. Haynes?" a woman's voice asked.

"Yeah, yeah, Haynes. How can I help you?"

"Mr. Jack Haynes?" she asked.

"Yeah, Jack Haynes. Go on, sister."

"Are you the brother of Lou Harris?"

Jack paused, not knowing what to say. He had changed his last name a long time ago, when he was being sought by the FBI. "Who wants to know?" he finally asked.

"I . . . I have some bad news. Are you Lou's brother?"

"What happened?" Jack asked. His fingers tightened involuntarily around the receiver.

"Are you his brother?" she asked again.

"Who wants to know?"

"My name is Maggie," the woman replied. "Maggie Thorton. I'm a friend of Lou's."

"Okay, okay, I'm his brother. What happened?" There was a pause. Jack jiggled the hook. "Hello?"

"It's very bad news."

"Go on," said Jack.

"I . . . I don't know if I can."

"Come on. Spit it out, sister."

"Lou's dead," she blurted.

Jack felt his heart drop. "What happened?"

"The police say he was murdered."

Jack did not know what to think. "Is this a joke?"

There was silence at the other end. "Please, don't even say that," he finally heard.

"Okay, okay. Where'd this happen?" asked Jack.

"Here in Washington," she replied. "At a ballpark."

"What ballpark?"

"Griffith Stadium."

Jack frowned. "Who killed him?"

"They don't know. I thought I should let you know. It's . . . it's . . . "

Sensing she was about to cry, Jack soothed, "Okay, okay, calm down, sister. Tell me, when did this happen?"

"The police said four days ago."

"Four days ago? And you're just calling me now?"

"I just found out myself," she answered. "It's a long story."

Jack pulled the chair out from the desk and sat down. "I got time."

"I can't talk over the phone," she snapped.

"Why not?"

There was silence at the other end. Jack again jiggled the hook. "Hello?"

Edwards walked up to Jack, shaking his head. "Haynes, everybody says it's your turn."

Jack glared at Edwards. "What the hell you talking about?"

Edwards' face turned red. "Hamburgers, Haynes, hamburgers."

Jack turned his attention back to the phone. "Hello?"

"That's all I have to say," he heard her say.

"Wait! Wait!" Jack shouted into the phone. He looked up at Edwards and moved the phone away from his mouth. "Get the hell out of here!" He placed the receiver back on his shoulder. "I just got a couple of questions. Did you go to the police station?"

"Of course I went to the police," she answered.

Jack turned around and lunged at the desk behind him. He grabbed a pen and a sheet of paper. "Do they have the guy?"

"The what?"

"The guy. Did they catch the guy?"

"No."

"Are there any suspects?"

There was a pause. "The police don't care," she finally said.

Edwards waved his arm and walked away.

"Why not?" Jack asked.

"Like I said, it's a long story."

Jack impatiently shook his head. "Where's this police station?"

"Here in Washington," she said.

"Yeah, yeah—where? What street?"

"The station's on Pomeroy Street. Why?"

Jack jotted down the name of the street. "And where d'you live?"

"Why?' she asked.

"I'll come down there if I can get away. When's the funeral?"

"We don't have money for a funeral," she replied. "But I live on 137 Elm Street here in D.C."

Jack's mind raced. "What's your name again?"

"Maggie Thorton," she yelled.

He could not think of anything else to ask. "Okay, thanks for the call." Jack threw down the receiver and brushed back his slick, sandy blonde hair. The familiar pain of guilt hit him as he walked back to his desk. He plopped down in his wooden chair, folded his arms, and stared at Ryan, still typing away. He reached for his phone and jiggled the hook. "Esther," he said, "get me Duffy."

* * *

"Final! Final! German troops advance in Poland! Read all about it!" the hawkers screamed outside Union Station in Washington D.C.

Jack turned his head away from their waving newspapers as he entered the main hall from the tracks, lugging a worn, brown leather suitcase in his left hand. He usually listened to the hawkers' yells to get a fix on what they would shout to sell papers. They worked through trial and error, starting by shouting the headline, then coming up with their own catchphrases if that didn't sell. They quickly discovered what persuaded people to buy. Jack had concluded long ago that editors could learn a lot from the hawkers.

Jack was too tired to pay attention now. The B&O train had been delayed in Charleston, making his journey from St. Louis last over thirty hours. He raked tired eyes across the hall, searching for an exit. *There.*

He pushed through the Roman arch at the station's main entrance, realizing only when he stepped outside that he'd forgotten to observe the station's interior. He had overheard a tourist on the train say that the station's interior was a national landmark, inspired by the Baths of Diocletian in ancient Rome. Jack had never heard of Diocletian and wondered what it meant. He was too exhausted to go back in and look.

The humid air hit Jack as soon as he walked out of the station. Dropping his bag at the taxi post, he pulled out a handkerchief and wiped his forehead. When a black Ford taxi scooted to the curb in front of him, he picked up the suitcase, opened the rear door, and awkwardly worked his tall, thin frame into the cab.

A middle-aged man wearing a black visor looked into his rearview mirror. "Where to, Mac?"

"You got hotels near Griffith Stadium?" asked Jack.

"Sure."

"Well then, that's where I'm going. Can you find me one that won't burn a hole in my pocket?"

The driver chuckled. "Depends on the size of your pocket, buddy."

"Do your best," said Jack.

The driver pulled down the lever on his meter and drove onto Massachusetts Avenue, entering light midday traffic. He reached forward and turned a dial on a Philco car radio bolted to the bottom of the dashboard. Jack rolled his eyes as the cab filled with music, and he recognized the song—"Jeepers Creepers" by Al Donohue, one of the biggest hits of the year.

> *Jeepers Creepers, where'd ya get those peepers,*
> *Jeepers Creepers, where'd ya get those eyes?*
> *Gosh all git up. How'd they get so lit up,*
> *Gosh all git up. How they get that size?*

He did not understand why the song was so popular. The words were dumb and the tune was flat. He rolled down the window and tried to think of something else. The hawkers' shouts came to mind; several days ago, Germany had invaded Poland, and England and France had both declared war on Germany. It was a big story, but it would not have been his anyway. The *St. Louis Herald* was not nearly as big as some other nationally known papers, but it did have several reporters totally dedicated to international affairs.

The cab turned abruptly in to the curb and stopped in front of a drab six-story building. The driver turned down the radio. "The service ain't so hot and the elevator's usually broken, but the rooms are clean," he said. "And you're just a stone's throw from the stadium."

Jack handed the man fifty cents and grabbed his bag. "Thanks a lot, buddy."

He checked into the Saratoga Hotel and the clerk handed him the key to a third floor room. The driver was right; he had to walk up three flights of stairs and carry his own bag. The room was not much larger than the length of its single bed, and it had only one window. But it did have a ceiling fan and it was clean.

Jack had planned to shave and bathe but he was too

tired. He removed his jacket and tie, flopped down on the bed with his shoes on, and promptly fell asleep.

* * *

Jack opened his eyes and contemplated a clear blue sky through the double-arched window, not sure for a moment where he was. Then he saw his suitcase on the floor and gazed around the undersized room until he realized he lay in a Washington hotel room. He turned his eyes to the clock on the bedside table and sat up in surprise; he had been asleep for over twenty hours.

He unpacked and shaved, then dreamed of a big breakfast as he showered. He had brought all three of his suits with him; they were not the most expensive, but they were acceptably fashionable, double breasted with long, broad lapels and square shoulders. He eyed the charcoal, speckled gray, and midnight blue suits, at last choosing the charcoal one. He studied a map of Washington as he dressed.

Suddenly anxious to get going, he left the hotel without eating. He considered getting a taxi but decided to save his money. As he started the half-hour walk to the police station at 371 Pomeroy Street, Jack wondered what he would tell the police. Would he let them know he was Lou's brother? He decided not to take the chance. He would tell them he was a Washington newspaperman.

Jack had not seen Lou since their mother died. Eight years ago, when Jack was nineteen years old and Lou was only thirteen, their mother had collapsed in a soup line. When the ambulance arrived, they found a pool of blood beneath her. They took her to a local hospital, where she was pronounced dead on arrival. The doctors said she had died of bleeding from the uterus. Jack suddenly had some hard choices to make: take custody of his brother or send him to an orphanage. With neither the money nor the know-how to take care of Lou, Jack relinquished custody of his brother. Lou went first to a foster home and later to an orphanage.

Jack pushed those thoughts aside when he found the police station, a red brick building with white columns framing the main entrance. He entered and found a young policeman sitting behind a tall wooden counter, his eyes glued to a magazine. Jack looked at the cover: *The Adventures of Dick Tracy, Detective #707*. Chuckling, the officer reached for a sandwich, still reading.

Jack cleared his throat. "Excuse me, where would I find Homicide?"

"Second floor," the policeman said without looking up.

Jack found the stairs and climbed them to the second floor, then scanned the doors beyond the landing until he saw the one with *Homicide* painted on the glass in scratched gold letters. The large room he entered reminded him of the newsroom back at the *Herald*, with its stale smoke and banging typewriters.

A young police officer sat behind an old wooden counter, scribbling notes on some paper. He looked up. "Yeah, how can I do ya?" he asked.

"Hi; Jack Haynes, *Washington Chronicle*. Can I speak to someone about the Lou Harris investigation?"

"Have a seat," the officer replied, and picked up a phone.

Within minutes, a middle-aged man with white hair appeared, his pear-shaped form clad in plain clothes. He leaned his elbows on the counter and stared at Jack. "Yeah, I'm Lieutenant Warner; what do ya want?"

"Hi, Lieutenant. Jack Haynes with the *Washington Chronicle*. I wanted to ask you if there is anything new with the Lou Harris investigation."

"You're with the *Chronicle*?" Warner scowled doubtfully at him. "How come I never seen you before?"

"Well, I'm new, Lieutenant. New with the *Chronicle*—not new in the newspaper game. What's with the Harris murder?"

Lieutenant Warner snickered. "Well if you're new, the first thing you got to learn is that the force isn't gonna stand on its head for every red bum full of dandruff."

Jack was taken back. "What do you mean, red?" he asked.

"Harris was a red and they're always in hot water. Why's the *Chronicle* so interested in a red?"

"How do you know he was red?"

"What? You joking?" Warner exclaimed. "Tell your editor to stop sending boys down here who are wet behind the ears."

"Okay, you're right," Jack quickly replied. He pulled out a pen and a pad of paper. "Can you tell me what you know of the murder so far?"

"Are you kidding me?" replied Warner. "Ask your friends at the paper."

Jack was not surprised by this remark. Reporters had to establish relationships with the police before they gave away information. But Jack was determined to press on. "Like I said, I'm new, Lieutenant. They want to see what I can come up with by myself." Jack winced inwardly at his pathetic response, but it was the only thing that came into his head.

Warner laughed. "Ain't that special. And I'm supposed to help you with your Easter egg hunt?" The other officer behind the counter chuckled as well.

Jack's facial muscles tensed. "I'm the bridge between you and the public, Lieutenant. I was sent here for an update on an investigation. Now, what are going to tell the public?"

"I never thought I would see the *Chronicle* go down the toilet," Warner answered.

"You got any suspects?" Jack pressed.

"I suspect everyone," he countered.

"Can you at least give me a quick lowdown on what you got so far?"

Warner shrugged.

"Come on, Lieutenant. I gotta go back with something."

Warner yawned and stretched. "Well, you got a red stabbed in the men's room at Griffith Stadium during a Senators game—broad daylight. Stabbed once in the back. He was alone. No witnesses." Warner took a step back, pointed to the zipper on his pants and chuckled. "His fly was open. The red was stabbed in the back when he was pissing!"

"You got anything new at all to add to that?" asked Jack.

"Yeah, here's something new," sneered Warner. "The investigation's getting older." He turned and walked away from the counter.

* * *

Jack walked down Elm Street, mulling over what he'd learned while he looked for house number 137. Lou had never told him he was with the communist party. All Jack knew was that Lou had been working in a Washington hardware store ever since he moved from Baltimore two years prior. Jack could not help thinking that none of this would have happened, had he taken custody of his brother years ago. They both would have stayed in Baltimore. Jack would never have had all those problems in Detroit, either.

Jack spotted the house, a three-story brick rowhouse just off Elm Street, and paused to examine the names on the postboxes before descending a dirty stairway to the door of a basement apartment. Double-checking the name on the door, he knocked.

The door cracked open. A tall, blonde-haired woman in her early thirties peeked out. "Yes?"

"Miss Thorton?"

"Yes?"

"I'm Jack Haynes, Lou's brother—"

Her blue eyes widened and she flung the door wide open. "Come in."

Jack entered a small, dimly lit living room and removed his black fedora. "Have a seat," she said as she reached for the hat.

Jack looked around and sat down on a worn cloth sofa. The only light came from the two basement windows in the front wall. Dirty plates sat on the coffee table and clothes were scattered on the floor. Jack glanced at the posters and photos on walls covered in dingy white paper that curled up at the edges. He saw no pictures of his brother, nor anything that would suggest he'd been here.

The woman placed the hat in a closet by the door and turned to Jack. Her curly blonde hair had dark roots and she wore a beige rayon street dress. Her shoulders drooped; she struck Jack as someone who was naturally lazy.

"Miss Thorton—"

"Call me Maggie," she interrupted and sat down herself.

"Maggie, I brought some money with me for a proper funeral."

Maggie shook her head. It's too late. They already buried him."

Jack's eyes narrowed. "You mean . . . he was buried like a pauper?"

"It wasn't like that," said Maggie, settling back on the sofa. "The city buried him. He has a headstone. I was there; it was proper."

Jack didn't like this, but he let it go. "How did you get my number?" he asked.

"I called your uncle in Towson. He told me where you work."

He nodded. "Maggie, I just went to the police station to ask about the investigation."

"What'd they say?"

Jack shook his head. "They don't seem to be working on it at all."

Maggie frowned. "No kidding. I wouldn't be surprised if they were involved in it."

"What do you mean?" he asked.

She crossed her legs. "They're out to get people like Lou."

"Was Lou with the communist party?"

She waved a casual hand. "Sure. That was no secret. Lou was a member for years."

"You think that had something to do with his murder?"

"It had to. Why else would someone kill him? He wasn't robbed."

"The police said he was knifed once in the back," said Jack. "Is that what you heard?"

"That's right," she replied. "At Griffith Stadium, during a baseball game. But there's more to it than that."

Jack sat forward. "Go on."

"Lou went to Griffith Stadium to meet with some workers."

"What workers?"

Maggie sighed. "You know about sit-down strikes?"

"I heard of them. I never covered them. Not my area."

"The first one was in General Motors a couple of years ago, in Flint. Big success. Bosses hate sit-in strikes. They're afraid to resort to violence against the workers—worried it will damage the machines and the products. There's a lot of other reasons sit-downs work. Workers are right there so they're not afraid scabs will come in and replace them. It also makes the owners' spies useless."

"Are you with the communist party?" asked Jack and then suddenly wondered if he should have asked.

Maggie hesitated. "Sure," she finally replied.

"So who were these workers?" Jack asked.

Maggie stared into the air. Her mouth opened but nothing came out. She suddenly frowned. A tear trickled down her cheek.

"I'm sorry," said Jack. "If you want to stop talking about it . . . "

She wiped away the tear. "No, it's okay." She swallowed. "Lou was supposed to give advice to some textile workers from Virginia. He was gonna tell them how to do a sit-in successfully. He was supposed to meet them at Griffith Stadium."

"Why Griffith Stadium?"

Maggie sniffled and reached for a hankie on the coffee table. "We meet in public places. Cafeterias, movie theaters, sports arenas. It's safer." She wiped her nose and continued. "Industry hires thugs to do away with people like Lou."

"Where were these textile workers from?" he asked.

"Gullane Textiles."

"Where's that?"

"Northern Virginia."

"Did you tell the police this?" asked Jack.

Maggie shrugged. "I did," she said, her voice heavy with resignation. "They couldn't care less. They even said something like: well, then he had it comin'."

An awkward pause followed. Jack looked around the room.

"Want something to drink?" Maggie asked.

"No, I'm okay," said Jack.

"Do you have a place to stay?"

He nodded. "I'm at the Saratoga Hotel on Larch Street."

Maggie brushed at her hair, tucking back some drooping locks. "If you missed the funeral, then why are you here?"

"I want to find out what happened," Jack answered.

"That won't be easy," Maggie said as she reached for a pack of Camels on the coffee table.

"Where was he taken?" asked Jack. "I mean, his body."

"His body? City Hospital. And it was in the morgue for two days before those bastards told anybody."

"How did you find out?" he asked.

"The police came here. My address was in his wallet. Like I said, he wasn't robbed." She offered Jack a cigarette but he waved it off.

"So where did Lou work?" asked Jack.

"In a hardware store."

"Which one?"

"Hubbard Hardware on Hubbard Road." She pulled a cigarette from the pack and reached toward the coffee table for a book of matches.

Jack absently watched her tuck the cigarette between her lips and strike a match. "Where are Lou's things?"

Maggie lit the cigarette and waved the match to extinguish its small flame. "They're still here," she said as she exhaled. "I got 'em in the bedroom. You want 'em? You can have 'em. I may want to keep a few things. You know—some of his things have a special meaning to me."

Jack nodded. "You can keep them. I was just thinking of going through them for a trace of what happened."

Maggie frowned. "I'll tell you right now, the answer's in his work, not his stuff."

Although she seemed lazy, Jack suspected she had a sharp mind. "What was the name of that mill?" he asked. "The one in Virginia?"

"Gullane Textiles. Why?"

"It might be the key," he said.

Maggie carelessly flicked the ash from her cigarette into a glass ashtray on the coffee table. "Did Lou contact you lately? Tell you anything?"

Jack shook his head. He wondered how much Lou

had told her. Did she know he had abandoned Lou at the age of thirteen? Did she know Lou had written to him repeatedly and Jack almost never answered the letters? "No," he answered. "I haven't been in touch with him for years."

Maggie rose and subtly brushed her hip with her left hand. "You know, you don't have to stay in a hotel. I have room here."

Jack glanced at her hand, wondering if the offer was more than friendly. "Thanks a million. I may take you up on it if my funds run dry."

Maggie stood thinking. "You know, you ought to meet Lou's friends. I don't know . . . if you're going to look into this, maybe you would learn something."

Jack nodded. "Sounds good to me."

As Maggie walked to an end table, Jack caught himself studying her hourglass figure. She bent over and reached for a scrap of paper and a pen, then scribbled something. "We're planning to meet the day after tomorrow. The Waverly Cafeteria on 3rd Street. Ten a.m. This is the address," she said as she returned and handed the paper to Jack.

"Thanks," Jack said, studying the address. He looked up. "When was the last time you saw Lou?"

Maggie sat back down and folded her arms. "That day. He left for the stadium after we had a late breakfast."

"Did he seem nervous?"

Maggie shook her head. "Nah. He's met with workers a thousand times."

"Notice anything unusual in the last few days before he died?"

She picked her cigarette back up from the ashtray.

"No. I would have told you. This whole thing came out of the blue."

* * *

Towson was just a few miles north of Baltimore. The town was a serene mixture of stone houses and wooden double houses with the occasional mansion. Jack had taken a bus from Baltimore and got off at the stop for the Maryland State Teachers College of Towson. Walking past the college, he turned right onto Summer Drive, where his uncle lived. Jack had not been on the quiet side street since he'd lived there, years ago.

It was his uncle, Mike Harris, who hid Jack from the FBI back in 1932. After Jack's mother died, Jack had gone to Michigan hoping to find work in an auto plant, but they were not hiring. He ended up working for the Mob, distributing alcohol to speakeasies in downtown Detroit. Prohibition agents had raided the speakeasy where he was making a delivery, and he was arrested. After being booked, fingerprinted, and photographed, he escaped during transport.

That, he now realized, was stupid. He would have been quickly released, but he'd made himself a fugitive. Prohibition agents from the Justice Department handed over Jack's file to the Treasury Department's Prohibition Bureau. Several years later, the two agencies combined to form the FBI. When Jack found out the United States Bureau of Investigation had published his photo in their law enforcement bulletin, *Fugitives Wanted by the Police*, he'd headed for Florida.

Jack walked up to the weathered gray country house where his uncle lived and rapped on the front door. A large, heavyset man in his early sixties swung open the door; "Come on in," he muttered when he saw Jack.

Jack removed his fedora as he entered the parlor, sniffing at the pervading smell of dust and mold. The old horse walked over to a worn brown leather couch and bent to toss newspapers off its cushions. "Take a load off your feet."

Jack sat on the couch and placed his hat on his knees.

"What's the dope?" Uncle Mike asked. "Find anything out?"

"Not yet. It looks like the police aren't carrying out much of an investigation."

"A bunch of crummy fatheads," Uncle Mike grumbled as he sat down in an old leather chair and folded his arms. "Fills me full of rotgut." The old man shook a big head that was now almost completely bald, making it seem even bigger. "Still, it ain't surprising. You could see it coming." He pointed a finger at Jack. "And I told him!"

"Did you know Lou was red?" asked Jack.

Uncle Mike snickered. "Are you kidding me? Sure, I knew. Everybody on the docks knew. Sometimes I had to pretend I didn't know him."

"Did you see him after he moved to D.C.?"

"Sure; he'd come here to Baltimore every time there was a strike in the city. Usually had some commie newspapers with him."

"You warned Lou?" asked Jack. "What did you tell him?"

"Forty years on the docks. Forty years and you think I don't know what's going on? Reds like Lou are small fry for these people, and I told him."

"What you tell him?" Jack repeated.

"I told him he was asking for it," Uncle Mike said, nodding knowingly.

Jack sat silent, not knowing what to say next.

"Where you stayin', anyway?" Uncle Mike asked.

Jack sat up. The question made it seem as if his uncle was willing to take him in if needed. "A hotel in Washington," he answered, and realized that, although Uncle Mike had refused to take custody of Lou when their mother died, both Jack and Lou had ended up living with him at some point.

Jack never made it to Florida when he was running from the FBI. He'd stopped in Baltimore to confront his uncle, to demand the reason why he hadn't taken them in when their mother died. Jack felt guilty for not taking care of Lou, but why had Uncle Mike not stepped in? Uncle Mike reluctantly admitted he had a drinking problem in those days, and it would have been hell for the boys. Feeling bad, he convinced Jack not to go to Florida, but to instead stay with him and work on the docks.

Jack worked side by side with his uncle for almost a year. Every day, Jack passed the Towson college on his way to and from work. One day, he walked into the main building and asked about admission. He ended up taking two courses in journalism, and decided to join the newspaper game. Fearing he was too close to Washington and the FBI, he moved to St. Louis, where he got a job with the *Herald*.

"I didn't know Lou was red," said Jack. "I hadn't talked to him in a long time. What do you think made him turn red?"

Uncle Mike's eyebrows rose. "It was those damn priests in the orphanage!"

"The priests?"

"Filled him with all these cockamamie ideas about social justice."

Jack thought this was a little crazy. Still, he was relieved to hear that his uncle wasn't blaming Jack for what happened. "Still, the priests?" Jack asked doubtfully.

"Lou told me so! Your brother told me so himself—how communism was the extension of Christianity into the workplace!"

Jack frowned. He couldn't see the connection. "How's that?"

"I don't know." Uncle Mike shrugged. "Something about the meek inheriting the Earth. Stuff like that."

"Never thought of Lou as an idealist," said Jack. "I still think of him as a little kid."

"Don't get me wrong," said Uncle Mike. "I got nothing against the priests. But a red idealist working on the docks?" He chuckled sardonically. "You got to be kidding me. You got the bosses. You got the Mob. I told him half a dozen times to leave the docks. Never listened to a word I said."

Jack thought he detected a hint of guilt in his uncle's tone. "Turns out the police don't have much interest in chasing down a red's killer," he said.

"They don't want to piss into the wind," said Uncle Mike.

"What do you mean?"

"Who knows where it would lead?" Uncle Mike replied. "A guy supporting workers' rights has a lot of enemies."

"Like who?"

"Like the thugs factory bosses hire. You think the flatfoots want to start investigating industry? Don't make me laugh." Uncle Mike rose. "Want a beer?"

"No thanks." Jack watched him amble toward the kitchen. "When was the last time you saw him?"

"Let's see . . . " the old man mused as he left the parlor.

Jack looked around the room. Nothing had changed. The same photographs of family members covered the walls. Even the same piece of peeling wallpaper curled away from the wall in the far corner of the room.

"It was in the late spring," Uncle Mike called from the kitchen. He returned a moment later with a bottle of Bohemian beer. "May or June, maybe. He stayed here for a few nights. That's when they went on strike at Stoddert's."

"The mill down by the bay?"

Uncle Mike gulped a mouthful of beer, then belched. "That's right."

"Did he say anything unusual?"

The old man looked at him. "Like what?"

"Like anything that would tie in with his murder?" asked Jack. "Did he say if anyone was after him?"

Uncle Mike shook his head, reaching for a newspaper folded on a table by his chair. "Nah, I would have remembered something like that." He unfolded the paper. "Who do you like in the fight?"

"What fight?" asked Jack.

Uncle Mike favored him with an incredulous stare. "Are you kidding me? The Louis-Pastor fight."

Of course—his uncle was a big boxing fan. Jack had forgotten about the fight. Joe Louis would be fighting Bob Pastor next week in Detroit for the world championship. "Haven't given it much thought," he admitted.

"Louis won by decision last time," Uncle Mike said,

studying the paper. He shook his head. "He won't be so lucky this time."

Jack pulled out his cigarettes and offered one to his uncle but the old horse brushed it off. "I'm thinking of staying in D.C. for a while," Jack said.

Uncle Mike looked at him, eyebrows raised. "What for?"

"I ain't letting this go. Someone's paying for this."

Uncle Mike shook his head, still regarding Jack with a mildly alarmed expression. "You'd be screwing with your life, Jack. Better drop it whether you like it or not."

"That bad?"

"Reds got a lot of enemies. And it's not just the bosses and the Mob. You got the feds, and we got Nazi spies here. You know that?"

"No."

"We got them here and even more in Washington. Feds can't even keep up with them; these krauts are everywhere."

"How do you know that?" asked Jack.

"Like I said. Forty years on the docks. I keep my ears and eyes open." He rose. "Want another beer?"

Jack chuckled; he'd never had a beer. "Who you think did Lou in?" he asked.

"I got no idea," Uncle Mike said.

"Where would you look?" asked Jack.

"I wouldn't look."

"Come on, Uncle Mike, cough it up," Jack wheedled.

His uncle stood there thinking, his expression pained, as if he were at odds with his conscience. "I really don't know what to say. The docks have changed in the past few years. I thought it was bad when I began as a young man.

Now it's crazy." He raised his arms in a helpless gesture. "It could be anyone."

* * *

Jack thought of taking the train straight back to Washington, but something niggled at his conscience, and he decided to visit St. Mary's Industrial School for Boys. He had never seen the Baltimore orphanage where Lou had been taken. As he walked by the school's stone walls, he thought of the foster home where Lou had stayed. He'd never been there, either. He ducked his head. *What the hell was wrong with me?*

As he rounded the corner of the stone wall, he looked up. The school's chapel rose before him, a modest structure made of white stone, with a wooden steeple. His legs brought him to the chapel doors and he stopped, staring at the sign on the door. He pulled the door open and peered inside. The smell of incense wafted from the dark interior. He made out a thin, elderly man wiping a pew with a piece of cloth.

The man twisted his head to look his way as Jack stepped inside. "You here for confession?" he asked.

"Yeah," Jack answered.

"It's over."

"The sign says three to five," Jack said.

"It's five-fifteen," the man responded. He tucked the cloth in his back pocket. "I guess I can still call the priest. You want that?"

Jack nodded, reaching for the pack of Lucky Strikes in his jacket pocket. "Thanks, pal."

They both existed the chapel. Jack lit his cigarette and stood on the steps, watching the man disappear around the corner of the chapel. An elderly priest appeared a few minutes later and barely acknowledged Jack's presence as he walked by. Jack threw the cigarette to the ground and followed the priest into the chapel.

"Bless me father, for I have sinned," Jack said as he entered the booth. "It's been a long time since my last confession."

The priest coughed. "How long?"

Jack hesitated. He had no idea. "I guess when I was a kid."

"What do you need to confess?" asked the priest.

Jack thought of his working for the Mob and the extramarital sex he'd had. But that was not why he was there. "Father," he said, "I feel really bad about what I did to my brother."

"Go on."

"He was here at St. Mary's. He lived in your orphanage."

"What happened?" asked the priest.

"He was murdered," answered Jack.

"And you are guilty of this?"

"No, no. I'm not the one who did him in. I screwed up because I could have taken custody of him. Our mother died. We could have stayed together but . . . I didn't want to be bothered. So he came to live here in the orphanage."

"How long ago was this?" the priest asked.

Jack scratched his nose. "I don't know. Almost ten years ago. I think Lou was about thirteen."

"Louis Harris?" the man asked. "You mean Dutch?"

Jack had never heard of his brother being called Dutch. "I don't know about Dutch. His name was Lou Harris."

"Murdered at Griffith Stadium?" asked the priest.

"Yeah, that's him. Why do you call him Dutch?"

"That's what we called him."

"Why?"

"I'm . . . I'm not sure," the priest replied. "But sure, I remember Dutch. He was a good boy. Yeah, we all heard he was murdered." The priest coughed again. "So you blame yourself for his death?"

Jack thought for a second. "I blame myself for abandoning him."

"How old were you?"

"Nineteen."

The priest grunted. "No one expects a nineteen-year-old to take care of a minor."

"But I could have," Jack said.

"How would this have prevented his death?"

"Lou got mixed up with communists and the bosses on the docks. That's what killed him."

"So Dutch did turn to the communists," the priest said. "Are you sure?"

"Damn sure," said Jack, and then realized what he'd said. "Sorry, father."

"It's okay. I read Dutch was a communist in the paper but I didn't believe it." He sighed, saying nothing for a long moment. "Well I'll be," he finally said. "When did he turn to the communists?"

"I don't know," Jack said. "Years ago. I didn't see him for a long time."

"Do you know who killed him?" the priest asked.

"That's what I'm trying to figure out. That's why I came to D.C."

"Tell me this," said the priest. "How could you have stopped him from being murdered?"

Jack was taken back by the question. "Well . . . I could have placed him on a different path," he finally said.

The priest sighed. "Young man, you may be guilty of not caring enough for your brother, but you are not guilty for his death. You must not blame yourself for this. It is simply not true."

"There is something else," Jack said slowly. This was something Jack had always tried to avoid in his head. It occasionally managed to creep into his consciousness, usually at the worst times.

"Yes?" the priest finally said into the silence.

"Before my brother got here, he was in a foster home. They beat him," said Jack. "They beat him daily."

"How do you know this? Did he tell you?"

"No," Jack mumbled. "I found out later from my uncle." He put his head down and fought back tears. It was not the news of the beating itself that hurt Jack the most, but the knowledge that Lou must have been constantly wondering *where is Jack?*

The priest sighed. "I know how you must feel."

"And I know . . . " Jack swallowed. "I know in my heart my mother would have wanted me to take care of Lou." He cleared his throat. The silence returned.

"And . . . and I let them both down," Jack said into it.

"No, no, no. You mustn't think like that," said the priest. "No one can predict the future. You could not have known the foster parents were rotten. And Dutch could have turned out to be a hero for the workers. But someone killed him. How could you have seen this coming?"

Jack did not answer.

"This is what you do," the priest continued. "Pray for the souls of your mother and brother."

Jack did not find the words comforting. He could have predicted the priest's response. "Yes, father," he answered, his voice wooden.

"And good luck in your pursuit."

"Meaning what?" asked Jack.

"Find the bastards that killed him," the priest said and pushed the window closed.

* * *

Gardner's Diner on Pennsylvania Avenue was different from the diners in St. Louis. The counter was the same, but instead of tables and chairs, this diner had booths. They reminded Jack of the kind of booths one would find on a passenger train; they allowed for much greater privacy than could be found in a typical St. Louis diner. Jack sat alone in a booth and slowly ate a turkey sandwich, pausing now and then to sip at a cup of hot coffee. He occasionally glanced at the newspaper he had open on the table, but he was really thinking of Lou.

He could not help wondering if things would have been different, had he taken custody of his brother. *Uncle Mike was right*, he thought. *Lou went from a Catholic orphanage to the docks and turned red for justice.* Jack thought it was the Depression, probably more than anything, that made people turn red. Despite the sadness of these events, Jack somehow felt better after talking to the priest. It had given him a sense of calm he had not experienced in a long time.

When he left the diner, he walked down Pennsylvania Avenue with in no particular destination in mind. A light drizzle developed and he tucked his hands in the pockets of his gray trench coat. Head down, he passed by a series of pawnshops, too preoccupied to notice the displays. What made him go to the orphanage? Catching a glimpse of an American flag, he raised his head, then stopped. He stood before a post office. He ran his fingers through his hair, thinking. Then his legs took him inside the post office, and he said to the gray-haired clerk standing behind the counter, "Get me St. Louis, Muriel-3945."

The elderly clerk didn't lift his eyes from his newspaper. "A lot of static today. Can't guarantee ya a good connection. Storms out west, ya know."

"I'll take my chances," said Jack.

The clerk shrugged. "You've been warned. I got to charge ya, no matter what."

"Sure, sure."

"Number three," the clerk said, pointing to one of the booths.

Jack struggled a moment with the stiff glass door, then got it open and entered the booth. The air within was hot and stale. He left the door open, pulled out his handkerchief, and wiped his forehead. Jack knew he was about to risk his job. Then again, there was that incident with the mayor; he had Duffy over a barrel. Still, Duffy might decide he'd had enough.

The clerk suddenly looked up and signaled. Jack picked up the receiver and heard a man's voice: "Yeah?"

"Get me Duffy in desk-copy," said Jack.

"Hold on."

The clerk was right. The static was high; the connection sounded like a radio between stations. He heard another man's voice: "Petersen here."

"This is Haynes. Throw Duffy on the wire."

"Who?"

"It's me, Haynes—Haynes!" Jack yelled over the interference. "Give me Duffy."

"Hold on."

Jack thought of closing the door but decided he needed the air. A minute of static passed without anyone at the other end. Jack rapped his knuckles against the booth's glass. He was paying plenty just to hear static.

"Haynes?" he suddenly heard.

"Boss?"

"It's me, Petersen. Duffy's busy," the man answered. "He can't come to the phone."

"This is important, damn it!" Jack yelled. "Get him on the wire!"

"I-said-he-was-busy," Petersen repeated.

Jack wondered if this meant he had gotten the ax. He took a deep breath. "Listen, Petersen, I'm calling long distance, from Washington. If I tell you it's important, it's important. Tell him he talks to me or I talk about the mayor. Now get him on the wire or you'll have to deal with me."

There was a pause. "Duffy's stewed," said Petersen.

"What do you mean?"

"Oiled to the gills," Petersen replied. "A couple of his old friends from Chicago are in town and they've been drinking in his office for hours."

Jack sighed. "Well, when he's sobered up, tell him I have to stay in Washington for a while."

"What's going on, Haynes?" Petersen asked. "You on a story?"

"What story?" Jack snapped. "I got business to take care of."

"You in trouble?"

"No, nothing like that. I got family business."

"Duffy's not going to like it, Haynes."

"That's tough," said Jack.

"Okay, it's your neck, not mine."

"Duffy owes me and he knows it," Jack said. "Seeya."
Jack put down the receiver and left the booth.

When he left the post office, he went in search of a branch of the National Bank of Washington. He filled out a form to have his life savings of $185 transferred from St. Louis to the Washington bank.

* * *

Jack caught glimpses of Griffith Stadium as he walked down Larch Street. As an adult, he had tried repeatedly to suppress his boyish excitement when he saw a major league ballpark, but it never worked. Whether it was in St. Louis or Washington, he found the sight just as exciting as when he was a child. He was grinning when he turned onto Georgia Avenue. The entire right side of the structure stretched before him, its whitewashed façade pocked with multiple arched entrances.

The buildings in the neighborhood were mostly one-story structures and the stadium towered over them as if it were a dwelling of great importance. The adult in Jack realized that this was not a building where laws were made or where higher education was taught; it merely enclosed a field of grass where men played a game. Realizing this did nothing to quench the thrill that ran through him at the sight.

Jack pulled fifty cents from his pants pocket and handed it to the attendant. The Washington Senators were playing the New York Yankees in a September day game. He entered Griffith Stadium and walked down a passage parallel to the right field line, looking for either hawkers or park attendants to interview. But when he passed a walkway leading to the field, his legs brought him instead to the field entrance.

He stood there, examining first the field and then the stands. The game was between innings with both teams in their respective dugouts. The stadium itself, he thought, was very similar to Sportsman's Park in St. Louis, where the Browns played. Both parks were two-tiered and could hold about thirty thousand fans. The main difference in Griffith was the bleachers and the greater number of advertisements.

Jack stared at a field he had never seen, one he had become emotionally attached to years ago. Griffith Stadium was the site of what Jack considered one of the greatest World Series of all time. In 1924, when Jack was a teenager, the New York Giants played the Washington Senators for the trophy. The series was tied at three games apiece and the final game was held at this stadium on the tenth of October. The excitement had spread all the way to Baltimore and Jack, like many boys, constructed his own crystal radio from scraps so he could follow the games.

He remembered the day of the final game. He'd been sitting on the cement steps of his row house, trying to fix his crystal set.

"Can I listen now?" asked eight-year-old Lou. He sat next to Jack, a slingshot clutched in his hand.

"I'm telling you for the last time, it's busted," Jack growled. "You gotta wait."

A number of neighborhood kids sat on the steps of their apartment buildings holding tiny speakers to their ears. The sound produced by the crystal radios was barely audible and sometimes faded away completely, but it made them all feel part of the action. Jack's radio had been working fine until the sixth inning, when the diode separated from the magnet wire. He struggled to make the connection, but the wire would not cooperate.

"Let Mom try and fix it," said Lou.

"Cut it out, will you?" Jack muttered. "You gotta wait. Besides, Mom's busy."

Jack looked around. He could not hear the action, but he could tell from the expressions on the other kids' faces that the Senators were still losing. He turned and looked at Jim McGraw, who sat on his front steps across the street. "What's going on?" Jack yelled.

"We're still losing," Jim called back. "Three to one."

"What inning?" asked Jack.

"The eighth."

Jack looked down at his radio. The problem was, the wire he was using was not pliable. No matter how much he tried to bend it to fit the diode, the wire would pop off. "Lou," he said. "Go inside and ask Mom for some sticky tape."

"What for?" asked Lou.

"Just do it," Jack replied.

As Lou ran off, some of the boys jumped up and cheered. Jack looked at Jim McGraw. "What happened?" he yelled, but Jim didn't hear.

He looked down the street, where boys had gathered, yelling and smiling.

"What happened?" Jack shouted.

One of the boys put down his earpiece. "We just scored. Two runs. We're tied."

"How'd it happen?" yelled Jack.

"We got two men on," the boy replied. "Harris comes

up and hits a grounder to third. But the ball bounced over the guy's head. Ain't it a scream?"

Jack cursed his radio. Lou ran out, one grubby hand holding a roll of tape. He handed it to Jack, who quickly taped the magnet wires to the diode. He put the speaker to his ear. "Lou," he said, grinning, "I got the game back."

"Can I listen now, Jack?" asked Lou.

Jack shook his head. "In a minute."

A boy stuck his head outside a second-story window. "Hey guys!" he yelled. "Mr. Thomas said we could listen in here!"

Boys scrambled toward the row house. Mr. Thomas was the owner of a vacuum tube radio, a Radiola, and the sound it produced could fill a large room.

Jack rose. "Come on, Lou."

They ran up the stairs to the second-floor apartment. The door was wide open, revealing a living room packed with boys wearing tee shirts, jeans, baseball caps, and sneakers. They sat on the floor wide-eyed, as if in a trance. Jack and Lou crawled in and found an empty spot near a corner.

The radio announcer described a fidgety Walter Johnson on the mound waiting to start the ninth inning. Jack could hear the crowd roar with every pitch. He imagined how exciting it must be to actually be in the stadium, witnessing the event with one's own eyes and ears.

Johnson held the tie. The broadcast cut to a tumble of commercials promoting everything from Bohemian Beer to Bromo-Seltzer. When two boys started fighting, Mr. Thomas finally made his presence known. "I told you," he said, rising from a chair against the far wall, "you can stay as long as you're quiet." The elderly man reached for his wooden cane and slowly limped between the boys until he disappeared into another room.

The game went into extra innings. The Senators managed to load the bases with nobody out in the bottom of the twelfth inning. Earl McNeely came to bat and another grounder was hit at the Giant third baseman. Again it took a bad hop, allowing the runner at third to score. The Senators won the World Series four games to three. The boys sprang up, shouting and jumping in delight.

Young Lou tugged on Jack's tee shirt. "What happened?"

"Don't you get it?" Jack exclaimed. "We won!"

"How?" asked Lou.

Mr. Thomas appeared and waved his cane at the door. "That's it, boys," he said. "Off ya go."

"How'd we win?" Lou repeated.

"The guy scored from third," answered Jack.

"How'd he do that?"

"Don't you get it? The ball went over the third baseman's head."

"What was the score?" asked Lou.

Years later, Jack would tease Lou about that, how he had listened to the World Series on a good radio and then asked who won and what the score was. The players now ran onto the field, jarring Jack out of his memories. He glanced at the crowd. Attendance was sparse; the Senators were way out of the pennant race while the Yankees were looking for another championship.

Jack turned around and walked back to the main passageway, thinking again of his brother. Lou had been taken to the same orphanage that gave Babe Ruth a home. After listening to the priests' stories, the Babe had become

Lou's favorite player. The Babe even visited the orphanage once, and Lou met him. Lou wrote Uncle Mike that it was the best day of his life.

Jack walked up to a short man selling programs from behind an old wooden stand. "Hiya, pal; Jack Haynes of the *Washington Chronicle*. I heard a guy was knifed here about two weeks ago. You know anything about that?"

The man's eyes shifted but he didn't look up. "Sure, that's no secret. You want a program?"

"Yep." Jack reached into his pocket and produced a nickel. "You know where it happened? I heard it was the men's room. Know which one?"

The man pulled the nickel in from the countertop. "Just off first base. Everybody knows that."

Jack continued down the passage, ignoring the hawkers screaming their wares. He glanced to his left every time he passed a walkway to the seats. The game had resumed and through the corner of his eye, he saw figures running on the field whenever the ball was hit. He avoided the temptation to watch the game, walking purposefully past the openings until he found the men's room down the first base line.

Entering slowly, he looked around the dimly lit room. A ceiling fan slowly circled the acrid smell of urine through the air. To his right were five urinals and to his left, three toilets. There was a dark stain beneath the center urinal. *Probably Lou's blood,* he realized with a jolt. He examined the walls—no windows, no other exit. He turned and left.

A vendor yelled about his hot roasted peanuts just outside the restroom. Jack approached the man. "One bag, mister." The gray-haired man scooped up some peanuts and placed them in a bag. Jack accepted the bag and handed the old man a nickel. "You know anything about the murder that happened here a couple a weeks ago?" he asked.

The man shrugged. "Yeah, yeah. I just don't get people. They come to the ballpark and instead of enjoying the game, they wanna go to the spot where some poor fellow was stabbed. Tell me, why? What's the attraction?"

"I ain't a fan," said Jack. "I'm doing a little investigating."

The man threw the nickel into an old cigar box. "You're a little late, ain't ya?"

Jack pulled a five-dollar bill from his pocket and placed it on the counter. "I just got some questions. The guy was my brother."

The man stared at the five-dollar bill. "Your brother?" He pushed the bill back toward Jack. "Save your money, mister." He reached for another paper bag and began slowly filling it with peanuts. His expression was vacant, as if he were deep in thought. "It's like I told the police and the feds," he said.

"The feds? You mean the FBI?"

The man nodded. "Yeah, sure. It happened during the game. The guy who got it—I mean your brother—was walking with this other fellow. They walked together talking for about ten minutes and then separated. A few minutes later, I heard another guy yelling. He was running down the passage screaming for the cops. Then a crowd gathered outside the men's room."

Jack recalled that Lieutenant Warner said Lou was alone. "What'd this other guy look like?"

"You know, that guy that got killed—I mean your brother—I had seen him before," said the peanut vendor, ignoring the question. "I thought he was a reporter. But I never told the cops."

"Why not?" asked Jack.

"They never asked. Didn't even occur to me until they left. Can you believe it? Washington police and the FBI question me for half an hour, and nobody asks me if I had seen the guy before. Ain't that a laugh?"

Jack tipped his head to one side. "Why did you think my brother was a reporter?"

"'Cause he used to come in here with a camera in his arms. Then I realized he wasn't a news guy. You see, reporters use the Larch Street entrance to get to the press box. This guy always came in from Georgia Avenue."

"Did he have a camera that day?"

The man shook his head. "I don't remember."

"The guy who was with my brother; what did he look like?" asked Jack.

The man shrugged. "Average looking guy. Wore a boater. That's all I noticed."

"A boater? You mean a straw hat?"

"Yeah."

"What else was he wearing?" asked Jack.

"A brown or black suit—I don't know, nothing un-usual."

The guy doesn't sound like a textile worker, Jack thought.

"Oh yeah, the boater," said the man. "There was something funny about it. It had a red band."

"What's so funny about that?"

"You ever see one before?" the old man asked. "Think about it. Blue or black are the only color bands I see around here. A red band tells me the guy's from out of town."

"I guess so," said Jack. "And my brother? What was he wearing?"

"I don't remember. Nothing unusual either; a dark suit."

"Remember anything else?" Jack pressed.

The man shook his head. "Nah, that was it. The only exciting day this whole season, the way this team is playing. You could—" He stopped abruptly, as if he realized he'd said something he'd regret.

"Thanks," said Jack and walked away.

He caught a glimpse of the field through a passage and could not resist the temptation. *I'll just watch one out,* he told himself. He walked down the passage until he could see the entire playing field from the first base line. He glanced at the scoreboard; the Senators were losing 5–2 in the bottom of the eighth with no outs.

A large sign just to the right of the scoreboard featured an illustration of a pretty young woman smiling and holding a bar of soap. The sign read: *The Washington Senators Use Lifebuoy Soap.* Jack saw scribbling at the bottom of the sign but could not make out the words. He took several steps forward and squinted until the words came in focus. *And they still stink!* someone had written.

Chuckling, Jack dropped his eyes to examine the contour of the center field wall. He had repeatedly heard the announcers on the radio complain about the wall and now he saw for himself—the wall detoured around a group of houses and, of all things, a tree that stuck out into the playing field.

The next batter approached the plate and Jack caught the player's number: four. *Taffy Wright, the outfielder.* Jack looked at the mound and made out Red Ruffing, the right-handed Yankee ace.

Jack was most familiar with the St. Louis Browns, but he knew the players in this game. Wright was one of the better Senator hitters, batting over 300. Although Wright threw right-handed, he batted left-handed, making it harder for the pitcher. But he was facing Ruffing with an ERA below 3.00; Jack thought Wright was clearly outmatched. He glanced at first base and saw a player he didn't recognize; it seemed strange not to see Gehrig holding the bag. The Yankee legend had been a fixture at first base for years but was sidelined earlier in the season with some sort of mysterious problem with his nerves.

The pitch came in: a curve taken for a strike. Wright glanced at the umpire and shook his head. He prepared for the next pitch: another curve taken, strike two. Jack smirked. *Wright's looking for a fastball but Ruffing doesn't want to give it to him. Ruffing's coming in with another curve, I can feel it.* Ruffing went into his motion. Wright's weight went back and he swung with all his might, looking for that fastball. Instead, Wright swung through a curve ball for strike three. Jack chuckled and headed out of the ballpark.

* * *

Jack took the stairs down to the basement cafeteria, where he looked around for Maggie. He spotted her at a corner table, sitting with three young men.

"Jack," Maggie greeted him as he approached, "these are some friends of mine; they were Lou's friends, too." She pointed in turn to the men sitting at the table. "Jack, this is Hans, Ray, and Tom."

Jack nodded and sat down.

The man named Tom shook his head as he raised his

glass of tea and paused with it just below his prominent chin. "There's no point in trying to disrupt the assembly line," he said, obviously resuming a conversation Jack's arrival had interrupted. "The workers have to become organized before any stoppage is attempted."

Jack studied Tom as he spoke. He appeared to be in his late twenties. His clothes were old and appeared a size too small for his thin frame. He sat with the stoop-shouldered posture of someone who habitually accommodated shorter people, and Jack suspected that, if he stood, Tom would be a tall man.

A petite young woman dressed in a white cafeteria uniform came to the table and sat down. The man named Ray turned his boyish face to look at her intently. His shaggy brown hair and thick-lensed glasses gave him a distracted air, but the eyes the glasses magnified were piercing. He struck Jack as someone sensitive and in-formed.

The cafeteria girl wore a look of disgust on her swarthy face as she tossed a newspaper onto the table. The headline *Red Army Invades Poland* confronted them.

Ray glanced at the paper and looked away. "We know."

"Molotov signs a nonaggression with the fascists and now they divide a nation?" she protested, her agitation making her brown bob sway as she looked at those around the table.

Jack did not follow events in Europe closely, but he did know about the Molotov-Ribbentrop Pact. A month earlier, the Germans and Communist Russia had stunned the world when they announced the signing of a non-aggression pact. It also provided for neutrality by one country should the other become involved in a war with a "a third power." The move stunned even Germany's allies, Italy and Japan. Not only did those two powers consider Germany's act a pact with Satan, but, to add insult to injury, they had been left in the dark and knew nothing about the negotiations prior to the announcement. Then, on September 1st, Germany invaded Western Poland. And just the other day, when the Polish troops had all been mobilized west, the Soviets invaded Eastern Poland.

Ray sighed as if he found the woman's comment annoying. "Sue, this is hardly the time to discuss this. Wait until the meeting."

"We're meeting now, aren't we?" she countered.

Ray turned his attention to Tom. "The workers at Rencke *are* organized," he said. "They picked that redheaded guy as their leader and almost all of them are for it."

Maggie turned to the cafeteria worker. "Sue, this is Jack, Lou's brother."

Jack examined Sue's face as he extended his hand to her. It had gentle lines and a warm expression; she struck him as someone who was naturally sincere.

"Jack just got here," said Maggie to everyone. "He's from St. Louis."

Ray stood and extended his hand to Jack in formal introduction. "Ray Ogren. Your brother was a good man."

Jack shook his hand. "Thank you."

Tom also rose and extended his arm. As Jack had suspected, he was tall, topping Ray by a foot. "Tom Murdock."

The man named Hans, a thirtyish, heavyset man, rose next, and bowed. "Hans Guter. It is a pleasure to meet you and it was a pleasure to know your brother," he said in a thick accent Jack could not place. He nodded.

Maggie tipped her head back to say to them, "Jack came to find out what happened to Lou."

Hans reached for his glass of tea as they resumed their seats. "Unfortunately, Lou was not the first or the last victim. They will do anything to stop the workers from uniting."

Maggie looked at Jack. "It's true. They're killing more and more of our people. And there's never a decent investigation."

"Lou was the second member of our nucleus to be killed this year," added Hans.

"Who was the other?" asked Jack.

They all turned and looked at Ray Ogren. Ray thought for a second and said, "A man named Albert Collins, one of the oldest party members."

"Was he working together with Lou on something?" asked Jack.

Ray punched his glasses back on his nose with his forefinger, and shook his head. "Not that I know of."

Jack caught himself leaning forward. "How was he killed? Was he knifed in the back like Lou?"

Hans' prominent red nose seemed to inch forward as he also leaned in to the table. "He was shot."

"In an alleyway," added Ray.

Maggie rose. "I'm going to get a cup of tea. Want some tea or coffee, Jack?"

"No, thanks." Jack turned to the others. "The project Lou was working on, this textile mill. Anybody else ever meet with these people?"

Ray shook his head. "No, Lou was working on that one alone. I don't think any of us have any contacts there."

"Where exactly is this mill? Anybody know?"

"Gullane Textiles is in Virginia," answered Ray. "A place called Burr Hill." He turned to Sue. "Sue, you're from Virginia. Know where Burr Hill is?"

Sue shook her head. "I'm not from Virginia."

Ray appeared confused. "But you—"

"I did live there once," she added. "For a couple of years. It's not far from Fredricksburg. About fifty miles south of D.C."

"Who went with Lou to Griffith Stadium that day?" asked Jack, steering the conversation back on track.

"He went alone, as far as I know," answered Ray.

"We usually meet contacts individually," added Tom.

Ray glared at Tom, who looked away.

Ray seems unhappy with Tom's loose tongue, Jack noted, then said aloud, "Did he ever meet the guy from the mill?"

"We don't know," Ray said.

"Who do you guys suspect did it?" asked Jack.

Ray shrugged. "It may have been goons from the mill. On the other hand, it might have been someone who had been following Lou for weeks. We just don't know. We have a lot of enemies."

"Like who?" asked Jack.

Ray tilted his head forward. "We are surrounded by fascists," he answered. "The factory bosses, the FBI, the Nazis. They're all fascists. They all want us dead." He removed his glasses and rubbed his nose. "Jack, if you're thinking of investigating this, you should talk to Petrov."

"Who's that?" asked Jack.

"He's our security officer," Ray said, replacing his

glasses. "He asked us all the questions you just did and a lot more. Maybe he can help you."

Jack glanced at Maggie as she returned with a cup and saucer and sat down, then returned his attention to Ray as he placed his arms on the table, palms down.

He looked intently at Jack. "I know murders such as these are hard to take, particularly when it involves a relative. It's a chance we all agree to take. But one thing remains clear. The revolution is inevitable and will succeed, despite these killings. Remember, chickens are counted in the fall."

This last comment sounded phony to Jack. If he thought he could comfort Jack by telling him the revolution would succeed, he was way off base.

Tom nodded in agreement and Hans raised his glass. "Here, here. To the revolution."

Tom turned to Jack and smiled. "We are having our weekly sorrow meeting tomorrow. Want to join us?"

"Sorrow meeting?" asked Jack.

Hans chuckled. "It's when we share our misery."

Tom raised his left hand and pointed his pinky up. "We have a few. Want to join us?"

"Sure," said Jack, then turned to Ray. "How can I meet this guy, Petrov?"

Ray sat in thought. "I can arrange a meeting," he finally said. "I'll let Maggie know the time and place."

* * *

"What's a nucleus?" asked Jack as he and Maggie left the Waverly Cafeteria together and walked down 3rd Street. "What did that guy mean: a member of our nucleus?"

Maggie put her head down. "I'm not sure how much I can tell you," she whispered. They walked in silence until Maggie finally said, "We're organized into small groups. We call them nuclei. There are street nuclei and factory nuclei. The street nuclei are made up of party members that live in a small city area. Factory nuclei are all communists in one shop."

"So Tom, Ray, you—you're all part of the same nucleus?"

"That's right," she answered and looked up at Jack. "Jack, there's something I haven't told you. Lou was putting together a list. A list of party members who had recently died."

Jack frowned. "What was he going to do with the list?"

"Lou thought he could prove they were murdered and that the murders were all linked," she said.

"Where's this list?"

"I don't know. I was hoping he mailed it to you or something," she said. "Did he?"

"No," replied Jack. He thought of the orphanage in Baltimore. "You know, I didn't see Lou for years. We were separated when our mother died. I don't know if he told you."

"I know," she said. "I know all about the orphanage. You know, he actually liked it there. Can you believe it? Liking priests?" She folded her arms. "Taking lessons on social justice from Catholic priests! What a joke!"

"Why's that?" asked Jack.

"I don't want to get into all that," she said. "Let's just say I didn't smoke their opium."

Maggie's response sounded peculiar to Jack, but he let

it go. He was more intrigued by this list. "You think the list had something to do with his murder?"

"I don't know," she said. "It's certainly possible. On the other hand, he may have been killed for trying to organize the workers in the Virginia mill."

Jack put his hands in his jacket pockets as they continued down 3rd Street. "So what's your story?" he asked. "Where you from?"

Maggie looked at the ground. "I'm from Kentucky. Surprised?" She glanced up at him. "It was the Depression. We couldn't pay the mortgage so they evicted my whole family." She smirked. "We ended up living in an old, broken-down bus on my grandmother's land . . . and my father and my four brothers left looking for work." She sighed. "I never heard from them again. So there it is."

Maggie's story was not uncommon. Jack had heard it a thousand times. "So how did you end up in D.C.?"

"I got a job as a waitress in a diner. Not just any diner. It was on U.S. 25. Ever hear of it? It's one of the major roads in Kentucky. I met a lot of people, listened to their stories, their heartbreaks. Then one night, some reds came by the diner. They were on their way to support a strike in Tennessee. They sat at their booth for hours, eating, talking. They invited me to sit down with them and started asking me about my job. Can you believe it?"

"What did they want to know?" asked Jack.

"My wages. My hours. How much time I got for my breaks. You know, I thought they were the most interesting people I had ever met. They invited me to their camp and I went. They saw I was interested in their cause and convinced me the real political action was in Washington. They gave me a name to look up if I ever decided to go. So, here I am."

"How did you meet Lou?"

"At a party meeting." She glanced at Jack. You don't think that's romantic, do you?"

Jack tilted his head in thought. "Well . . . I guess not."

"To someone dedicated to the cause, it's very romantic."

Jack did not care anything about this. "Lou have a camera?" he asked.

"Yeah, why?"

"Because a guy at Griffith Stadium told me he used to see Lou with a camera."

Maggie turned her head. "You went to Griffith Stadium?"

"I sure did."

"Why?"

"It would have been dumb not to. What was Lou taking pictures of? You know?"

"I have no idea," she answered.

"Did he have a collection of photos?" Jack asked.

Maggie thought for a second. "Not that I know of. Lou used to take pictures at factories whenever the workers won a fight against management. But he didn't keep the photos. He would give them out like they were trophies."

"Where's the camera now? You have it?"

"It's probably with the rest of his things, back in the apartment."

They reached the corner and waited for the light to change. "Chickens are counted in the fall," Jack said slowly. "What the hell does that mean?"

She gave him a quizzical look. "What?"

"One of the guys said that. Chickens are counted in the fall."

Maggie chuckled. "Which one? Hans?"

"I don't remember," Jack admitted.

"It means you don't count how many chicks are hatched, but how many grow up to be chickens. He was trying to say that in the end, we will win."

The light changed and they headed across the street. "Never heard that saying before," said Jack.

"It's a Russian proverb," Maggie answered. "We follow the Russian example whenever we can. They know how to get things done."

* * *

Jack walked down the stairs to the basement of City Hospital, then searched the empty corridor until he found a door bearing a *Morgue* sign. He opened the heavy wooden door and peered inside.

A young, crew-cut man wearing white scrubs was mopping the floor. He looked up. "How can I help ya, buddy?"

Jack removed his fedora. "Hi, Jack Haynes of the *Washington Chronicle*. How can I get some information on an autopsy performed here?"

The man propped the mop against an autopsy table. "You got to go upstairs. You got to go to the Superintendent's Office."

Jack grimaced. "The thing is, I don't want to get caught up in red tape. I just want to find out what happened to my brother."

"Your brother?"

"Yeah, I'm a newspaper guy but I'm here about my brother. He was murdered."

The man shook his head. "Yeah, well, you still got to go upstairs."

Jack had covered a number of murder investigations for the *St. Louis Herald*. He had dealt with morgue attendants, and knew they could be talked into cooperating. "Look, pal," he said. "I know you do a lot of cases. I cover murders for my paper, so I know. But this was my brother; it's different. I don't want to spend the day filling out some lousy forms. I just need to know a couple of things."

The man pushed the metal bucket against the wall with his foot. "So what was his name?"

"Lou Harris. He was the guy murdered at Griffith Stadium."

"Oh yeah," the man said. "The baseball murder. I remember that one. Ton of feds here for that one."

"Feds?" Jack prompted.

"Yeah. The FBI. There were, like, five of them. They were here for the entire autopsy."

"Why?"

The man shrugged. "Don't know. They never tell me stuff like that. Anyway, if you want to know more, maybe you should talk to the coroner. It was Dr. Fields. He was pissed off during the entire thing. The feds wouldn't leave him alone. Kept asking him questions."

"What questions?"

"The usual. Who knifed him? Was it a hobo full of bum gin, or a pro?"

"What'd the doc say?" asked Jack.

The man hesitated. "Maybe I should get the doc." He turned and walked toward the door, saying, "Wait here."

A thin man in his mid-forties eventually appeared. He also wore white scrubs, and sported a black moustache. As he approached Jack, he tilted his head in curiosity. "I'm Dr. Fields. How can I help you?"

"Hello, doctor," said Jack. "I wanted to ask you about the Griffith Stadium murder. The guy was my brother."

The coroner halted midway to the door where Jack stood and folded his arms. "I'm sorry. I can't discuss my cases like this. If you need information, I suggest you go upstairs and speak with the superintendent. He has an office upstairs."

"Come on, doc. He was my brother. I just want to get the lowdown."

"I'm sorry, it's the law," said the coroner. He turned around and left the morgue.

Jack put his hat back on and sighed. *Guy's a stiff,* he thought; *always gotta play it by the book.*

The morgue attendant had returned; now he reached for his mop. "Hey buddy," he said, "I can tell you one thing I remember about it."

Jack had been turning to leave. He stopped and looked back at the attendant. "Yeah? What's that?"

"I remember during the autopsy, what the doc told the feds. He said it was probably a professional job. The guy stuck the knife in so it hit the back of the heart where the big pipes come in—between the seventh and eighth ribs on the left side; the knife went straight into the heart. Caused massive hemorrhage. The killer was either left-handed and very lucky or he knew exactly what he was doing. I wouldn't bet it was by chance."

Jack smiled grimly. "Thanks, pal," he said, and left the morgue.

* * *

Hubbard Hardware & Seed was located in a small wooden building just off Hubbard Road, in the eastern part of the city. Jack had taken the bus Maggie had told him was Lou's daily ride. He opened the store's door, revealing a poorly lit showroom smelling of sawdust and grease and dominated by counters and shelving that stretched to a high ceiling. The old wooden floor creaked as Jack entered.

"Hey pal," he said to a teenage boy sweeping the floor against the far wall, "is there someone here I can talk to about Lou Harris?"

The boy looked up and fixed his red apron. "Lou?"

"Yeah, Lou Harris. He used to work here."

"I know. But he's . . . " The boy turned his head toward the back. "Mr. Gibbs!"

A slight man, stooped with age and wearing a brown sweater and cap, appeared in a doorway behind a counter running along the back wall. He banged a clay pipe against his palm and stared at Jack without speaking.

"Excuse me, sir," said Jack. "Can I ask you a few questions about Lou Harris?"

The man glanced at Jack's clothes. "You with the police?"

"No, I'm Lou's brother. You got a minute?"

The man folded his arms and leaned against the counter. "I didn't know Lou had a brother."

"Well, I live in St. Louis. We hadn't seen each other for a long time. Can I ask you a few questions?"

The man did not immediately answer. He stared at Jack as if attempting to formulate an opinion. "Jimmy," he finally said to the stock boy, "why don't you take your break?"

The boy removed his apron and left. Jack pulled out a pad of paper and a pen. When the man stared at the pad, Jack said, "Sorry, I'm a newspaperman—force of habit. I don't have to take notes if it bothers you."

The man shrugged. "I don't care. You got some proof, some ID?"

Jack hesitated. "Well, yes. But you see, I got a different last name. My last name is Haynes, not Harris."

"Why's that?"

"It's a long story, sir. I . . . I had problems with the law. But I can prove to you I know Lou like no one else."

The man straightened, arms still crossed. "Go ahead."

Jack tried to think fast. "Lou was from Baltimore. He worked on the docks with his uncle. That's my Uncle Mike. He lives in Towson. Lou was a big Babe Ruth fan. He met the Babe once at St. Mary's Orphanage. He must have told you that. His girlfriend was Maggie, Maggie Thorton."

"Okay, okay," the man said, dropping his arms. "So, what you want to know?"

"Anything unusual happen before Lou was murdered?"

"Like what?"

Jack put away the pad. "Did Lou act unusual before died? Did he seem worried or anything?"

The man shook his head. "No."

"Did Lou work the day he was murdered?"

"No, it was his day off."

"Did you know he was going to the ballpark?"

"No, he didn't say."

Jack thought a moment. "Did Lou ever have any visitors, here to the store?"

"No . . . no." He hesitated, as if he wanted to change the focus. "You know, Lou was a good man. Honest, hardworking. Some of the things they are saying about him are nonsense."

"Like what?"

"Like this crazy stuff that Lou was a red."

"Where'd you hear that?" asked Jack.

"The cops. And then the newspaper when he died." He cleared his throat in disgust. "*Commie Cockroach Squashed at the Griffith* was the headline in the paper—the lousy baboons."

"Were the feds here?" asked Jack.

"Yeah, they came here early one morning."

"What'd they ask you?"

The man banged his pipe against his hand before placing it on the wooden counter. "The same things you are. I really didn't have anything to tell them. They asked me if I knew Lou was with the communist party. I told them it was ridiculous."

Jack folded his arms and looked at the floor with a sigh. "Let me level with you. I'm looking for Lou's killer." He met the old man's gaze. "Anything you know you think will help me?"

The man shook his head. "I wish I did. But I can't help you there. The poor kid. To be cut up like a dog." He looked up at Jack. "You have my sympathies, young man."

"Well, I guess I have no more questions," said Jack. "Thank you, sir."

The man turned and brushed ashes off the counter. "You're welcome."

Jack walked out of the store and paused on the sidewalk to pat his pockets in search of his cigarettes. He spotted the teenage stock boy sitting on a log against the store's left wall. The kid was in need of a haircut, Jack noted; his curly red hair crept over his forehead and his sideburns were below his ears. Jack approached him and pulled out his pack of Lucky Strikes. "You smoke?" he asked.

The boy stared at the pack of cigarettes. "Sometimes," he answered.

Jack waved the pack. "Go ahead and take one."

The boy rose and removed a cigarette from the pack. Jack pulled out a box of matches. He lit a match and offered it.

The kid shook his head. "No thanks, mister. I'm gonna save it for later."

"What was your name again?" asked Jack.

"Jimmy."

"I'm Jack." He offered his hand and they shook.

Jack lit a cigarette for himself. "Did you know Lou?" he asked.

The boy put the cigarette over his right ear and sat back down. "Yeah, sure I did."

Jack exhaled a cloud of smoke. "Well, I'm his brother. How long did you know him?"

"Not as long as you," Jimmy quipped.

Jack chuckled and sat down on the same log, a foot away from the teenager. He leaned forward, cupping the cigarette in the palm of his left hand. "I've come here, all the way from St. Louis, to find out what happened to my brother. You got anything I might want to know?"

Jimmy shook his head. "Not really."

"What did you think of Lou?"

Jimmy reached for the red apron draped over the log beside him and placed it on his knees. "Lou was swell," he answered. "We used to go on deliveries together."

"Deliveries?" prompted Jack.

"Sure," said Jimmy. He jerked his chin toward the rear of the building. "See that old Lionel Ford truck in the back?"

Jack twisted sideways to look and made out a rusty black truck that had to be twenty years old. "Yeah."

"Lou and I used to deliver the large orders in that truck. Lou drove and I helped unload. But now, old man Gibbs has a new a new guy delivering and I just stay in the store."

"Gibbs?" asked Jack.

"The owner," Jimmy answered. "The guy you met in the store." He stared at Jack's cigarette. "Ah, what the hell," he said, pulling the cigarette out of his hair. He leaned toward Jack to light his cigarette off of Jack's.

"You know," said Jimmy, exhaling smoke, "we had some crazy times in that truck." He laughed. "You know, mister, some guy used to follow us when we were on delivery."

That brought Jack's head around. "Yeah? Who?"

Jimmy shook his head. "I don't know. At first, Lou thought it was funny." He flicked an ash and chuckled. "He used to drive around the block in circles just to drive the guy nuts."

"Who was this guy?" asked Jack.

"We never found out. Must have been in the money. Had a brand new Ford sedan."

"Did Lou ever tell you who he thought it might be?"

"No," answered Jimmy. "But I'll tell ya, the last couple of days—I mean before Lou died—he was kind of nervous when we drove. Kept checkin' out that rearview mirror. He wasn't laughing anymore."

"Like he saw it coming?" asked Jack.

"Yeah . . . " answered Jimmy. "That's what I've been wonderin'."

* * *

Jack swung the heavy glass door open and was overcome by smoke. He squinted through the haze, looking for Maggie's friends. Spotting Tom and some others, he made his way between tables to the back of the hall. He arrived in time to see the man with the heavy accent, Hans, down a shot of liquor, then exhale slowly.

Tom raised his arms, a cigarette in his left hand. "What does Ray say?" he asked Hans. "Why is there no contact?"

Hans spotted Jack and tapped Tom on the shoulder. Tom looked up and smiled. "Jack Harris, how good of you to come." He pointed to a chair. "Sit, sit down. Join us."

Jack nodded and pulled a wooden chair over to the corner of the table between Tom and Hans. Besides these two men, there were three others at the table that Jack had not met. Two were engaged in a chess game and the third studied the board from the side.

Tom pointed at the others. "Jack, these are some friends of ours. Fredrick, Gene, and Ryszard. This is Jack Harris."

Jack was about to extend his hand to the chess players, but they did not look up. Only the observer, Ryszard, rose and shook hands with Jack.

"Actually, it's Jack Haynes," said Jack.

"Another American," mumbled one of the chess players.

Hans turned to the chess player. "What do expect to find in America?"

Tom signaled for the waiter. "Another round," he yelled. "And more water." He turned to Jack. "Have you ever had Russian vodka?"

Jack shook his head. "Not unless Russians make moonshine in Kentucky."

Hans laughed. "He has Lou's sense of humor! You can tell they are brothers!"

Tom pulled Jack by the arm and whispered into his ear, "If there was justice, Ryszard would be recognized as a national hero."

"What do you mean?" asked Jack.

"Ryszard was key in the sit-down strikes in Flint, Michigan, a couple of years ago," Tom explained. "You know, when United Auto Workers was founded. First he helped the workers organize, then he supported them for weeks. Brought them food and barrels of coal so they could stay warm. One day, he delivered over a thousand loaves of bread to Plant Number One. To this day, none of us know how he did it. If you ask him, he just laughs."

"Jack!" yelled Hans. He jerked his chin toward a man in his late thirties who leaned over the chessboard. "You play chess? Gene is one of the top chess players around. He was once the champion of the Omsk Province."

Under a worker's cap pulled over his brow, Gene's small, dark eyes peered at Hans over a pugnacious nose. "I still champion of Omsk," he said in a Slavic accent. "No one beat me."

Not large, Jack thought, *but a forceful man.*

The waiter arrived with a bottle of vodka and put

down a shot glass for Jack. He poured everyone a drink and walked away.

Jack was about to answer Hans' question about chess when Hans raised his shot glass.

"Another toast to the revolution?" asked Ryszard. "Enough is enough."

Hans shook his head. "No, no. This one is for Lou." He raised the glass even higher. "To Lou."

All the men raised their glasses. "To Lou!" they yelled in unison.

Jack threw the shot into the back of his throat. It felt smooth at first, but as it went down, the drink kicked back. He shuddered.

The others noticed. Tom looked for the waiter. "Where's that water?" he yelled.

Hans turned to Ryszard. "Jack is here to look into Lou's murder. He wants to find out who took care of him."

Ryszard put down his shot glass and sighed. "That's not an easy task, given the circumstances. I would say it's impossible." The waiter appeared with a pitcher of water. "Bring back the bottle," he told the waiter. "And leave it on the table."

The waiter nodded and left.

"Jack strikes me as me someone very determined," said Hans to everyone. "The way Lou was."

Ryszard reached for a pack of Camels lying on the table. "Good luck," he murmured as he offered everyone a cigarette. Jack was the only one who accepted.

Eyes on Ryszard, Jack asked, "Did you know my brother?"

Ryszard glanced at Jack and then struck a match. "I met him once or twice."

"Ryszard isn't from our nucleus," Tom told Jack. "He's from another in D.C. We meet once in a while."

Ryszard reached over to Jack with the match in hand. Jack puffed his cigarette alight and nodded in appreciation. Exhaling the smoke through his nose, he asked Ryszard, "What does that mean? Why do you think finding Lou's killer is impossible?"

Ryszard lit his own cigarette. "There's nobody to back us up. We've seen this before. He's not the first to die for the cause."

The waiter returned with the bottle of vodka. He placed it in the center of the table and walked away. Hans reached for the bottle and poured everyone a drink.

Tom raised his glass. "To Lou and the revolution."

Everyone swung their shot glasses down in one swoop. Hans exhaled in satisfaction. He slammed his palms on the table and turned to Tom. "Do they still have those marinated mushrooms here?"

Tom shrugged. "Ask the waiter." He reached for the bottle and filled all the shot glasses again.

Jack kept his focus on Ryszard. "You know anything about Gullane Textiles in Virginia?"

"I know Lou met someone from that plant at Griffith Stadium," answered Ryszard.

Jack drew on his Camel. It was bitter, lacking the sweetness of his Lucky Strikes. "How do you know they met?" he asked. "I heard the meeting never took place."

Ryszard turned his palms up dismissively. "Well, I don't know if they actually met. But that's why he was there."

Hans raised his shot glass and looked at the others. Tom and Ryszard quickly reached for their glasses. Jack stared at his shot glass, again filled with vodka. *Oh brother, another one?* They all drank up and Jack waited for the kick, but it didn't come this time.

He turned to Ryszard. "You have any idea why the FBI would follow Lou into Griffith Stadium?"

As one, the men turned their heads to Jack. "The FBI was there?" asked Tom.

Jack nodded, hiding his satisfaction, and put out his cigarette. "Yeah, and I can prove it."

Hans raised his hands. "Well, there you go," he said. "That answers everything." He kept his right arm raised to draw the waiter's attention.

Tom turned to Jack. "Did you ever meet with Petrov?"

Jack shook his head. "No. I'm still waiting for a meeting."

"You have to meet with Petrov," insisted Tom. "I'm sure he can answer some of your questions."

Jack began to feel as if his body were floating. He looked down at his shot glass. *These guys are trying to get me drunk*, he suddenly realized.

The waiter arrived. "Get us another bottle, my good man!" yelled Hans. "You have those mushrooms?"

The waiter nodded. "For everyone?" he asked.

"Of course!" said Hans.

The waiter left. Jack picked up the vodka bottle and stared at the red label. The letters *CCCP* were stamped at the top, and underneath, *SSSR-Lux*. "What does that mean, SSSR-Lux?" he asked.

"It means it's the best," said Hans. He took the bottle from Jack. "See for yourself." He prepared to pour the last of its contents into Jack's shot glass.

Jack put his hand over the glass. "No, no. That's enough for me."

The men laughed. "What are you talking about?" asked a smiling Hans. "The night is young."

Tom leaned toward Jack. "How do you know the FBI were at Griffith Stadium?"

"I have witnesses placing them there," Jack replied.

"You seem passionate about this, Jack," said Tom. "But if there's no official interest in an investigation, nothing will happen."

"Maybe," Jack countered, "maybe not. I'm a newspaper guy; I've seen this before. It's just a question of knowing how to put pressure on the police."

"And how are you going to do that?" asked Tom.

"If I were a news guy here in Washington, it would be easy. I'd pound them with the pulp. But there are other ways."

Tom raised his eyebrows in curiosity. "Like what?"

"Like pitting one against the other."

"Who against who?"

Jack had thought this through. "You have the cops, you have the FBI, and you have the company goons. You make it seem as if one is trying to point to the other, and someone will crack."

"You have to meet with Petrov," Tom repeated firmly.

Gene moved a chess piece across the board and sat back. "Check mate," he said.

The others laughed. Hans turned to Jack. "Look at that. He plays us without a queen and he still wins!"

The waiter arrived with a new bottle of the SSSR vodka, a bowl of marinated mushrooms, and a stack of small plates. Hans opened the bottle and poured everyone a drink. He raised his shot glass. "To Lou's dreams!" he yelled.

Jack reached for the vodka, but he took only a small sip as they all downed the vodka in their glasses.

Hans reached for the mushrooms. "You would think the Americans would have caviar in their bars," he said as he handed out the plates to the others.

Ryszard grabbed his plate and reached for a fork. "I prefer mushrooms, if they're marinated the right way."

Hans shook his head. "The salt in caviar is good for you. Sea salt is the purest."

Jack asked Hans as he accepted a plate, "Where are you from, anyway?"

Hans didn't immediately reply. He had just popped a mushroom into his mouth and was savoring the moment, chewing with his eyes closed. He nodded. "These are excellent," he murmured. He reached for a napkin. "I am from the motherland," he said at last. "Russia."

From the corner of his eye, Jack saw a short man in glasses approaching. He turned his head, saw it was Ray. Hans also noticed and scanned the nearby tables for an empty chair. Ray nodded to everyone at the table, wearing a slight smile. Hans pulled a chair up to Ray's legs and he sat.

"Ray, is it true we lost contact with the workers in Ellicott City?"

Ray's shoulders dropped and he snickered. He punched his glasses back on his nose and shook his head. "Tom," he said slowly and deliberately, "as you must know, we do not discuss our affairs in front of those who are not party members."

The two chess players snickered as well.

Hans reached for the bottle and poured everyone a drink. Ray however, refused. "I will have coffee," he muttered to Hans.

Tom continued to look at Ray. He appeared upset by Ray's comment. "The unrest in Ellicott City is no secret," he told Ray. "It has been covered by every major newspaper."

Hans nodded, the movement exaggerated. "Yes, yes," he said. "But I see Ray's point. Our efforts are a different matter."

Ignoring both Tom and Hans, Ray looked at Jack with his piercing eyes. "Jack, did Maggie tell you that Lou made a list . . . a list of casualties?"

This is it, thought Jack. *This is the reason for the booze.* He shook his head. "Yeah, she asked me something about that. But the list is news to me. What do you think it means?"

Hans raised his shot glass and sniffed the contents. "Lou never completed the project," he said. "If we don't find his list, all his efforts were for nothing."

"So you want to continue his work?" asked Jack.

Tom nodded and raised his shot glass. "To Lou's work," he said.

They downed the vodka and Hans wiped his chin. "Lou's project was important. They are targeting us more and more. We have to prove it."

Jack left his glass on the table. His head had started to spin.

Staring at Jack's shot glass, Hans urged, "Come, come, drink up."

Jack shook his head. "That's enough for me," he said. "I'll have some coffee, like Ray."

* * *

"The FBI does not grant interviews to the papers," said

the secretary, a thin, middle-aged woman with pointed glasses and brown hair streaked with gray. "We put out press releases and schedule press conferences when we have something to report. If you think an agent is going to come down here and fill you in, you're wasting your time."

Jack flopped back into the wooden chair in the main lobby of the FBI headquarters. He wondered whether he should walk out or pull the trigger. He'd felt some apprehension when he walked into the building. There was always the chance he would be recognized. But it was too late now.

He leaned forward and stared at the woman. "Maybe I got something the agency wants to know."

She hiked her shoulders in a so-what gesture and continued with her typing.

"Lady, listen to me. I want to talk to someone about the Lou Harris investigation. The guy murdered in the ballpark. I may have something they want to know."

The woman sighed in resignation and picked up her phone. She jiggled the hook. "Sally, I got a tipster here on a murder case. A newspaper guy." She looked at Jack. "What was the name?"

"Lou Harris," he replied.

"Lou Harris," she repeated and put down the phone. "Cool your heels," she told Jack. "It may be a while."

Jack sat back in the chair and took a deep breath. *What are the odds?* he thought. *What are the odds someone could recognize my face? They must have warrants out on thousands of men.*

A tall man wearing a black suit eventually appeared and stared at Jack with curiosity. He escorted Jack to a side room containing a plain wooden table and several chairs. "How can I help you?" he asked as they both sat down.

Jack cleared his throat. "My name is Jack Haynes. I'm with the *Washington Chronicle*. I was wondering if you cared to comment on the Lou Harris investigation."

The man shook his head. "That name you gave the secretary—Lou Harris—well, there's no such case in our records. Where'd this murder occur?"

"Here in D.C.," said Jack, managing to hide his surprise.

"Then I suggest you go to the Washington police and ask them."

"But I know you're involved in the case. You had a bunch of agents at his autopsy."

The man leaned over the table toward Jack. "That's simply not true."

Jack reached into his trench coat pocket and pulled out a pen and a pad of paper. "Now I know I got a story," he said.

The FBI man appeared about to speak but stopped abruptly, looking thoughtful. "Wait here," he said, and left.

Jack slowly exhaled. *There's no need to worry,* he told himself. *These bums don't know who I am.* He wondered why the FBI had attended the autopsy. *If they were involved in the murder, you would think they'd stay away from the morgue. On the other hand, they might attend just to pressure the coroner to make sure his report is in their favor.*

Another man appeared at the door. He wore an off-brown suit and had tufts of gray around the ears. "Mr. Haynes?" he asked.

Jack nodded.

"Hello. I'm Special Agent Wayne Mullen." He lifted

his square jaw. "Let me see your press identification papers."

Jack reached inside his jacket as if searching for identification. He patted his chest. "I must have left it at the hotel," he said.

"Hotel? I thought you're working here in D.C.," Mullen said.

Realizing he had screwed up, Jack tried to think quickly. "I just did a story at the Saratoga Hotel. I must have left my ID there."

The man pulled back one of the wooden chairs and awkwardly folded his tall frame onto it. "How can I help you?"

"I'm just wondering why the FBI attends the autopsy of a murdered red and then denies it."

"We checked our records. We have no investigation going on for this Lou Harris. Someone must have given you a bum steer."

Jack shook his head. "No, no. I got a reliable witness. Places your agents there."

Mullen shrugged. "What hospital was this?"

"City Hospital, here in D.C."

"Look, maybe some agents were there on some other case. Maybe the case they were involved in was over and they stood there in conversation. Or maybe they were in the morgue waiting for their case to start. Who knows? You ever been in a morgue? It's one case after another."

Jack decided to pull the trigger again. "You know about a list this Lou Harris had put together?"

Mullen stared at Jack with a stony face. "What kind of list?"

"Apparently this guy Harris had some sort of list. I hear a lot of people want it."

Mullen leaned slightly forward. "You have this list?" he asked.

Ha! He took the bait, Jack thought. *He knows about Lou and the list.* "I only got a list of questions," he said. "And it's getting longer."

The FBI man stared at Jack for a long second. "We all got questions. So what?"

"You know about a list?" Jack pressed.

Mullen frowned. "I already told you. We are not investigating the name you gave us and I certainly know nothing about a list."

"Then why did you ask me if I have it?" asked Jack.

Mullen scowled. "Get the hell out of here."

* * *

"Want bread?" asked Maggie. She tipped the ladle, pouring Jack a bowl of steaming potato soup. The kitchen in her apartment was small, with barely enough room for two at the table.

"Sure, thanks," said Jack. He picked up his spoon and started working on the soup, still mulling over his meeting earlier in the day.

Mullen's involved in this, he thought. *I got the feds at the stadium and in the morgue. When I waltz into the FBI headquarters, they call a second guy to see me and he asks me if I got the list.*

Pausing to blow on the soup in his spoon, Jack looked at Maggie. "If Lou was walking with this guy wearing a boater, he must have known him and trusted him," he said. "I'll bet the guy either killed Lou or led him into the hands of the killer."

Maggie gripped half a loaf of bread in her hand. She

cut off a slice with a small knife before asking, "You think the guy wearing the boater was the contact from that mill?"

"He doesn't sound like a worker," answered Jack. "Not wearing that boater. If he wasn't the contact from the mill, he might have pretended to bump into Lou while Lou was waiting for the contact."

Maggie handed Jack a thick slice of bread and shook her head. "Who knows?" She sounded resigned.

"You sure Lou didn't say anything about meeting anyone else?"

She removed her apron, revealing a white blouse and a long, pleated blue skirt. "I'm positive. I would have remembered that."

"It's possible industry is killing union organizers and the cops and the FBI are in on it," said Jack.

"I wouldn't be surprised," Maggie agreed.

"They found out Lou was putting together a list of murdered activists and they took care of him," Jack continued.

"A lot of companies hire these thugs," said Maggie. "They call them detective agencies, but they're really terror groups."

"Has anyone from your group gone down and talked to these workers in the mill?" asked Jack.

"Not that I know of."

"Why not?"

Maggie shrugged. "How's that gonna help?"

"To find out if they actually met Lou, find out if this textile mill hires goons to do their dirty work."

"I guess it wouldn't hurt," said Maggie. "But after a murder like this, I imagine everybody would clam up."

"I think I may pay that place a visit," said Jack matter-of-factly. "I would need someone to go with me from the party for credibility." He waited for her to volunteer, but she remained silent.

"They won't talk to a newspaper guy," he added.

He kept waiting, but she just stood there, cutting another slice of bread.

"Didn't that girl Sue say she was from Virginia?" he finally asked.

Maggie shook her head. "Sue's out."

"What do you mean?"

"She's in hot water with the party," said Maggie.

"Why's that?"

"Too independent. I think they're gonna dump her."

"In that case, why don't you come with me?" he asked.

Maggie frowned. "I would need Ray's okay. I can't just do it on my own."

"Well, then . . . can you ask him?"

"Sure," she answered. She looked up, met his gaze and held it for a long moment. Jack couldn't read her expression. She seemed to be weighing him. Then she deliberately set down the knife and walked behind his chair. A moment later he felt her hands settle on his shoulders. Their weight felt first alien, then soothing. His eyelids drooped as she began rubbing the muscles in his shoulders and neck, smoothing away the tension and replacing it with an acute awareness of the warmth and pressure of her fingers. "You know, Lou used to talk about you," she whispered.

It had been a while since Jack had felt a woman's tender touch. For a long second, he had forgotten the subject of their conversation.

"He used to tell me things about you," she added.

Jack wondered what she meant by that. "What'd he say?" he mumbled.

"He'd tell me how you used to teach him."

"Teach him what?"

She slipped her right hand down his chest and stroked gentle circles. "About everything," she murmured.

Everything? thought Jack, tensing involuntarily. *Does she know I abandoned him?* "Well, did he tell you I could have stayed with him, but I took off?"

He felt her hair brushing back and forth against his neck as she shook her head. "No," she said, her voice still soft. "He used to tell me about the two of you growing up in Baltimore. Lot of kids on your street, from what I heard."

Jack chuckled. "Yeah, our gang was okay."

Maggie traced fingers across the back of Jack's neck; it felt good, and he settled back again to enjoy it. "He used to tell me how you taught him everything from sneaking into the movies to playing baseball," she said. "And how you two snuck into the ballpark to watch games."

Her tone was curious; it almost sounded as if she was talking down to him. But he could only think of the fingers on his neck. "Yeah, we had some fun."

Maggie pushed her hand beneath Jack's collar and stroked his upper back with her fingers. Jack closed his eyes, letting his mind wander back to his old row house in Baltimore. He and Lou had spent most of their time on the front steps, either playing with the neighborhood kids or waiting for their mother to come home from work.

Jack opened his eyes. "You ever here of anyone calling Lou 'Dutch'?"

"Oh yeah," answered Maggie. "That's what the priests

used to call him. He didn't like it that much. He liked being called Lou."

"Why did they call him Dutch?"

"Because when Lou got to the orphanage, he had one of those haircuts—you know, with the hair cut the same all around the head, like a Dutch boy."

"So what did he tell you about the priests?"

"It's like I said the other day. He liked the brothers. Took their lessons to heart." She snickered. "Lou thought Christianity held the key for justice in the workplace."

"So what's wrong with that?" asked Jack.

"Nothing, except that if you believe in that, then the logical extension is that Christian leaders decide what's justice. And that's what they've been doing for two thousand years—telling people what they should think." She pulled her hand away. "Telling them what sinners they are and that their only redemption is through them."

"Lou ever tell you about the foster home he was in before he got to the orphanage?" Jack asked as Maggie stepped back over to her chair. He missed her fingers on his back.

"No." Maggie sat down, leaned back, and folded her arms. "Still, I got to admit, the priests did put Lou on the right track. That is, they told him to look for social justice. You know what Lou once told me?"

"What?"

"He said the first time he thought of equal distribution of wealth was when he was giving out food to the unemployed."

Jack raised his eyebrows. "Lou worked in a soup line?"

"No, not in a soup kitchen. The brothers gave out food when they could and the boys helped. Lou told me about these poor men with their tired faces and ragged clothes. How they didn't have a dime to their name. Many of them with kids."

That was a sight Jack did not want to imagine. There were rough times in St. Louis, too. Jack realized with a twinge of shame that he had always ignored the penniless. There was always the chance that if the paychecks stopped coming, he could be next. "Yeah," he said. "Rough times for a lot of folks."

"And just down the street from the orphanage there was a fancy restaurant with stuffed shirts stuffing their faces. Those were the exact words Lou used," she said, nodding to herself. "Stuffed shirts stuffing their faces."

Jack nodded. "I can imagine how Lou felt."

Maggie suddenly stood. "What time is it?"

Jack had no idea. He shrugged.

"I almost forgot; there's a concert on that I want to hear," she said, running into the parlor.

Jack finished the last of his soup and followed her into the room. He removed a robe and a blouse from the couch and sat down to examine the radio, a Marconi combination record player and radio. *That's a nice piece of equipment for someone who couldn't afford to pay for a funeral,* he thought.

Maggie turned the dial until he heard classical music. She turned and studied his face, as if trying to determine if he was impressed. "Do you recognize it?" she asked.

Jack shook his head. "No."

Maggie chuckled. "It's Mozart. Symphony No. 26. One of my favorites." She started for the kitchen. "Want a beer?" she called back.

"Sure," he answered. As she disappeared into the

kitchen, he sat back on the couch and felt his muscles relax.

"This broadcast is coming all the way from New York City," she yelled from the kitchen. "Can you believe that?"

"It's amazing," he replied, though his mind still lingered on the way she had caressed him. He had not experienced this sort of intimacy in a long time.

She returned with the beer. "Do you like Mozart?" she asked as she handed it to him.

Jack shrugged. "I don't listen to classical music."

Maggie sat down on the couch beside him and folded her leg up on the cushion. "That's too bad. It ennobles one."

She sounded like one of those pretentious rich women in the movies. He took a sip of the Bohemian Beer. "I'm surprised you like it," he said. "I mean, isn't it the music of rich people? What you call the bourgeois?"

Maggie let out a cackle and lifted her chin. "No, quite the opposite. The music of Mozart is one of the highest achievements of man. It wasn't appreciated in its time. Much like the science of communism in our time."

Jack was not convinced. "I don't know. I always associate that kind of music with phony rich people."

Maggie stared at him. Her facial muscles tightened. Jack realized he had hit a raw nerve. "Well, maybe it's because you don't know how to appreciate beauty," she said, her voice stiff.

With that one cheap shot, the intimacy Jack had felt just seconds ago vanished. He leaned forward, rested his elbows on his knees, and studied the label on his beer. "Maybe. Or maybe I just think it's phony."

The broadcast faded and Maggie rose and walked

over to fiddle with the radio. Jack could not help staring at her figure.

"Well, I guess it's not surprising," she said, her back still to him, "from a newspaper guy from St. Louis."

Jack found himself on his feet without realizing he'd stood. "What's that supposed to mean?" he asked, voice rough.

Maggie shrugged as she turned the radio's dial. "Nothing."

Now she was starting to sound like a snob herself. He took several steps toward her. "Do I get you right?" he asked. "A waitress from a Kentucky diner is calling me a hick?"

Maggie turned away from the radio and glared at Jack. "There's nothing wrong with being a waitress in a Kentucky diner," she snapped.

"And there's nothing wrong with being a newspaper man from St. Louis," he countered.

She opened her mouth as if about to reply, then, with a fleeting look of surprise, she shut it again. Jack stood waiting to see what she would do next. His nerve endings thrummed with adrenaline, and he realized it wasn't the argument that was stimulating his senses.

Maggie put her head down and started for the kitchen. "Want another beer?" she asked, voice carefully neutral.

As she passed, Jack grabbed her by the arm and pulled her into his arms. He felt her body trembling. Not only did she not resist, but she looked up, lips parted as if to let him know she was willing. He bent, mouth hovering over hers for a second, and then he pressed his lips to hers. Her mouth was soft and warm, her tongue aggressive. His hand lingered on her skirt, cupping her bottom and caressing her hips.

She broke off the kiss and stared at him. There was an expression in her eyes he was not sure how to interpret, until she took him by the hands and led him toward her bedroom. The room itself was tiny, with only one small window near the ceiling covered by a curtain that left the room almost totally dark.

Jack nuzzled her neck and then searched for her lips as she undressed him. He undressed her, his hands roaming over her skin, enjoying its warmth and softness. They moved onto the bed, kissing and caressing until Jack could take it no more, and they joined. When his body shuddered, Maggie grabbed him tightly, held him as he took several deep breaths. He rolled onto his back, and Maggie jumped to her knees and hovered over him. She smiled and brushed his hair off his forehead with her hand.

"Not bad for a hick," she quipped.

* * *

"The crazed, the idiotic, and the poor!" someone yelled. Jack had been staring at the pavement as he walked down the street, but the exclamation brought his head up. A man wearing a three-piece single-breasted suit stood on the sidewalk in front of a group of tourists, pointing to an open space between row houses. "This was the location of the Washington Asylum," he continued with authority. "A popular tourist attraction of the nineteenth century. Here the wretched syphilitics spent the last days of their lives."

Jack shook his head as he walked by the crowd, wondering why tourists would be attracted to such a place. His thoughts returned to the Sampson story, one of Jack's greatest achievements as a reporter. Bill Sampson had been the owner of a successful luggage store in St. Louis. When a young woman employed in his store was murdered, Jack was put on the story. The police nabbed the killer, but Jack suspected from the beginning that Sampson was somehow involved. He'd tricked Sampson into admitting he knew the killer by bluffing during an interview; he told Sampson that the killer had admitted to police that Sampson was in the car when he drove away from the store with the body in the trunk. When Sampson quickly replied that it was ridiculous, the man didn't even know how to drive, Jack knew he had him. He asked Sampson how he knew this, and the man melted and ended up confessing to the police that he'd hired the man to kill the woman after an affair with her went bad. He was hoping to use the same tactic on the cop, Warner, and bluff something he could use out of him.

He spotted a newsstand and bought a copy of the *Washington Chronicle*, then flipped through the pages until he came to the paper's masthead. He went through the list: president, vice president, production manager, circulation director. Finally he found the managing editor: Wallis Gardner. He tossed the paper into a garbage can and turned onto Pomeroy Street, heading toward the police station.

The officer behind the counter was the same young cop who'd been there on Jack's first visit, and he was reading the same comic book: *The Adventures of Dick Tracy, Detective #707*. Chuckling as he passed the desk, Jack ran up the stairs to the second floor and asked at the counter for Lieutenant Warner. As he waited, he wondered how long it would take the young cop downstairs to finish reading one comic book.

The pear shaped Lieutenant Warner appeared at the door, wiping his lips.

"Sorry to bother you again Lieutenant," said Jack. "I'm the guy from the *Chronicle* who was here last week. Remember?"

Warner didn't react. He looked puzzled.

"Old man Gardner is giving me a hard time about this case. He thinks we have a chance to break it wide open. I mean that guy who was killed at the ballpark. Are you willing to comment on this red's involvement in the bank robberies?"

Warner frowned, still confused. "Red in a baseball park?"

"You know," said Jack, "Lou Harris, murdered at Griffith Stadium."

"Oh, yeah. Lou Harris." His expression cleared and he nodded. "But I never heard anything about no robberies."

"First I thought it was just two banks here in town, but then I got the dope from the feds," said Jack. "There was a third bank in Virginia."

"The feds?"

"Yeah, the FBI. What was that fed's name?" Jack grimaced, snapping his fingers repeatedly, as if in thought. "I got it on the tip of my tongue."

"You mean Mullen? Wayne Mullen?"

"Yeah, that's it. Mullen. He says this red fits the description in all three jobs." Jack pulled his pad from his coat pocket. "Anyway, are you willing to comment on this Lou Harris' involvement in the robberies?"

"Why the hell is Mullen telling you shit I don't know?" the lieutenant blurted.

Jack shrugged. "When was the last time you spoke to Agent Mullen?"

"Hell, I don't know," said Warner. "When did Mullen tell you this?"

Jack pretended to scribble on his pad, but he actually only jotted down an exclamation point; Warner knew Mullen, and that was significant. He looked up. "Just yesterday. Is this a combined investigation between D.C. and the feds?"

Warner slowly shook his head. "I got no comment."

"Come on, Lieutenant. This is a great story. It would get Gardner off my back. And it would put a feather in the force's cap as well."

Warner's eyes narrowed. "What you mean?"

Jack spread his arms and feigned excitement. "D.C.'s finest combining forces with the FBI? It's great!"

Warner's face flushed red. He pointed his finger at Jack. "Listen to me, punk. I don't want to see your face in here again. You got that? Now get out of here."

Jack knew he had hit a nerve. "Okay, but I ain't givin' up that easy," he said as he turned. "I got a job to do, you know," he muttered as he walked away.

✳ ✳ ✳

Jack threw what was left of his cigarette onto the pavement and walked down the stairs into the Waverly Cafeteria. A large flock of tourists was lined up at the counter, so he thrust his hands in his trench coat and joined the queue. The wait suited him fine; he'd have a chance to look for Sue. Maggie still seemed reluctant to go to the textile mill in Virginia and he did not want to push her. Sue was the logical choice to accompany him.

Not only did she know the area, but she seemed to be the independent type, willing to act without anyone's permission.

He scanned the smoke-filled hall as the line slowly shuffled forward. Finally he spotted Sue clearing dishes from a table near the far wall. Leaving the line, he wove between the tables and stopped on the other side of the table she was clearing.

"Hi, remember me?" he asked.

Sue looked up and smiled. "Sure, you're Lou's brother."

"I was wondering if I could have a word with you about Lou."

She hesitated and glanced toward the kitchen. "I guess I can take a quick break. Sit down."

They sat down at the table, looking at one another over the dirty dishes. Jack inched forward on his chair. "Lou was killed when he was trying to meet a worker from this mill in Virginia, you know that?"

She shrugged. "Sure. That's no secret."

"Well, I'm surprised none of you visited this mill to find something out," he said.

"That's not up to me," she replied.

"I'm going there, but I can't go alone."

She raised a brow. "Why not?"

"They won't open up to a newspaper guy."

She glanced toward the kitchen. "So what is it you want?"

"Would you be willing to go with me?"

Sue sighed. "Does Ray know about this?"

"Why?"

"That's how we work."

"It's none of my business," said Jack, "but I hear you're in hot water with the party."

She snickered. "Who told you that, Maggie?"

"Well, I . . . "

"It's okay," she said. "You don't have to answer." She glanced again toward the kitchen and quickly rose. "Yeah, that's true. I guess I'm out."

"What happened?" Jack asked.

Sue picked up a plate and scraped what was left of a bacon and egg breakfast onto another plate. "We're better off not talking about it," she said.

"Would you need Ray's permission to go?" he asked.

"He's the head of the nucleus," she answered.

"If you're out, do Ray and the others really matter?" asked Jack.

Sue kept her eyes on the table as she started stacking the dirty dishes. "It's not just that."

"Then what?" Jack pressed.

She looked at him. "It's just that I'm sick of the whole thing. Meeting, plotting, negotiating, spying, and what does it lead to?"

"I'm not plotting anything," said Jack. "All I want is justice for my brother."

She looked toward the kitchen and sat back down with her eyes on Jack. "No one will tell you anything if you go down there," she said. "Even if the workers know something, they won't spill it to a stranger—even to a member."

"Did you like Lou?" he asked.

She blinked. "What?"

"Were you fond of him?"

Sue shrugged. "Of course I liked him. Lou had a good heart. That's not easy to find."

The gentle way she said "Lou had a good heart" mesmerized Jack. For a second, he forgot what he was after. "So, isn't it worth a try?" he finally asked. "For Lou?"

Sue stared at the dishes in silence.

"I came all the way from St. Louis to look into this," continued Jack. "All I'm asking is that you take a quick ride on a train with me to northern Virginia. I'll pay."

As Jack stared at her, waiting for her answer, he thought of what she had just said. For some strange reason, he was surprised to hear that his little brother had established his own life in the adult world. It seemed from what everyone was saying that Lou had touched others in a way that Jack had been unable to do.

She finally looked up and smiled. "You're a good salesman."

Hoping his silence would get to her, Jack did not respond.

"Okay," she finally said. "I'll go with you. I'll do it for Lou."

Jack returned her smile. "Great. I know Lou would appreciate this."

As Sue started to rise, Jack extended his arm to her. "Wait—there's something else I wanted to ask you."

She sat back down, widening her eyes in curiosity.

"What was between Maggie and Lou?" he asked. "I mean, were they in love, or was it some sort of partnership to support the party?"

Sue brushed her hair back and chuckled. "They were a funny couple. Always arguing, even in front of other people."

"So they were a couple?" he asked.

"Yeah, they were," she answered. Her eyes slid away. "But . . ."

"But what?"

She looked at him. "They weren't a good match. Not by any means."

"Why do you say that?" asked Jack.

She responded with a faraway smile. "I don't know . . . I just don't know what he saw in her. Lou needed much more than someone like Maggie was able to give."

Had Sue been in love with Lou? he wondered. Aloud he said, "I guess it doesn't matter now."

Sue sighed and rose. "I guess not." She lifted a stack of dishes off the table and pressed the stack against her hip.

Jack rose as well. "So, when are you free to go to Virginia?"

* * *

Jack thought about what Sue had said about Maggie as he pulled himself up the handrail, climbing the stairs to his hotel room on the third floor. Had she and Lou loved one another? Had Sue loved Lou? He shook his head. "Doesn't matter anymore anyway," he muttered. But there was so much, he was realizing, that he didn't know about his brother.

Stopping before his door to reach into his pocket for the key, he noticed the crack of light under the door and paused with his hand on the knob. Slowly releasing the knob, he tipped his head toward the door and listened. Voices.

Without thinking, he lunged at the door handle and swung the door open. Three men stood in the room; they turned their heads toward him as the door slammed open.

"What the hell is this?" Jack barked, taking in his possessions strewn over the floor, the open dresser drawers, and the mattress propped against the wall.

A man wearing a black overcoat grabbed a handful of Jack's trench coat and yanked him into the room. A second man slipped behind and kicked the door closed, then walked over to stand before Jack. He was tall; he towered above Jack as he gazed at him for a long second. Jack stared at the man's thin black moustache, wondering what was coming.

The man grinned just before his fist hit Jack square in the stomach, sending him to the floor. Jack lay there, gasping for air, but he could not breathe. The man swung his foot back, and another blow to the stomach followed. Senseless with pain, Jack lay on the floor, squirming.

The man in the black overcoat moved to stand over him. "Where is it?" he demanded.

Someone pulled Jack's hair, yanking his head upward. "Well?" Jack heard.

Blinking tears of pain, Jack tried to pull the hand off his scalp, but agony kept him curled around his stomach. Someone else spoke; Jack couldn't make out the words. His belly loosened and he sucked in air, then exhaled. "Where's what?" he managed to get out.

"No games," said the man in the black coat. "Give it to us."

"What the hell are you talking about?" Jack wheezed.

A blow to his chest drove the breath from his body again.

The third intruder had been standing against the window. He had not moved, but now Jack saw him approach from the corner of his eye as he lay there, sucking in air. He stood over Jack with his hands in his pants pockets, his teeth working a toothpick in his mouth. "Mr. Haynes," he finally said, "you must know why we are here."

Jack shook his head. "Tell me."

"You have a list, Mr. Haynes," said the man with the toothpick. "And some photographs."

"I don't have any list," Jack moaned.

The man in the black overcoat pulled a knife from his pocket and looked at the man with the toothpick. "So?"

The man with the toothpick shook his head. "No, Mr. Haynes will help us." He turned to Jack. "Mr. Haynes. It is very important that you give us the list and anything else you have."

"I don't even know what you're talking about," Jack answered. "What kind of list?"

The man jerked his chin toward the one with the knife. "My friend here is getting impatient."

Jack shook his head. "If I had something, I would give it to you."

The man in the black overcoat kicked Jack in the head, and a sheet of white pain blinded him. Another kick, in the ribs. Jack felt something snap in his chest, then intense pain shot through his right side.

"It's very simple, Mr. Haynes," said the man with the toothpick. "You give us what you have and we leave. We're in no hurry—we can stay here all night." He walked over to a chair against the wall and sat down. "All night, Mr. Haynes."

Jack managed to get on his hands and knees and looked up. The man with the toothpick leaned back in his chair and smiled. Jack squinted at him. A brown suit of some heavy fabric hung on his thin frame, and a cheap-looking fedora covered greasy black hair. He played with the toothpick in his mouth.

"Your brother put together a list and took some photographs. Give them to us and we leave. It's that simple."

They'd kill him if he didn't do something. But he could barely breathe—pain stabbed his chest when he tried to inhale. He glanced at the door; it was only a few feet away and still partially open. He looked back into the room and saw the mattress against the wall. "The mattress," he whispered. "The undersurface . . . in the lining."

The man in the black coat walked up to the mattress and held up his knife. "Look out," he said to the others. He stabbed the knife into the mattress at one corner and pulled the knife down, tearing it open. As he started ripping out the straw, the other two joined him. All three began pulling the stuffing out of the mattress until straw covered the floor.

Jack watched the men absorbed in their quest. *Now or never,* he decided. Taking a deep breath, he lunged for the door. His right shoulder grazed the doorframe as he rolled out into the corridor. He tried to rise, but did not have the strength. Scrambling on all fours, he managed to make it to the staircase and scrabbled down the steps, one hand clutching his chest. Behind him, one of the men yelled something.

Jack's face slammed against the wall of the stairway. He lifted his left arm and grabbed the rail, pulled himself partway upright, and swung around to the next set of stairs. He tried to stand, but pain seared through his midriff; he squatted on the top step, staring at the steps below him. He could hear his panting breath echoing in the stairwell, and below that, footsteps on the landing above. He dove forward and rolled.

"No! No!" someone yelled behind him. "Let him go."

Jack continued rolling until he thudded onto plush carpeting. He pushed himself to his hands and knees and crawled blindly, gasping for air, still caring only about getting away. Finally he looked up; he was in the lobby.

* * *

Jack took the last sip of whiskey from the shot glass and sighed as it burned down the back of his throat. Maggie refilled the glass and sat down across from him at her kitchen table. "You better not go back there," she said. "They may still be there waiting for you."

Jack shifted, felt a spasm of pain in the right side of his chest, and grimaced. "I'm not staying there anymore," he told her. "They've got my things in storage. That son of a bitch hotel manager wanted me to pay for the damage. I told him I'd sue. 'Where the hell was your house detective?' I asked. 'Thugs walk into my room and beat the shit out of me, all on his watch, and you want me to pay for the damage?'"

"So, what happened?"

"He got the message and agreed to hold my things until I pick them up."

Maggie lifted a wet rag from a bowl and wrung out the excess water. "I hate to see you like this," she said as she held the rag against Jack's swollen right cheek. Jack slipped his hand under hers to hold the rag, enjoying its soothing coolness.

Maggie knelt in front of him and lay her head in his lap. Lifting his right hand, she pressed it to her lips, kissing the back of his hand repeatedly before turning it over. She pressed her right cheek into the palm of his hand. "I've got to go to work," she said. "There's stew in the icebox and bread in the cupboard. It's kind of stale, but you can dip it in the stew."

"Where do you work, anyway?" asked Jack.

"Delaware Bus Lines," she said as she rose. "I do the evening shift at the station." She walked out into the living room and opened the closet door. "By the way, I saw Ray. He set up a meeting for you with Petrov—Tuesday, one forty-five, at the Royal Theater."

"And where's that?"

"Right off of Connecticut Avenue. You meet in the main lobby. One forty-five will be between shows. Traffic should be adequate."

It struck Jack that she recited the time and place without thinking twice. She had been well trained by the party. "How will I know him?" he asked.

"He'll find you," she answered. She fixed her layered skirt and threw her brown cloak over her shoulders. "You can play the radio if you want," she added. "I'll be back just after midnight. Don't take up all of the bed." Smiling, she left the apartment.

Jack swallowed the whiskey in his glass in one gulp and thought of the thugs in the hotel room. The list Lou had put together had to be a bombshell. It may have been the reason he was killed. So where was it?

Jack slowly rose to his feet. The pain in his chest made him squirm, but he managed to walk out of the kitchen. Entering the bedroom, he looked around; no sign of Lou's possessions. He opened the closet, saw men's clothes on some of the hangers, pushed against the wall. *Those have to be Lou's jackets.* Pulling the hangers toward him, Jack went through the pockets. He was about to give up when he felt a folded piece of paper in the inside pocket of an old brown jacket against the wall. He pulled the scrap of paper out, straightened it, and read its contents:

e) The organizer is responsible for attendance and the activity of the captains of the nuclei; the captain in turn is responsible for the attendance and activities of his nucleus.

f) Meetings are to start on time and last less than two hours. This means the agenda must be well prepared by buro before the meeting.

g) No minutes are to be kept during the meeting. The captain will make notes immediately after the meeting to insure that all decisions are carried out.

h) No records are to be kept in headquarters; every record should be taken away from the premises after the day's activities.

i) It is absolutely imperative that all records be removed from a headquarters before the initiation of a demonstration. This also includes typewriters and mimeographs. In the event that the typewriter cannot be removed and as a last resort, the ribbon should be stripped off the typewriter and destroyed as soon as possible.

The list of instructions went on and on. Jack put the

paper back in the jacket and examined the inside pocket. He saw another sheet of paper, folded over several times. Jack pulled it out and unfolded it—a letter, over a year old:

July 28, 1938

Dear Dutch,

Thank you for your letter of June the sixteenth. I am glad to hear all is fine with you in Washington. As you may have heard, there have been large downpours in Baltimore over the past few days and unfortunately our canteen was flooded. The boys have been forced to eat their meals in the gymnasium. This not only disrupts their sports activities but also forces the cooks to carry their huge pots of food up a flight of stairs and through the corridors to the other side of the building. God willing, the water damage will be repaired soon and things will return to their normal chaotic self.

The argument you presented in your last letter is unconvincing. I must preface my point by stating that I am impressed by the amount of study you have done on your own. Now, then: I must state that I still do not agree with your view that communism represents a natural result of human progress based on lessons from capitalism and Christianity. To conclude that communism represents an extension of Christianity in the workplace is fundamentally flawed.

Whereas participation in Christianity is voluntary, any social organization that forces all members of its society to participate in its structure, such as communism, is by definition a mandatory participation and therefore a form of slavery.

Still more, from a pragmatic point of view, communism will never work because of the "weak link phenomenon." You may have come across this in your readings. As you know, any social network is only as good as its weakest link— that is, where the chain will be first to break. In communism, members of society are forced to participate even if they do not believe in the cause. Do you believe such a network can compete against a religious organization such as the Roman Catholic Church, where all participation is voluntary and a great majority believe in its cause? Certainly not. I will grant you that a communist society may succeed if all participation is voluntary and its ideology respected by all participants. But such a society can only succeed on a small scale, such as on a farm or a small island. This ideology certainly cannot succeed for all humanity. I believe the purges and famines in the Soviet Union prove my point.

On the other hand, I do agree with the point you raise about the Jesuits. Through the centuries, many have indeed studied the Jesuits in an attempt to uncover the secrets behind their success, sometimes with the

*worst intentions. But there is one point you
have overlooked in your argument. Not only
was their participation voluntary, but they
did not seek rewards in this world. This
separates them from any organization planning for immediate worldly success. Think
about that.*

*I agree with you that the boys should
have gotten a summer break, but I am told
most classes are way behind in the curricu-
lum. Still, most of the kids do get to play
baseball in the afternoons.*

*We all miss you here, Dutch. Keep in
touch.*

*Sincerely,
Father Douglas McFarland
St. Mary's Industrial School for Boys.*

It was clear to Jack that this Father McFarland knew
Lou much better than the priest Jack had met in the
confessional. This priest not only knew Lou was a communist, but also freely exchanged views on the subject.

As Jack placed the letter back in the pocket, he made
out a large brown box on the floor of the closet. He
thought of bending over, but decided it would be less
painful to get down on his knees. Carefully lowering
himself to the floor, he pulled out the box and flipped
back the cardboard flaps on its top.

The contents were a jumble. On the top of the heap
was a framed photo of workers in a factory. Jack studied
the faces and spotted a smiling Lou on the periphery. It
appeared the workers had just won a battle against man-

agement. Jack pushed the photo aside, revealing several dime novels and two leather-bound books underneath. He went through the pages of each book but found nothing of interest. Stacking the books on the floor beside him, he lifted out and examined the remainder of the box's contents. Nothing unusual: a tin containing some tobacco, handkerchiefs, a lighter, a folded knife, and under those, copies of communist newspapers.

Jack found the camera when he pulled out the newspapers. He picked it up, recognized it as a Kodak Regent folding camera with a coupled range finder. His searching fingers found the latch to unfold the camera and pulled. When he found the hook to unlock the chamber, he pulled the cardboard box aside, shuffled into the closet, and closed the door. In the total darkness, he unlocked the chamber and felt inside with his fingers. The camera was empty; there was no film in its interior. He opened the door, put the camera aside, and pulled the box toward him again.

On the bottom of the box he found Lou's old baseball glove: a brown Rawlings glove his mother had bought Lou at a pawnshop. He pulled out the glove, pushed his left hand into it, and tried to suppress a sudden wave of emotion. Closing his eyes, he pressed the glove against his nose to smell the leather. The day Lou came home with the glove was a day Jack would never forget. He'd been a teenager, and Lou was only eight years old.

* * *

The door flew open. Lou ran up to the kitchen table. "Look, Jack!" he yelled. "A Billy Doak's."

Immersed in his math homework, Jack did not pay attention. "Leave me alone, will you? I got stuff to do."

Lou pounded his fist into the glove. "Want to play catch?"

The thud of a fist hitting the leather got through to Jack. He looked up. Lou was holding a Bill Doak-style brown leather glove. The glove was not new, but it was in good shape. It was a full adult size, and dwarfed Lou's small hand.

"Where'd you get that?" asked Jack.

"Mom got it for me. Want to play catch?"

Stunned, Jack could only stare at Lou. *How'd he get a glove?* They had no money, not even to pay the rent, and there was Lou, smiling ear to ear, holding a glove much better than his own.

The door to the apartment swung back open. "Help me with this, Jack," his mother said as she let the two bags she carried slip from her thin arms onto the floor.

Jack slowly rose from his chair, still wondering how this could have happened. As he picked up the bags and walked them over to the kitchen table, his eyes returned to Lou and the glove. He remembered Lou's question. "Nah, I ain't got time now."

His mother removed her coat and put on a stained white apron. "You bring up the coal like I asked you to?"

Jack had completely forgotten. "I was just gonna do it now," he replied.

"Momma," yelled Lou, "I'm gonna go show Tommy."

She pulled her brown hair back and tucked it up into a bob. "You be back for dinner," she told Lou as he ran out.

Jack pulled a sack of oatmeal and a loaf of day-old bread his mother had gotten from the mission out of the bag. "How . . . how did Lou get that glove?" he asked.

"I got it at Thatcher's Pawn Shop," his mother said casually, reaching under the counter to pull out a large pot.

"But how did you get the money?" he asked.

"Remember that brooch Aunt Sophia gave me?" she asked, filling the pot with water.

"Yeah."

"Well, I pawned it."

Jack could not help thinking that he should get the Bill Doak glove and that Lou could have his old one. After all, he was older. "But . . . but why does he get it?" he asked, and then wondered whether he should have asked.

She put down the pot and turned to look at Jack with her tired eyes. She smiled sadly as she approached him. "Jack, that's all that Lou ever gets. Old things. He wears your old clothes. He plays with your old fire engine." She lifted her hand to Jack's head and caressed his hair. "Don't you think that just once, just once, Lou could have something that's not a hand-me-down from you?"

"I guess," he answered. He sat back down to his math homework and tried to think this over. He could not concentrate on the math problems. It just didn't feel right for Lou to get the glove. Not only was Jack older, but the glove was too big for Lou. Not to mention that Jack was a much better baseball player.

As the oatmeal started to cook, his mother sat down at the table. "You know what I heard the other day? I heard you broke a window at Cybulski's Bakery. Is it true?"

Jack was not sure whether he should admit it. He

decided not to say anything, and bent his head over the math problem he was working on.

"Never heard of someone your age hitting the ball that far," she continued. "You must have some swing."

He looked up at his mother. She looked back at him with a coy smile. Jack could not help but chuckle. It was a smile he would never forget.

* * *

Now, Jack put his hand into Lou's glove and thought of his brother. Lou had slept with the glove beneath his head. He'd never let Jack touch the glove. *Because Lou used it to hide his money, whenever he had any,* Jack thought with a smile. Then he paused, staring at the glove. *He hid stuff in it.* Removing his left hand from the glove, Jack inserted his right hand, palm up. He felt the upper lining with his fingertips; sure enough, there was something in the lining of the opening for the pinky. He worked his right forefinger into the space for the fifth finger and felt something shaped like a cigarette. Wiggling the tip of his finger to the apex of the space, he found the slit. *This was where Lou kept his money.* He worked the object out with his finger and pulled it out of the glove.

It was paper, rolled tightly so that it resembled a cigarette and tied with string. He sat on the floor and examined the roll, then pulled the string off and unrolled the paper to reveal a list of names. Some were written in blue ink, others in black; he recognized Lou's handwriting:

James Fredricks, Department of Justice,

special assistant to the Attorney General of the United States.

Timothy Keens, Department of Labor. Wage and Hour Division.

Rex Hart, Legal Staff, National Labor Relations Board.

Michael White, National Youth Administration.

David Hallion, National Labor Relations Board.

Joseph Gregory, General Counsel of the C.I.O.

Milton Walton, State Department.

The list went on to name a total of fifteen individuals; all appeared to have worked for the federal government. Jack slid back to the wall and sighed. *Were all these people members of the CPUSA—the American Communist Party?*

He picked up the glove, placed it on his left hand, and stared at the opposite wall.

Industry would not have murdered people working for the government. Why would they? *Did their own government kill them? Was it the FBI?*

He pounded his right fist into the glove as he thought, and heard a crack. Removing his hand from the glove, he folded it with both hands, felt resistance. There was something in the inner lining. He worked his hand in but did not find an opening. Tucking the glove under his left arm, he used both arms to push himself to his feet. A spasm of pain shot through his chest as he straightened up, making him gasp. Clutching his chest, he slowly walked back to the kitchen and looked for a knife.

He cut open the inner lining of the glove and inserted two fingers; they touched something that felt like cellophane. He carefully pulled it out of the glove; and recognized a collection of photographic negatives, taped together. Jack tore off the tape and held one of the negatives up to the light. He couldn't make out much. Placing the negatives on the kitchen table next to the list, he shuffled back into the bedroom to return the glove to the cardboard box.

* * *

Sue blew on her hands and rubbed them together. "You want to get out of here?"

Jack had his own hands shoved into his pockets. He looked at Sue and shrugged. "Let's give it another hour," he said. "Maybe they have to wait for their break."

They stood just outside the fence of the Gullane Textile Mill in Burr Hill, Virginia. The rain had stopped, but it was still a cold, gray day. When the morning work shift had arrived, they'd told several workers who they were and what they wanted to discuss. That was over two hours ago, but no one came out to talk to them.

Jack stared at the smoke coming out of a chimney at the plant's center, slipping one hand inside his coat to rub absently at his chest. It was still sore. "You think you can get their trust?" he asked.

Sue shrugged. "I can only tell them who I am."

Jack spotted a worker approaching, a man in his mid-thirties clad in blue overalls. He walked through the gate and stopped in front of Jack. "Yeah, what do you want?" he asked.

"Hi, buddy," said Jack. "My name is Jack. I'm the brother of the guy who was murdered in the baseball park in Washington—Lou Harris. I heard he met with some of you guys at the park before he died. I wanted to find out what you guys know."

The worker shook his head. "Never heard of the guy."

Jack frowned. "He met with a labor leader from this plant. You know who that is?"

The worker spit on the ground. "We got no leaders," he sneered. "I don't even know what you're talking about."

Sue took a deep breath. "Sir, my name is Sue Pinkerton. I've been with the CPUSA for four years. We know Lou was to meet with at least one of you earlier this month and he was murdered at the point of contact. All we have is a couple of questions."

The man put his hands in his pockets. "Like what?" he asked.

"Like did you people actually meet with him?" asked Jack. "And did anybody see anything? See anyone else with Lou?"

The man turned to Sue. "Who did you say you were with?"

"The CPUSA, the American Communist Party. We help workers organize and Lou Harris was trying to help you guys. You must have heard something about it."

The man thought for a second. "I don't know nothing."

Jack and Sue looked at each other in resignation.

The man scratched his chin. "Look, even if I knew something about a meeting, it don't matter now. And I don't know nothing about how this guy died—nothing."

Jack felt his face flush. "Harris died for you guys! Is this how you thank him?"

The worker shrugged. "I got a plant full of guys with their own stories."

"But their stories don't end with death, do they?" countered Jack.

"What about the meeting?" asked Sue, her tone calmer.

The man looked away. "There was no meeting. It never got that far."

"How far did it go?" she asked.

"Look." The worker pointed at both of them for emphasis. "I told you all I know. Everything I know, and that's nothing. You got it?"

Jack's shoulders drooped. "Well . . . thanks anyway, pal."

The worker looked past Jack and his eyes widened. "Shit, it's Cromwell."

Jack turned around. A black Ford sedan approached them. "Who's that?" he asked.

"He owns the Chesapeake Security Agency," the worker answered. "They're goons. I'm going back in. Look—I'm sorry about Harris, but forget about all this. It won't lead to nothing."

As the worker walked back to the gate, the sedan pulled up to the curb beside Jack and Sue. The back door opened and an obese, middle-aged man stepped out and walked over to Sue and Jack. He wore a charcoal-colored, double-breasted business suit and an expensive-looking, dark gray fedora. As he drew closer, Jack noted his large red nose and oily face.

"What y'all doing here?" Cromwell asked in a southern drawl.

"What's it to ya, pal?" Jack countered.

The car's front doors swung open and two other men

in business suits got out. The fat man didn't look at them. He continued to stare into Jack's eyes. "You're on private property. I make it my business."

"We're out for a stroll," said Jack. "Nice day, ain't it?"

The fat man turned to his colleagues and chuckled. "We got a comedian here, fellas."

One of Cromwell's men nodded. The cigarette dangling from the corner of his mouth bobbed as he said, "He's awful funny, Mr. Cromwell."

Cromwell turned back to Jack. He wasn't smiling. "I want an answer."

Jack shrugged. "Look pal, if we wandered onto private property, well . . . we didn't know. We'll get out of here." He took Sue by the arm. "Come on, honey, let's go."

Cromwell jerked his chin and his men grabbed Jack's arms and pulled them behind him. Sauntering up to Jack, Cromwell smiled. Then he put his fist into Jack's stomach. Jack doubled over.

"Stop it!" yelled Sue.

"What are you doing here?" growled Cromwell. "Who sent you here?"

Jack's mouth gaped as he tried to catch his breath. "I'm with the Washington Senators," he wheezed. "We want to know why you're killing our fans."

Cromwell frowned. His men pulled Jack upright. Cromwell hit Jack in the stomach again. "Who sent you here?"

The breath left Jack's chest. He tried to gasp for air, but he couldn't get any in.

"We didn't do anything!" yelled Sue. "Let us go or you're in big trouble."

Cromwell chuckled. "With who? The commies? Stay out of this, sister."

"I'm calling the police!" Sue yelled.

"Go ahead and call," said Cromwell. He turned to Jack. "You're either gonna spit out words I want to hear, or you'll spit out some teeth, fella. It's up to you."

Jack finally managed several breaths. "Okay, okay," he whispered. "Mullen sent us. He's under pressure to make an investigation."

Cromwell thought for a second. "You're with Mullen? What investigation?"

"Tell these guys to let go," said Jack.

Cromwell jerked his chin and Jack's arms fell to his sides. "Go on," said Cromwell.

"You know they murdered a red at the baseball park in Washington. Mullen just has to make it look like he put in an effort. So he sent us here." Jack waited, watching for Cromwell's reaction, whether he'd take the bait.

Cromwell stood thinking. "Reds are always asking for it," he said. "Who's putting pressure on Mullen?"

"How do I know?" said Jack. "I'm small fry. Now, let us get out of here."

Cromwell waved his arm. "Who's keeping you?"

Sue grabbed Jack by the arm. "Come on," she said.

Holding his chest, Jack let Sue lead him away.

"So that's it? Don't you have any questions?" called Cromwell.

Jack slowly turned around, grimacing as his chest twinged. "Do you know who killed Lou Harris?"

"No," answered Cromwell.

"Well then, there we go," said Jack. "That's good enough for me. I'm done." He turned back to take Sue's arm. "Come on."

"Is this a joke?" Cromwell asked.

"I came down here and we talked," said Jack with his back to Cromwell. "That's all I need to report to Mullen. And I'll tell him how hospitable you were." He continued forward, ignoring the pain that each step triggered in his chest and stomach.

"Who's Mullen?" Sue asked Jack in a whisper.

"Quiet, not now," Jack murmured, concentrating on walking normally.

When they were a safe distance from Cromwell and his men, Jack looked at Sue. "Mullen's with the FBI," he said. "I think I hit the jackpot."

"Why's that?" she asked.

"Cromwell knew about Mullen, and I got the feeling he knew about Lou's murder. Did you feel that?"

She frowned. "I'm not sure."

They continued walking until they reached the bus stop. There, Sue turned toward him and caressed his cheek. "You okay?" she asked.

Jack smiled through the pain. "I'll live." He put his hand on her back and rubbed it gently. "Thanks for coming down here with me."

✻ ✻ ✻

The room at the Worthington Hotel on Larch Street was larger than the one at the Saratoga, and the elevator worked. Just two blocks farther away from Griffith Stadium, the hotel was well situated and on a main avenue. The rate for the room was actually less than at the previous hotel, and Jack wondered whether the taxi driver who had picked him up from the train station that day had been getting a kickback from the Saratoga.

Jack sat on the bed with his back against the bedpost and a deck of playing cards in his hands, thinking. Every few moments, he plucked a card from the top of the deck and flipped it toward his hat, lying upside-down on the floor against the wall. When he'd thrown all but the last card, he turned to pick up the pad of paper lying beside him on the bed. He had written down three names: Warner, Mullen, Cromwell.

He rubbed his forehead, trying to think the whole thing through. The peanut vendor at the ballpark and the morgue attendant had both asserted the presence of the feds—in the stadium and at the morgue. Both the thug Cromwell and the cop Warner knew of Mullen. So the fed at the ballpark may have been Mullen, or someone under Mullen's control. Mullen had shown interest in Lou's list. And soon after he'd told Mullen he knew about the list, Jack got beat up in his hotel room by thugs who were looking for the list.

Jack tossed the last card at the hat. *These bastards are all in on it together,* he thought.

He threw the pad on the bed, rose, and crossed to the desk against the wall beside his hat. Lifting the bottle of whiskey he had purchased at the corner store, he checked its level (half full) and then poured a tall drink into a glass of rapidly melting ice that sat on the desk next to a jug of lukewarm water. He added a splash of water and then, drink in hand, he moved over to the window.

Although it was late September, the trees in Washington showed no signs of turning color. Jack decided he did not like Washington. The streets were wide and impersonal. The white stone government buildings seemed pretentious and contrasted eerily with the hobos combing the streets.

Sipping his whiskey, Jack watched the cars making their way along the street below and wondered what was new at the paper in St. Louis. Ryan was probably riding the Dyson story and he could imagine Duffy trying to convince his bosses to run Dyson headlines instead of going with the war in Europe.

Jack cautiously lifted his right arm over his head, pleased that he was finally able to do so without too much pain. His chest still hurt when he inhaled deeply and to this day, he did not know whether he had broken a rib. His mind returned to the puzzle of Lou's death. How did it all tie together?

Leaning over, he retrieved the pad from the bed and paused to find the pen he'd left on the night table. He set his glass on the window sill and wrote the word *list* next to the three names. In parentheses, he added the words *government employees.* The list, to his knowledge, only meant something to Mullen. The deaths themselves, he thought, had to be recorded somewhere—as police reports, autopsy findings, obituaries. Jack drew an arrow to the name *Mullen* and another arrow to the word *list.* These, he decided, would be his points of attack.

He stared at Mullen's name. *This son of a bitch,* he thought, *is the only one I've caught lying so far.* He felt his heart beat faster as he circled Mullen's name. *This is the son of a bitch who's going to pay.*

* * *

The sign over the Royal Theater read *Stagecoach, starring John Wayne* in large, black letters on a lit background. Jack entered the theater lobby. It appeared that the matinee had just finished; as Maggie had said, there was plenty of traffic, with some patrons leaving and others just arriving.

Jack sat down on a plush red velvet chair and reached for his cigarettes. Before he was able to withdraw the pack from his coat pocket, a well-dressed man in his mid-forties approached him. "Mr. Haynes?" asked the man in an eastern European accent.

Jack nodded, studying the short, stocky man. He had a commanding face with prominent cheekbones, and a bushy moustache that reminded Jack of the pictures he had seen of Stalin. "Yes. Mr. Petrov?"

The man sat down next to Jack and extended his hand. "Vladimir Petrov." He crossed his legs and glanced around before whispering, "I think it is safe to speak. First, allow me to offer you my condolences. I knew your brother for several years and he was a dedicated member of the party. I share in the pain of your loss. Now, let me tell you what I heard and you say if it is correct. Is that satisfactory?"

Jack nodded.

"You are Jack Haynes, the brother of Lou Harris. You have come from St. Louis to find out what had happened to your brother. Is this correct?"

Jack nodded again.

"Your brother was murdered at Griffith Stadium," Petrov continued, "on a day when he was to meet with textile workers from Virginia."

"That's correct," Jack answered.

"And you wanted to meet with me for more information."

"Bingo," muttered Jack.

Petrov tipped his head, his expression quizzical. "I am sorry?"

Jack realized Petrov was not familiar with the slang. "I mean, exactly."

"Whenever a comrade in our organization falls, a full investigation is performed and a report produced for the First Secretary. In the case of your brother, I am responsible for the examination and it is currently in progress." Petrov paused to scan the main entrance. His eyes darted back and forth as he studied the patrons moving through the lobby. Satisfied that he was not being observed, he turned back to Jack. "Your brother's case is currently classified as unsolved with strong suggestion."

"What does that mean?" asked Jack.

"I have heard you suspect that American federal agents are involved and you are quite correct. They were at the sports arena when the murder occurred."

"And at the morgue when they did his autopsy," said Jack.

Petrov nodded. "But you have to understand, this knifing in a men's room is not the method of the FBI."

"So what are you saying?"

"In all probability, the FBI was there for support—backup, if you will."

"Backup for who?"

Petrov leaned back with an air of satisfaction. "Ah, now that is the question. Theoretically, it could have been any number of factory bosses, maybe even the Mob. But the FBI would not work with just anyone. This must have been a foremost important group."

Resting his hands on his knees, Jack leaned forward. "There's a boss who keeps the workers in line at the textile factory in Virginia. His name is Cromwell."

Petrov made a face and shook his head. "No, no. He

is—how you Americans say—small fry. The FBI would not work with such a party."

"So, who?" Jack asked.

"You may not know," said Petrov. "Lou's responsibilities changed shortly before he was killed. He was given an assignment much more important than the textile mill in Virginia."

"Like what?"

"Unfortunately, I cannot tell you for security reasons. But I can tell you this—it has to do with a major industry in the northeast." Petrov also leaned forward and dropped his voice. "Now, listen to me very carefully. Some time ago, your brother told me he suspected the deaths of a number of party members were linked. Some were reported as deaths due to natural causes, others as accidents, and one or two as outright murders. He was to put together a list for me the next time I came to Washington."

"So you don't live here?" asked Jack.

Petrov shook his head. "No. I have come from New York to meet with you. As I said, we take these matters very seriously."

"So if you're a security officer and you don't live here, who investigated the deaths on Lou's list?"

Petrov raised his eyebrows. "So there is a list?"

Jack tried to think fast. "That's what I've been told," he said. "Maggie, that guy named Ray—that's what they said."

Petrov nodded, seeming satisfied. "To answer your question, deaths due to natural causes or accidents are not investigated. As to the two murders, they remain unsolved."

"So, let's say you find Lou's killer. What will you do to them?"

"First answer me this," said Petrov. "Are you sure you have no idea where this list is? Maybe he mentioned something to you. Think back, if you can."

Jack shrugged. "No, I don't know. I've given it a lot of thought. The others asked me too. Besides, what's the big deal? Do your own polling. How hard would it be to find out which of your members died recently in the D.C. area?"

Petrov's expression hinted at a smile. "Perhaps you do not realize the size of our organization. It would be starting from scratch."

Jack returned to his earlier question. "So, what would you do to Lou's killer?"

Petrov looked down and lowered his voice. "Perhaps it seems callous to you, but we do nothing. It is for informational purposes only."

"So why do you bother?"

"Information is power," Petrov replied.

Jack shook his head, frowning. "Nothing, huh? That's just great."

"In the meantime," Petrov said, "my investigation will continue. It is only proper that I inform you of my findings. Maggie will serve as contact. I must ask you not to attempt conducting your own investigation."

"Look, pal," Jack growled, "I didn't come all the way to Washington to see the monuments. I'm staying in D.C. until I find out what happened."

Petrov nodded reluctantly. "Very well, but I must ask you to stay clear and not interfere with our work. This is a complicated situation."

"I bet."

Petrov leaned forward. "I do not mean to sound—

how you say—mean spirited, Mr. Haynes, but this is not a business for an amateur."

Jack nodded. "I understand," he said solemnly, and thought, *Telling an American newspaperman to back off a story is the surest way to pique his interest.*

* * *

Jack walked through the cemetery with his fedora in his hand, wondering how he would react when he finally saw the grave. When he found it, the burst of emotion he was afraid of never came. Instead, he tried to remember what he'd felt when he was nineteen years old, and his mother had just died. Why didn't he want Lou to stay with him? Was it only because, like many big brothers, he considered the young brother a nuisance? Or would Lou's presence have constantly reminded him that he had not looked for work hard enough, forcing his mother to stand countless hours in soup lines?

All of this ran through his mind as he examined the headstone, a simple block of granite. Lou's full name and the dates of his birth and death were printed in black ink on a small wooden board attached to the stone. The earth over the grave was still fresh, which instilled in Jack the gnawing feeling that he had just missed his chance to meet Lou as an adult. Had he arrived in Washington just several weeks earlier, not only would he have had the chance to get to know Lou, but more importantly, he would have had the chance to apologize for leaving him with strangers when he was just a kid. But Jack had come too late, and nothing would ever change that.

Jack looked around the rustic public cemetery. The sun had started to set, casting long shadows throughout the yard. He placed his hat back on his head and sighed. *It's pointless to torture myself like this,* he thought as he stared at the long fingers of shade stretching from each stone. *I still have a chance to get justice for Lou. And if I can expose what happened to Lou, it might help Lou's cause. Lou would be acknowledged as a martyr for his cause, a recognition he deserves.*

* * *

Leaning against a tree on Pennsylvania Avenue not far from the FBI headquarters, Jack pretended to read a folded copy of the *Washington Chronicle* while he watched the figures leaving the FBI building. Sooner or later, Mullen would have to come out.

Jack drew on his cigarette, thinking of the FBI agent as he inhaled its pungent smoke. The visit to the textile plant left no doubt, he decided; Mullen was the key. The cops, the vendor at Griffith Stadium, and Cromwell all knew something about Mullen; it could not be just coincidence. He was not convinced Petrov was right about Cromwell being small fry. Jack had found evidence of a connection between the fat man and the feds.

Jack glanced at his watch. He'd expected a mass exodus from the building at 4:00 p.m., but he was wrong; the tempo of people leaving had not picked up. *Maybe at 5:00*, he thought. *Another hour.* He opened the paper to the sports section and checked out the schedules and scores. The Washington Senators had left town to play the Chicago White Sox but would soon return to play his team, the St. Louis Browns. Jack glanced at the FBI building, then flipped through the rest of the paper. A small article on the second page caught his attention:

Machinists Cry Foul at New York Metals Plant (New York) – The nation's largest union of tool and die workers, The Union of American Machinists, which represents over one million employees, has accused New York City based Cox Metals Inc. of violating the National Labor Relations Board Act on the eve of a vote for unionization. According to union leaders and Peter Morgan, a union supporter at the plant, Cox Metals Inc. has been intimidating workers with threats of unemployment and even physical harm just days before the important vote. In response to this claim, company spokesman Ralph Dawson stated that this is just the latest false claim by the union in an attempt to stir up trouble at the company's plant.

It is unclear whether the union has filed or plans to file a complaint with the NLRB. The voting is scheduled for tomorrow, although union leaders have not ruled out the possibility of postponement. Rumors of a work stoppage at the plant could not be confirmed.

Jack wondered whether this had anything to do with Lou. He tore out the article, folded it, and placed it in his wallet. Again he glanced at his watch. Almost five. Shifting his gaze to the FBI headquarters, he saw a larger number of people leaving the building—the workday at the FBI was over. This first wave was mostly women, no doubt secretaries. Minutes later, men in business suits emerged through the building's main door. Jack kept his paper open, and his eyes on the entrance.

A tall figure wearing a boater and an off-brown suit caught Jack's eye. Although the man was over two hundred feet away, Jack made out Grey hair and a strong chin; they could belong to Mullen. Head down as if eyeing the white stones of the plaza, Jack tucked the newspaper under his arm and walked slowly toward the man. Twenty steps closer, there was no doubt: it was Wayne Mullen. And Mullen's boater had a red stripe. That was the color of the stripe that caught the peanut vendor's eye at Griffith Stadium.

Jack followed Mullen as he walked down Pennsylvania Avenue, swinging a black briefcase in his right hand. He looked at his watch and turned off Pennsylvania Avenue into a side street. Jack followed him for two blocks, and then ran up to him. "Hello there, Agent Mullen. Remember me? Jack Haynes of the *Washington Chronicle*."

Mullen raised his head and looked at Jack in surprise. "What do you want?"

"I want to know about the Lou Harris investigation."

"What is it you want to know?" asked Mullen.

"I want to know what you were doing at Griffith Stadium the day Harris was murdered."

"You're crazy," said Mullen.

Jack forced a chuckle. "I got a Washington cop who admits you're in on the investigation. I got a guy working at Griffith Stadium who places you with Harris when he was murdered. I got a thug working for Gullane Textiles in Virginia who knows you're in on it."

Mullen sneered. "Conducting your own investigation?"

"I sure am, and it all leads to you."

Mullen stopped and stared into Jack's eyes. "Ever been to Michigan?" he asked.

Jack had stopped as well; now he felt his stomach tighten. He stood there looking at Mullen, not knowing what to say.

Mullen placed his briefcase on the pavement and smiled. "I called the *Washington Chronicle*. They never heard of you. So we ran the fingerprints you left in the building. You're Jack Harris, Lou's brother. You're looking at two to five for bootlegging in Michigan and another five for escaping. So don't tell me you're calling the shots, you two-bit punk."

Jack felt his face flush as his rage built. He lifted his right arm and hit Mullen square on the jaw. Mullen doubled over. "You killed my brother, you son of a bitch!" yelled Jack. "And you're gonna pay for it."

Mullen jerked his head up, hitting Jack under the jaw. Jack's head snapped upward, and Mullen followed with a shot to Jack's stomach. Jack's breath gusted out; he staggered, then caught himself and raised his head. Lunging for Mullen, he grabbed his shoulders with both hands and let momentum carry them both to the ground. Jack managed to pin Mullen's shoulders against the ground and then punched him in the abdomen.

In a smooth, practiced move, Mullen's left arm shot up, hooking around Jack's throat to throw him off. Jack rolled and rose to find Mullen already on his feet. They stared at each other, panting.

Mullen braced his hands on his knees. "I didn't kill your brother," he gasped.

Jack rubbed his numb jaw, probing with his tongue

for lost teeth. "You, or one of your goons—but you're the one that's gonna pay."

"Listen to me! I didn't kill your brother, you dumb bastard!" grated Mullen.

Jack looked around to see if anyone had witnessed his assault on a federal agent; the street was empty. "Yeah, okay, I'm a fugitive," he said. "And I got nothing to lose."

"This is bullshit," said Mullen. "Come back to HQ with me."

"No way," said Jack.

Mullen straightened, holding his stomach. "You're coming with me. Otherwise, I'll put out a warrant for your arrest. Now, come on."

* * *

Mullen leaned back in his chair and folded his hands. He had led Jack into a small, poorly lit office in the FBI building. The room was cluttered with folders and stacks of paper crammed the desk and a small table against a side wall.

"When was the last time you saw your brother?" Mullen asked in a tone that suggested he was in control.

Jack crossed his arms. "What the hell you asking me that for? You were with him when he was murdered."

Mullen reached for a pouch of Beechnut tobacco on the desk in front of him. "Answer the question."

"Why should I?" Jack countered.

Mullen did not answer. Silence stretched. Jack stared at a framed photograph on the wall behind Mullen. The photo was signed; Jack wasn't sure, but it appeared to be a portrait shot of J. Edgar Hoover. Below this was a photograph of a middle-aged, overweight woman wearing an evening gown.

"I haven't seen him for years," Jack finally said, dropping his gaze to Mullen. "But I got a witness placing you at Griffith Stadium. What you gonna do? Bump me off, too?"

Mullen tucked a pinch of tobacco into his mouth. "Did he send you anything in the mail before he died?"

Jack eyed him. "You taking about the list?"

Mullen's mouth stopped moving. "What do you know about the list?"

Now Jack had no doubt. Not only the communists, but the feds were desperate to get Lou's list. "I know Lou was killed for it," he said. "We both know it will prove who killed him."

Mullen lifted a paper cup and spit tobacco juice into it. "So you don't have the list?" he asked.

"Your boys didn't find it in my hotel room, did they?" Jack shifted in his chair as if getting comfortable. "Well, I didn't say I did, and I didn't say I didn't."

"Don't get cute with me," answered Mullen. "I make one phone call, and you're going up the river."

Jack leaned forward and placed both hands on his knees. "We both know you're not going to do that. I'm your only hope of finding it."

Mullen rose and reached for a stack of folders on a shelf behind him. He pulled one out of the bunch, sat back down, and thumbed through the file. "So you were with the Mossey family? Biggest group in Michigan." He looked up. "He's dead, you know. Sam Mossey was gunned down years ago."

Jack shrugged. "I never even met him. I just delivered the booze."

Mullen dropped his eyes to the file. "So you punched an agent during the escape," he said. "That makes it even worse."

"I never touched anyone," said Jack. "I jumped out of the back of a truck at a sharp turn. If the agent with me had any guts, he would have jumped after me."

Mullen raised his head and smiled. "They didn't stop?"

"They stopped but it was too late. I rolled down a hill and ran into some woods."

Mullen chuckled. "Weren't you cuffed?"

"Yeah, I was cuffed. But I could still run. There were only three of them. They didn't have any dogs and they had four other prisoners on the truck they had to watch."

Mullen seemed amused. "That wouldn't happen here," he said.

Jack thought of the textile plant and the shots he took to the stomach. "Why would you be involved with someone like Cromwell?" he asked.

Mullen frowned. He threw the folder on his desk. "Who?"

"You know who I'm talking about," said Jack. "That goon down in Virginia. I may not be with the *Washington Chronicle*, but I am a newspaperman. The FBI scheming with factory thugs to kill commies? That's quite a story. I could make editor with a story like that."

Mullen spit into the cup again. "Yeah, I know. You're with the *St. Louis Herald*. There's no flies on us around here." Mullen slammed the cup on the desk and sighed. "I gotta admit, you got a lot of nerve, waltzing into FBI headquarters with your record." He folded his arms behind his head, studied Jack. "You're really on the hunt, aren't you? What is it you're hoping to find?"

Jack thought it curious that Mullen did not appear concerned with the possibility that he would go public. "I want to find out what happened to my brother," he said. "Ain't it obvious?"

Mullen dropped his arms and leaned forward. "I'm willing to make a deal. You get me the list and any photos you have, and I'll have your file destroyed. Otherwise, you're looking at at least five years in a federal penitentiary."

"How nice of you to be looking out for me," sneered Jack. "The list could put someone away for more than five years, couldn't it?"

Mullen toyed with the paper cup on his desk. "I'll give you some time to bring it to me. If you don't, we're bringing you in."

"How long you gonna give me?" asked Jack.

Mullen shrugged. "Until I get restless."

"That's no deal."

Mullen shrugged again. "And don't try and skip town," he said. "Like I said, no flies on us. Now get out of here."

* * *

"Who was that woman, the one with the shawl?" Maggie asked as she poured tea for Hans from a tarnished metal pot. The group sat in Maggie's parlor, digesting that night's party meeting.

Tom Murdock held up his glass as Maggie moved over to him with the pot. "She's from Richmond," he answered.

Jack was not in the mood for conversation. The party meeting was news to him; he'd come to Maggie's apartment expecting her to be alone. He sat on the couch with his arms folded, his brow puckered in thought, berating himself for blowing the whole thing with Mullen. Instead of finding out about Mullen's involvement through investigation and polite conversation, he'd confronted Mullen like an idiot. Rage had gotten the better of him. That had never happened when he was on a story for the newspaper.

"What was she doing at the meeting?" asked Maggie.

Jack glanced at her and his thoughts turned to what Sue had said about her and Lou. If they were not a good match, as Sue had claimed, why were they together? Was one using the other, or did they just argue a lot, the way many couples do?

Tom shrugged. "I guess just to say what she said."

"Why was she making such a big deal about it?" Hans Guter asked in his thick accent. "Terror has been used throughout history. It goes without saying that it's a necessary reality to advance the revolution."

"Maybe she was appealing to new members," Maggie mused.

Tom raised the glass to his lips but abruptly stopped. His eyebrows rose. "Maybe there has been some dissent in other nuclei! Maybe she was sent here to bring order!"

Jack caught Maggie glaring at Tom as she sat down. She seemed to be letting him know he was out of line.

Hans glanced at Jack. "Maybe we should discuss this some other time."

The room became silent.

Tom turned to Jack. "So, you find anything out about Lou?"

Jack frowned. "I met with Petrov."

Hans took a sip from his glass of tea. "Was the meeting, as you Americans say, fruitful?"

"We'll see," Jack answered. "I'm waiting for him to get back to me." He turned to Maggie. "Have you heard anything from Petrov?"

Maggie shook her head. "No."

Jack thought of the list and wondered whether he should tell them he'd found it. "I think the thugs at that textile plant are involved," he said. "And so is the FBI."

Both Tom and Hans jerked their heads toward Jack, but remained silent. "Not surprising," Hans finally muttered.

"Like I said the other day," Jack added, "I can place the FBI at the scene. And I can tie them to the thugs from that textile mill."

The group sat in silence. "Who are these witnesses?" Tom asked after a long moment.

"People who were at Griffith Stadium," Jack replied.

"Did you tell Petrov about this?" asked Hans.

Jack had to think for a second. "I guess so."

Hans looked at his watch. "It's getting late." He put down his glass and looked at Maggie. "Thank you, Maggie." He rose. "Come on, Tom."

The two men left the apartment. Jack sat back. "Hans is a Russian?" he asked.

Maggie nodded.

"But Hans is a German name."

"The name isn't real. It's just his code name."

"And Tom?"

"Tom's his real name," she answered, and laughed. "I know it's confusing. You get used to it."

"What's with the glasses?" asked Jack.

"What glasses?"

He nodded toward the glasses on the coffee table. "Why do they drink tea from glasses instead of cups?"

"It's just a Russian custom," she replied.

"But Tom isn't a Russian, is he?"

"No," Maggie answered with a sigh. "I guess he picked it up from the others."

Jack caught her eye. "And you? Is Maggie your real name?"

Maggie smiled and flopped over on the couch next to Jack. "Yes, I'm really Maggie. So, do you like my friends?"

The question caught Jack off guard. He had only thought of these people as potential leads, not as social contacts. "Sure," he heard himself say. "Hans is quite a character."

Maggie nodded. "Yeah, he's so . . . so full of life."

Yeah, he's full of it, alright, thought Jack.

"He has that European elegance," she continued. "Yet, he's not pretentious."

"These guys sure like their booze," Jack observed.

"That reminds me." Maggie propped herself up on one elbow. "Did you ever go to their sorrow meeting?"

Jack chuckled. "Yeah, that's what I mean."

"Who else was there?"

"Let's see. Hans and Tom, and some other guys I met for the first time. I didn't talk to them much. They were busy playing chess."

Maggie moved closer to Jack and crossed her legs. "Then Reznov must have been there," she said.

"I don't remember their names."

"Reznov, Gene Reznov. He's a chess champion. They always try to beat him, but they never do."

"Yeah, I think he was there."

"Reznov's funny," said Maggie. "When he gets nervous, he starts moving his jaw up and down. Then his shoulders move up and down."

Jack looked at her. "Like a tic? This guy didn't have tics."

She chuckled. "That's probably because he was winning." She raised Jack's hand to her lips and kissed the back of it.

Jack caressed her hair with his other hand. "What are Russians doing here?"

She turned over his hand and kissed the palm. "The Soviets sent over people to help us. They have more experience in helping workers." Her voice had grown throaty, soft, at odds with the words she spoke.

Jack gently lifted her chin with his forefinger and kissed her lips, still caressing her hair.

Maggie reached for his left hand and kissed the palm. "Jack," she whispered watching him with hooded eyes, "what would you say if I told you I've been a bad girl?"

"What do you mean?"

"I've done things I shouldn't have."

Jack drew a deep breath. "Like what?"

She rubbed her cheek against the palm of his hand. "What would you do with a bad girl?"

What the hell . . . ? "I don't know."

"Do you think bad girls should be spanked?" she asked, her lips quirking with a smile as she again kissed his palm.

Jack shrugged. "I guess that's one way to punish someone."

"I've been a very bad girl, Jack. I deserve to be spanked."

Jack did not respond. He stared at her in growing dismay.

"Jack, have you ever spanked anyone?"

"No." No longer finding her attentions to his hand sensual, he tugged it gently from her grasp.

She let go of his hand and ran her fingers under his shirt to stroke his abdomen. "Want to spank me?" she asked, then caught her lower lip between her teeth and looked at him.

"W-why do you say you've been bad?" he asked, thinking, *I am in way over my head—*

She raised her hips and slapped her buttocks with her right hand. "Come on, Jack. Spank me." She reached for his left hand and rubbed it slowly against her buttocks.

Jack's mind went blank. He'd heard that some adults enjoyed being spanked, but he had never come across one before. "Are you . . . are you joking?" he finally blurted.

Maggie lowered her head to the sofa, rubbed her neck, and sighed. "Haven't you ever wanted to spank a woman? I'm giving you the chance, Jack."

He drew back. "I'm not into that sort of thing, honey."

She took a deep breath and rose to her feet. "Your loss," she muttered, and left the parlor.

Jack could only stare after her.

* * *

Sitting in the booth at the post office, Jack jiggled the hook on the receiver. "Hello? Hello?"

He barely made out a man's voice on the other end, but he could not make out the words. Pulling the phone booth door open, he glared at the clerk, the same elderly man who had been behind the counter the last time he was there. "I can't hear a damn word!" Jack yelled.

The clerk didn't look up. "I only connect 'em," he answered. "I don't make 'em."

Jack put the receiver back to his ear. "Hello?"

"Ryan here," he finally heard.

"This is Haynes," said Jack. "I'm calling from Washington. I need to talk to Judy in Records."

"Haynes? Duffy's pissed off at you."

Jack sighed and sat back. "Why's that?"

"He said if you don't get your ass back to work right now, you'll be pounding the pavement."

Jack shook his head. "Oh yeah? Tell Duffy I'm still busy here. And remind him about Jenkins." The year prior, Duffy was about to be called in front of a congressional hearing to investigate his relationship with the mayor of St. Louis, George Jenkins. The mayor had been accused of collaborating with organized crime, and Duffy, of publishing false statements in his paper. Jack had saved Duffy's ass by giving a sworn statement asserting that he had received false information from an informant and that Duffy was just going with his reporter's story.

"Why you calling?" asked Ryan. "You want to talk to him?"

"I just told you. I want to talk to Judy in Records."

"Judy? You on a story?"

"Yeah," said Jack. "And it's bigger than your little brain can imagine."

Ryan laughed. "You stinkin' yellow belly! That'll be the day, when you can out-scoop me!"

"Just get me Judy," Jack sighed.

"Judy's hot on that new photographer," said Ryan. "You know that?"

"I could care less. Get me Judy."

"Listen to this," Ryan continued in his conversational tone. "Judy goes dancing with this guy after work and comes back the next day wearing the same dress. And she's dancing around the place singing out loud! Ain't that a scream?"

"Cut the stalling and throw her on the wire," Jack growled.

"Okay, okay, keep your shirt on," Ryan muttered.

It was hot in the booth. Jack opened the door for ventilation. He removed his hat and fanned his face. Finally he heard a woman's voice in the receiver: "Yeah?"

"Judy? It's me, Jack. Is that you, Judy?"

"Yeah, yeah, it's me," she replied. "How can I do ya?"

"Judy, I got a favor to ask."

"You calling long distance, Jack?" she asked.

"Yeah, yeah." Jack sat forward, fighting frustration. "I'm in Washington. Judy, I need some obituaries from Washington papers."

"Washington," the woman hummed. "I've been there . . . it's beautiful."

Jack realized there was something to what Ryan had said about Judy being on cloud nine. "Yeah, Judy, it's really nice. Now listen to me. This is very important. I got some names you gotta check out for me in the Washington papers."

"Are the cherry trees in blossom?" she asked.

"What?"

"The cherry trees. They're beautiful when they blossom."

Jack shook his head. "Judy, that's in the spring. It's September."

"Oh, that's right," she replied. "So, how can I help you?"

"Judy, I beg you. Try and focus for a minute. Okay?"

"Okay, okay, I'm focused," she snapped. "So, what do you want?"

"I need you to check out some obituaries from the Washington papers. I only need you to go back two years."

"Obituaries? I'd like to, Jack," she said, "but do you know how far behind I am? This war in Europe is driving me crazy. Wooden wants his stuff. Johnson wants his."

Jack lowered his voice. "Judy, please . . . this is important. I'm onto something big. When was the last time I ever asked you for something?"

"Listen to me," she countered. "I can't promise you anything. I'm all backed up."

"Come on, Judy. There's always something going on, always a job. But this is different. I'll make it up to you. I swear."

"I got a stack of requests here, and it's just getting bigger each day," Judy complained.

"Judy . . . this is personal. It's about my brother."

There was a pause. "So what are the names?" she asked.

"Hold on." Jack reached into his jacket pocket and pulled out his list. "You ready?"

"Yeah, yeah, go on."

"Okay, here goes: James Fredricks, Timothy Keens, Rex Hart, Michael White, David Hallion, and Joseph Gregory. All from Washington. How much time you want?"

There was another pause; Jack imagined Judy scribbling down names. "Give me forty-eight hours," she said.

"Great, Judy. Thanks again. I'll make it up to you. I'll call you the day after tomorrow." Jack put down the phone.

As he left the booth, he remembered that he'd wanted to ask Ryan what was new with the Dyson case. He shrugged. *Too late.* He approached the post office clerk. "Hey, buddy, you got a Virginia phone book?"

The man nodded, his eyes never leaving his paper. "So your connection got better?" he asked as he reached below the counter.

"Yeah, you did a great job," said Jack.

The clerk glanced at him. "It's not up to me, you know. That's the phone company's responsibility."

Jack smiled as he reached into his jacket pocket for his cigarettes. "Don't be so modest. Not everybody can read the funnies and connect two cities together all at the same time."

The clerk looked up and held his eyes this time. "Don't read the funnies. Gets me thinking too much." He rose and threw a dog-eared telephone book on the countertop. "Strange thing, asking someone for a list of obituaries," he added, shaking his head.

Jack reached for the book. "You're supposed to connect 'em, not tap 'em."

The man chuckled and returned to his chair.

Jack opened the book and searched for the address of the Chesapeake Security Agency.

* * *

"I always thought Pennsylvania Avenue was supposed

to be grand, "Jack said, examining the pawnshops and the bars they strolled past. Jack had invited Sue out to dinner. He'd told her it was to thank her for going down to Virginia with him, but it was really just so he could be with her again. He'd insisted that she pick out an expensive restaurant, but Sue wouldn't hear of it. Instead, she told him about her favorite spot, Duncan's Chicken Shack, off of 14th Street.

Sue smiled. "That's on the other side of the capital. On the west side."

"I was expecting statues and fountains, tall trees."

"First time in Washington? she asked archly.

Before Jack could answer, Sue suddenly moaned. Jack looked at her, then followed her eyes to a hobo lying on a wooden bench, fast asleep. "You see that?" she asked.

"See what?"

"On his chest."

Jack looked again and made out a medal pinned to the man's raggedy jacket. "Oh, yeah. So?"

"He wears it on purpose," she answered. "He's a World War veteran. He wants people to see this is how they're treating the veterans."

"You mean the way the government treats them?" asked Jack.

"That's right."

Jack frowned, puzzled. "How's that gonna help him?"

She looked at him, features softened with compassion, eyes wide. "What else can he do? I'll tell you something, though. I admire him."

"Why?"

"He's totally down on his luck. He's hit rock bottom. But he's still trying to tell the world something."

"I never would have thought of that," Jack admitted.

"And he's doing it peacefully. You have to admire that."

Who is this woman? thought Jack, watching the play of emotions on her face. *I see a hobo and she sees a noble man.*

"You ever hear of the Bonus Army?" Sue asked, one hand reaching absently for a heart-shaped locket resting on her breastbone.

"No."

Sue slid the gold ornament along its chain, back and forth, slowly, as if it were a habit. "The veterans once marched on the capital, demanding money. The poor guys were unemployed and wanted the money that had been promised to them."

The story suddenly rang a bell with Jack. "Oh, yeah, yeah," he said. "I know—federal troops came in."

Still clutching the golden heart, Sue nodded. "That's right. The senators called in the cavalry and then ran out of the capital through secret tunnels, like rats. It turned into a riot."

"Were you here then?" asked Jack.

"Six, seven years ago? Yeah. It was a sight I will never forget; guys in their old World War uniforms lying on this street, wounded and dying. It was that scene that got me involved."

"Why?"

She looked at him, her convictions puckering the skin between her brows. "Think about it. A soldier goes across the ocean to fight for his country. He comes home, can't get a job, and then gets shot by his own army on Pennsylvania Avenue."

"Is that when you joined the party?" he asked.

"Not right away," she answered. "But I couldn't get over that sight. Worst of all, I knew some of those politicians who called in the cavalry. I was part of the problem."

"You knew the senators? How?" Jack asked in surprise. How would a waitress know senators?"

Sue grimaced and looked away. "Let's just say I knew some of them. It was a couple of years later that I ended up a member."

Jack watched her face. He was seeing facets of this woman he'd never dreamed existed. "Regret joining?" he asked.

Sue shrugged. "Who knows? I guess I learned a lot. But was it worth it? Probably not."

"What's wrong with the party?" he asked.

She shook her head. "It's so autocratic. Party members are told what to do and they don't know why. One day we're told to support a group of workers and we do. The next day we're told to back off support and they don't tell us why."

"What happens if you ask?" asked Jack.

"It's considered disloyal," she answered wryly. She let go of the necklace. "They tell us to destroy property and we don't know why. It's all for the cause—that's all you ever hear."

"So you got sick of it?"

Sue nodded. "I sure did. You know, a friend of mine spends all his free time making fake birth certificates. Is that why you join the party? To make phony documents all day?"

Jack chuckled.

"It's not funny," she snapped. "They suck you in and you get stuck."

"Sounds like the Mob," he said, stepping off the curb.

Sue grabbed his arm. "Watch it!"

Jack stopped just as a bus pushed by on the street in front of him. "But you're leaving," he said. "I mean, they're kicking you out."

"That's the only way to leave. If you say you want out, they put pressure on you to stay. The only way out is to open your mouth and criticize them until they can't take you anymore."

The light turned and they started across the street. "So that whole thing you brought up about the Nazis and Soviets forming a pact was just an act?"

Sue shook her head. "No, no. That wasn't an act. It pissed a lot of us off."

"Have others left?" asked Jack.

"Sure," she answered. Then she looked at him. "You want to know how crazy it is? Party members who criticized the pact were actually accused of being Nazi spies."

This made no sense to Jack. "By who?"

"By the party leaders. They said only a Nazi spy would react that way, to keep his cover."

"That *is* crazy," Jack said. She was still holding his arm. He liked how her touch made him feel.

"Let's change the subject," Sue said as they made their way down the sidewalk on the other side. "I'm from Baltimore. Where are you from?"

Jack smiled. "I'm from Bal-mar too. Whereabouts in Bal-mar?"

"Woodbourne Avenue. You know where that is?"

"You mean north of Hopkins?" asked Jack.

"That's right."

"Ritzy!" he exclaimed. "I didn't know I was in the presence of royalty!"

Sue laughed and grabbed her necklace again. "I never heard Woodbourne Avenue called ritzy before. Where did you grow up?"

"A row house on Orleans Street," he answered. Still conscious of her arm around his, he tucked his elbow a little closer to his side. "Actually, when my mother died, Lou was taken to an orphanage near the harbor." He wondered how much Sue knew of Lou's life. "So, how does a girl from Woodbourne Avenue end up working in a cafeteria?" As soon as the words left his mouth, he realized he was being rude.

"My family lost everything in the Depression," she said, her tone subdued. Then her voice grew more animated as she changed the subject. "So you and Lou were orphans? I didn't know that."

"Well, I was already grown up when it happened." He felt his shoulders tense, as he braced for her next logical question. *How do I tell someone like her that I abandoned my brother?*

"So you're from Baltimore, and this is your first time in Washington?" she asked.

"That's right," he said, relieved.

She uttered a short laugh and gaped at him for a moment. "You've go to be kidding. I mean, didn't you ever come here with your school? On a field trip?"

Jack chuckled. "My school? I already told you, I grew up in a poor neighborhood."

Sue wiped a raindrop off her forehead. "Someone sneezed," she said.

"What do you mean?" Jack asked. He heard tiny

plunks as a couple of raindrops struck the brim of his fedora.

She smiled at him. "Someone sneezed and it started to rain. You never heard that when you lived in Baltimore?"

"No."

"We all used to say it. You know how it can start raining anytime at all in Baltimore."

"I guess it does get kind of humid. So, how long did you know Lou?"

"Couple of years, I guess," she replied with a shrug. "Did you know Lou was an active member of the communist party?"

Jack nodded. "I found out when I got here. So why were you so fond of Lou?"

Sue stared at the sidewalk as they walked. "It's like I told you. He was sincere; you could trust Lou." She looked up at Jack. "He was a big supporter of the Popular Front, you know."

Jack had heard of the Popular Front but did not know much about it. "How's that?"

Sue shrugged. She seemed puzzled by Jack's question. "He simply was." She wiped her forehead again. "Do you know anything about them? The Popular Front?"

"Not really."

"I thought it was a great idea—I still think it was a great proposal," she said. "The communists were always against the liberals and the socialists, but then they came out and said we should all unite against the fascists. They proposed a Popular Front. Lou supported it just as much as me."

"You know, I've been busy with my work," Jack admitted. "To tell you the truth, I don't know much about this stuff. What happened next?"

She looked up at Jack wide-eyed. "It was great," she answered. "An avalanche. Workers, writers, artists, thousands joined the Popular Front. Hollywood contributed tons of money. We even took control of major organizations like the American Labor Party, the Farmer Labor Party, the American Youth Congress . . . the League of American Writers, and—what's it called? The American League for Peace and Democracy."

"So what happened?" asked Jack.

She snickered cynically. "It was the pact with the Nazis." Her tone suggested that Jack should have figured that out for himself. "It was Stalin's agreement with Hitler; he blew it," she said. "When he formed that pact, the Front started to collapse. The CPUSA was told to stop criticizing the Nazis and focus on attacking the Americans as warmongers . . . like a lot of people are going to go for that."

"How did Lou react to this Nazi pact?" asked Jack.

"I don't know," she answered. "I don't think I even saw him after that."

"You know anything about Lou having some list?" he asked. "Everybody seems to want it."

Sue's reaction to the question was subdued. "I heard the others mention it once or twice, but I really don't know anything about it."

Jack nodded; besides the man in the hardware store, this was the first time since he'd arrived in D.C. that he believed someone wholeheartedly.

Sheets of rain suddenly came down. Sue uttered a mock scream and grabbed Jack's arm, pointing forward with her other hand. "Come on! Let's go!"

She pulled him under an awning, laughing. Jack noticed tendrils of her brown hair curling in the humid air to frame her face. "That veteran on the park bench is gonna get soaked," she said.

Jack stared into her brown eyes. She stopped laughing when their eyes met and put her head down as if suddenly shy. Jack lifted her chin with his finger. "Your hair looks great when it's wet," he murmured, and slowly leaned forward. He was close enough to feel the warmth of her lips when Sue shook her head ever so slightly and then jerked her head back. She looked away. Embarrassed and unsure what to think, Jack drew back as well. He looked at her and saw pain in her eyes.

Sue stared at the pouring rain, looking as though she was deep in thought. Jack turned and watched the rain hitting the cobblestones out on the road. It was not so much that he felt rejected, but more like he'd hit a raw nerve. "This is an awful lot of trouble to go to for some fried chicken," he said, keeping his tone light.

Sue giggled as if she was happy they'd returned to ordinary conversation. "You're right about that," she answered heartily. "Tell me, have you seen the monuments?"

"No."

"Then I have to show you the sights," she said firmly.

"Why?"

"It's your first time in town," she replied as if the reason was obvious. "You have to see them."

Jack shook his head. "I ain't some tourist."

Sue smiled. "Come on. The White House, the Washington Monument, Lincoln Memorial—you have to see them."

Jack shrugged. "Lou comes first."

* * *

Jack was not looking forward to this. The calm he had experienced after talking to the priest at St. Mary's Orphanage had long passed. In fact, he had put off the visit to the orphanage to interview Father McFarland twice already. But here he was, standing in front of the orphanage's main residence. The two-story building was U-shaped, with a central courtyard and walls thick with ivy, although Jack could still make out the light-hued brick and cast stone here and there beneath the foliage. Taking a deep breath, he approached the entrance under a rectory sign on the front of the right wing.

For some strange reason, the task of interviewing the priest reminded him of that terrible day when he'd visited Lou at the office of The Baltimore Children's Home Society, where Lou was taken when their mother died. It was there that he had seen Lou for the last time.

Jack paused with his hand on the latch, then reluctantly swung the heavy front door open and walked through the Roman arched entrance. The interior corridor was dark; as the door clicked closed behind him, Jack could not see a thing. He stood by the door until his eyes adjusted, finally making out a staircase to his left and a double door to his right. He knocked on the door and entered an office containing two wooden desks, both stacked with papers. No one was there. A door at the rear was open, revealing another office. He took several steps forward and tilted his head inside the door. The room contained rows of shelves and several more desks, but it also was unoccupied.

Behind Jack, the office's front door suddenly swung

open and a nun appeared in the doorframe. She wore a traditional black habit and carried a tin of Lipton Black Tea. Regarding Jack with baggy eyes within a wrinkled face, she asked, "Can I help you?"

Jack nodded. "Yes. Good day. I wanted to see Father McFarland."

She stood thinking for a moment. "Father McFarland? Is he expecting you?"

Jack hesitated. "Well, no. But I think he would want to speak with me. It concerns an old pupil of his."

"Yes, who?" she asked.

"Louis Harris."

"Dutch?" Her eyes lit up, but then her expression quickly changed, as if she was trying to convey that the request was routine. She bustled over to the front desk and set down the tin of tea. "I'll see if he's here," she said. "Have a seat. And your name?"

"Jack Haynes. I'm Dutch's brother."

The nun's eyes widened. "Wait here," she mumbled and left the office.

The fragile wooden chair squeaked as Jack sat down. He looked over his left shoulder and saw a large wooden cross on the wall. Below it, a calendar was heavily marked with hand-written notes on each day of September. Below the calendar, an end table held a small statue of Mother Mary and a figurine of the Eiffel Tower. Jack smiled at the combination and continued his scan of the room. On the far wall hung an oil painting, a portrait of a priest holding a prayer book; Jack wondered if it was the orphanage's founder.

Jack leaned his head back. His mind wandered back to the day he'd walked into the office of The Baltimore Children's Home Society, a week after their mother died.

The old building, with its large, echoing rooms, creaky floors, and high ceilings, gave Jack the creeps. He'd waited in the outer office, wondering if they had told Lou that he was going into foster care, that Jack had declined custody.

Lou finally appeared in the doorway. He was thirteen now, and had recently had a growth spurt; Jack couldn't get used to his sudden height. Lou looked curiously at Jack.

Jack was not sure how to start the conversation. He cleared his throat. "Well Lou, they told me they found a home for you."

Lou looked down. "Yeah, I know. They told me."

"Did they tell you where?" asked Jack.

Lou quickly looked up, brushing his curly brown hair with his fingers. "Why can't I go with you, Jack?" His voice was plaintive.

Jack shook his head, groping for something to say. "I—I can't take care of you, Lou. I don't even have a place to stay tonight."

That was the truth—at the apartment where their mother had raised them, Jack had admitted to the landlord that he would not be able to pay the rent. The landlord told Jack he could sell all their furniture and give Jack the money, provided he could keep a percentage. Jack had agreed; he'd ended up with fifty-two dollars.

Lou looked at Jack with wide eyes. "So where you goin', Jack?"

Jack shrugged. "Well, I got to find some work. I hear they're hiring in the plants up in Michigan."

Lou appeared confused. "Michigan? Why can't you stay here?"

Jack was afraid of Lou's eyes. He looked away. "I gotta go where the work is, Lou."

"I can go with you to Michigan, Jack," he said eagerly.

Jack shook his head again. "I can't take care of you, Lou. I wouldn't even know how."

Lou grimaced. "I don't need anyone taking care of me. I can take care of myself. Don't you know that?"

"It wouldn't work, Lou." Jack jerked his chin, vaguely indicating the offices elsewhere in the building, as he added, "Besides, they wouldn't like it, here."

"Who cares what they want?" Lou retorted.

Jack reached up and gently pushed Lou's shoulder. "Come on, Lou. It's for the best."

Lou turned his head away. "There's a game on the radio," he muttered. "I'm gonna go back inside."

"This is what Mom would have wanted," Jack blurted, but he was unconvinced by his own words.

Lou walked away without looking at Jack. "I'm gonna go listen to the game, Jack. See ya."

Jack lunged to his feet, groping in his pants pocket. He ran up and shoved a twenty-dollar bill into Lou's shirt pocket. Lou kept walking without acknowledging the gesture.

The nun reappeared, jerking Jack's mind back to the present. "You're in luck," she said. "Father McFarland is here—in the canteen. I'll take you there."

Jack rose and followed the nun to another wing of the building, where she led him down a flight of stairs and into the cafeteria. At the far end of the hall, a middle-aged man dressed in black sat at a short table together with two boys about ten years of age. Both wore black ties and brown sweaters. One boy with curly black hair had guilt written all over his face. The one with the crew cut stared at the ceiling as if he was not fazed at all. Jack imagined Lou sitting at the very same table while he was working for mobsters in Michigan.

"Would you boys want that?" Jack heard the priest ask as he approached. The two orphans shook their heads in unison. "Because that's exactly what I'm going to do if you boys steal one more time. You got that?" The boys nodded in unison.

"And stop calling us priests monkeys behind our backs," added the priest. "I know all about it." Both boys stared at him with their mouths sagging open. The priest waved his hand. "Off you go, now. Back to your class."

The boys jumped out of their chairs and ran off.

Jack did not expect this bluntness. The priest he had imagined from the letter was a thoughtful intellectual, not a man who scolded ten-year-olds for stealing.

The nun introduced Jack. The priest studied him carefully. "So you're Jack Haynes."

Jack nodded and pointed at a chair. "May I?"

The priest ran his fingers through his shock of white hair. "By all means."

Jack sat and folded his hands on the wooden table. "Did Lou tell you he had a brother?"

Father McFarland nodded. "Yes. He told me about your problems and how you changed your name."

"I don't want to beat around the bush, father. I came across a letter you wrote to Lou. It was clear the two of you . . . well, you seemed close, and exchanged thoughts freely."

The priest stared at Jack with penetrating brown eyes and nodded.

"I've come here from St. Louis to find out what happened."

The priest tilted his head. "Well, you know it was a murder, right?"

"Sure, I know that. I want to find the killer."

"Are you looking for revenge?" asked Father McFarland.

"I'm looking for justice," Jack answered. "I wanted to ask you if Lou gave you some sort of indication that he was worried."

"For his life?"

"Yes, exactly."

Father McFarland sat in thought. "That's hard to answer." He pushed his chair back and crossed his knees. "Dutch was always concerned about the opposition. He told me how he was being followed and threatened. A guy would come up to him from nowhere and ask him if he enjoyed having two legs that weren't broken. But Dutch always blew it off. He said they were just trying to intimidate him. He never gave in."

Jack crossed his legs as well, leaning back in his chair. "But somebody finally decided to go to the next step, didn't they?"

"They sure did," the priest answered.

"When was the last time you saw Lou?" asked Jack.

Father McFarland rubbed his chin. "Let's say you found the killer. What would you do?"

Jack immediately thought the question ridiculous. But then he remembered the priest's question on revenge. "I would contact the authorities," he quickly answered.

Father McFarland made a face; he did not seem satisfied. "You know, the Greeks have a saying. I'm not sure exactly how it translates, but it's more or less this: revenge does not heal wounds, but just the opposite—it keeps the wounds open and fills them with pus."

Jack should his head. What could he say to reassure the man? "Father, I'm not some sort of Al Capone type, running around with a tommy gun."

"I didn't say you were," the priest answered.

"I just want to know what happened to my brother."

The priest studied him for a moment. "Have you gone to the authorities?"

"I have," answered Jack. "They don't care because he was a red. They may even been in on it."

"I see your dilemma."

"When did you see him last?" Jack repeated.

"That would have been . . . June, in June. There was a strike on the bay, and Lou came here to support them."

"You remember anything about that meeting?" asked Jack.

"Hmm . . . " Father McFarland scratched his chin. "I think I did ask him if they were still threatening him. But I don't remember what he said."

How can you not remember something like that? Jack turned his head and watched steam wafting from the kitchen, trying to control his frustration. He caught the smell of fish and his stomach turned. He looked back at the priest. "Did he seem nervous?"

Father McFarland shook his head. "Not really. We spent most of the time talking about the mill. What was the name of that mill?" He frowned and tapped the table with his fingers. "Stoddert's, that it. The workers at Stoddert's carried out a sit-in strike and it was working. Dutch came here asking if the orphanage could spare some food. Unfortunately, we could not."

"Did he say anything about being threatened by the thugs at Stoddert's?" asked Jack.

"Ah, now I remember!" exclaimed Father McFarland, pointing his finger at Jack for emphasis. "When I asked him if he was being threatened, he said yes. And he was a little puzzled."

"By what?"

The priest almost smiled. "The guy who threatened him told him he breaks fireman's hoses for fun."

"What does that mean?"

"Dutch didn't know either," the priest answered. "I told him that a fireman's hose is old New York City slang."

"What does it mean?"

"A fireman's hose is a nose. The guy was saying he likes to break noses for fun."

Jack shrugged. "So what's so special about that?"

"I guess Lou was surprised that he was now being threatened by thugs from New York."

"Just because one guy is from New York?" asked Jack, his voice heavy with skepticism. "Maybe he moved down here."

"That's what I told him. But Lou said no. He said after this guy, there were more. And they all had New York accents."

Jack remembered that Petrov was from New York; he'd said something about Lou working on a project involving the northeast. "Remember anything else?"

"Not really," the priest answered. "He was totally engrossed by this strike at the mill. He didn't stay here long. Said he had a lot of things to do."

Jack nodded slow acceptance. "Did Lou ever tell you about the party?"

Father McFarland frowned. "No. And I never asked him. Our conversations on the subject of communism were always about its ideology. I think Dutch considered his membership in the party a subject too personal to discuss with me."

Jack put both palms on the table. Surely something useful must come of this trip? "You got anything else, father? Anything else that could help me?"

Father McFarland shook his head. "I wish I did," he answered. "Dutch didn't deserve this fate. But I must say, he knew what he was getting into. He got into the biggest fight there is. The outcome will decide the future of this nation."

Jack sighed and rose. "Thanks for your time, father."

The priest nodded and also rose.

Jack turned and started to walk away, but then he stopped and turned back around. "Father . . . tell me. Did Lou ever say anything about me?"

"Like what?"

"Well, you knew I had to change my name, so you probably know a lot more." Jack hesitated, then asked, "Was he mad at me?"

The priest took a moment to stretch his arms, then he shook his head. "Not as far as I know. He always spoke about you with fondness. But I felt . . . "

"What?" asked Jack.

"I'm not gonna mince words with you, Jack. I felt there was some sorrow."

Jack dropped his head. He knew exactly what the priest meant. He squinted, fighting off sudden tears. "Thank you, father," he muttered, and strode quickly from the cafeteria.

* * *

Sue slipped her arm through Jack's as they left the Paradise Movie Theater. They had attended a late afternoon showing of *Mr. Smith Goes to Washington* and the streets were now completely dark. She looked up. "Well? What did you think of the movie?"

Jack chuckled. "It was okay. I don't have to ask you what you thought. I didn't know you could laugh like that."

Sue smiled and shook her head. "I just love the way he looks at things."

"Who?"

"Capra. Frank Capra. Did you notice the credit at the beginning? He was the director."

Jack had never heard of Frank Capra. "No. I guess I missed it."

"He has such a warm view of humanity," she said, taking a deep breath. "It just fills my heart."

Jack welcomed Sue's tenderness, but he wanted to get his two cents in. "You got to admit, though," he said, "it's not realistic. I mean, you got a crooked senator who is so impressed with Jimmy Stewart's honesty that he admits to being a crook in front of the entire senate? Stuff like that never happens in real life."

Sue squeezed his arm. "But that's just it," she countered. "Capra's an idealist. He shows us what life could be like if we acted a certain way. If we trusted and respected one another."

The affectionate way she held his arm made Jack wonder if it was her way of saying that she regretted brushing off his kiss the last time they met. Her touch felt good. Still, he was not about to let it distract him from her argument. "But we know it's not like that in the real world," he insisted.

"But, don't you see?" she asked. "It's a vision. A vision of what is possible."

Jack shrugged. "I guess. I did like the girl. I mean, the way she supported Jimmy Stewart."

"I liked her too," Sue said. "You could say she was the force that made it all possible. It was her vision. She represented what Capra believes."

Jack thought Sue was right. In fact, the girl in the movie reminded Jack a little of Sue. Spotting a drugstore at the next corner, he jerked his chin toward it. "Want to stop for coffee?"

"Sure," she answered.

They stepped off the curb and crossed the street. "Find out anything about Lou?" asked Sue.

Jack wondered if he should tell her about the list and the negatives. "I'm working on it," he hedged.

Sue suddenly laughed. "Look at that sign!"

Jack looked up. A large Ex-Lax sign soared over the drugstore window.

"That will get your appetite going," she crowed.

"They probably never thought of that," he said.

When she'd stopped chuckling, she asked, "Find anything out on the creep down in Virginia?"

They were about to enter the drugstore. He stopped and turned toward her. "You mean the fat guy? Cromwell?"

"Yeah."

"I'm not through with him," Jack grated. Then he asked, "You ever hear of a guy named Petrov?"

Sue thought for a second. "Doesn't sound familiar."

"You sure? He's a security officer for the party. He said he came all the way from New York to meet with me."

Sue appeared surprised. "A security officer met with you? That's strange."

"Why?"

"They're a mysterious bunch," she answered. "I never met any of them and I was a member for years."

Jack opened the door to the drugstore. "Well, he's supposed to do his own investigation and keep me informed."

Sue made a face and shook her head. "He's not going to tell you anything. Believe me. They won't even tell the rest of us what they know," she said. Jack opened the door and she entered.

"Which reminds me," added Jack as he came in behind her, "Petrov said Lou was working on an assignment in the northeast. You know anything about that?"

Sue shook her head as they approached the soda fountain. "That's news to me."

A waitress appeared behind the counter. She brushed back her red hair and snapped her gum. "Yeah?"

"Two cups of coffee," said Jack as they sat down at the counter.

"That doesn't make sense," Sue continued. "Are you sure you understood him?"

"Positive," answered Jack. "He even said he was from New York."

"If Lou was given an assignment up north, what was he doing in D.C?"

Jack shook his head. "I don't know. Maybe he never got a chance to leave." As soon as the words left his mouth, Jack remembered what the priest had said. "Ah, wait—someone told me Lou was being threatened by New Yorkers."

"Where? Here or in New York?" asked Sue.

"I don't know," he said. "Maybe he was going back and forth. But you'd think that Maggie would have said something about that."

The waitress slid two cups on saucers across the counter and left.

Jack looked at Sue. "Anybody ever threaten you?"

"No. But I wasn't in the front line like Lou. They always kept me behind the scenes."

Jack glanced at Sue's cup of coffee. "Look at that," he said. "Your cup's half empty. That waitress isn't paying attention to her job. Let me call her."

Before he turned away, Sue shook her head. "No, no. It's okay. Maybe she's got things on her mind."

Jack raised his cup, wondering what to think of Petrov. He took a sip; the coffee was barely lukewarm. He grimaced and placed the cup back on the counter. "What did you think of the short before the movie?" he asked.

Sue giggled. "Don't tell me you like The Three Stooges."

"I can't help it," Jack answered, grinning sheepishly. "That guy Curly really cracks me up."

Sue continued to giggle. "Just when I was beginning to think you were a stuffed shirt conservative, you tell me you like The Three Stooges."

"So, what's wrong with that?" asked Jack.

"Nothing," Sue said, laughing, "if that's who you are."

Sue's smile was too infectious for Jack to feel insulted. "And what's that supposed to mean?" he asked, laughing himself.

Sue was in stitches. "Nothing, nothing. If the shoe fits . . ."

* * *

The sun hit Jack's eyes as he walked out of the photography shop on Pennsylvania Avenue. Ducking his head, he walked down the street, the envelope clutched in both hands, looking for a place to sit. After passing several row houses and an A&P grocery store, he spotted a park bench on the other side of the street where the sun would be at his back. He ran across the street, sat down on the bench, and opened the envelope, revealing a pack of black and white photographs and a small wrapper. He quickly opened the wrapper to make sure Lou's negatives were there, then turned his attention to the prints. They were sticky and still smelled of chemicals. He studied each photograph; they all showed two men, either sitting or walking together. Jack did not recognize them. He wondered if they were all from Lou's list.

An elderly man in a brown derby with a newspaper under his arm sat down next to Jack. Jack inched down the bench and tilted the photographs the other way. He studied them further, but they did not reveal any specific location.

The man in the brown derby opened his newspaper and shook his head. "Another war in Europe."

Jack ignored the man and continued examining the prints. He noticed something unusual—the photographs invariably showed two people, but one person was always the same: an older, distinguished-looking man whose suits looked expensive. His white hair was well groomed.

"They'll get us involved sooner or later," sighed the

man on the bench. He turned the paper to a new page. "Just like in '16."

Jack shrugged and slowly looked up. The man wore a freshly pressed, albeit old-fashioned, single-breasted suit. His head trembled slightly as he read.

"I guess so," said Jack, and suddenly wondered if he was being followed. He looked left and right but saw nothing unusual.

The man sighed again. "Tell me, why do they bother?"

Jack ignored him and turned his attention back to the photos. He stared at the image of the white-haired man, then tore the photo in half and placed the half with the white-haired man in his breast pocket. He stood. "Don't know, Pops," he said, and walked away.

Jack continued down Pennsylvania Avenue and turned onto Vermont Avenue. As soon as he'd turned the corner, he pressed his back to the façade of a row house and waited to see if there was someone behind him. Satisfied he was not being followed, Jack continued down the street until he saw the neon Greyhound sign of the bus station, a modern building with sleek, curved lines.

Jack made his way through the crowd and entered the lobby. Travelers gaped at a vast schedule board that dominated the space above the main hall. A man stood on a catwalk in front of the board, scribbling in the latest changes. Jack glanced at the two passages that led from the lobby, but saw no sign of lockers. He chose the passage to the left and walked briskly through the crowd.

A young woman wearing a pink dress with a V-shaped neckline and a ruffled collar pushed away from the wall as Jack passed and approached him, waving her left arm aggressively. "Hi, champ," she said. "Looking for a good time?"

Jack did not look at her. "Not today, sister. I'm all tied up."

As the woman walked away, Jack spotted a set of lockers against the wall farther up the corridor. He strode toward them, then turned around and leaned against a locker, glancing casually along the corridor in both directions to see if anyone was watching. Satisfied, he searched for and found an empty locker near the ground, and pushed a quarter into the slot. He removed the envelope containing the list, the negatives, and the prints from his jacket as he swung the door open, and slid them inside. Slamming the door closed, he pulled out the key.

❋ ❋ ❋

You ever see this guy?" asked Jack.

Maggie took the torn photograph and gazed at it. "No, never."

"Take a minute to think about it," Jack urged. "I think Lou may have known him."

She looked again, then looked up. "Nope, never seen him." She handed the photo back to Jack.

He knew that Maggie had not studied the photograph. She gave it only a fleeting look, as if it was not relevant. *You'd think,* he thought, *if she really cared about Lou, she would examine it intensely and try to recall if she'd had even the briefest encounter with the guy. Is she still upset that I refused to gratify her with punishment?* He looked at the photograph himself. "He doesn't look like a worker," Jack mumbled, studying the white-haired man who'd appeared in most of Lou's photographs.

153

Maggie rose from the sofa. "Where did you get it from?" she asked.

"I got lucky," said Jack.

"What do you mean?"

Jack shrugged. "Nothing. But this guy may hold the key." He looked at her. "Hear anything from Petrov?"

"No," she replied, and left for the kitchen.

Jack continued to stare at the photo. Why had Lou taken a series of photos with the white-haired man in each? Lou must have followed the guy and taken the photos to document his contacts. But why? Was the white-haired man the bait? The bait to lure everyone in? Did Cromwell and Mullen know this guy?

Maggie returned with two cups of hot tea.

"I wonder if this guy was the bait," he said.

"You're gonna have to tell me what you're talking about."

Jack looked up at her. "I suspect this guy knew the party members that were killed. I've got a feeling he led them into a trap."

"What makes you think that?" she asked as she held out one of the cups.

Jack took the tea from Maggie. "A hunch. Tell me, did Lou ever travel to the northeast, like to New York?"

"I can't be sure of that," she answered. "He would take off for days sometimes, meeting with workers here or there. But New York doesn't ring a bell."

"How many party members do you know of that died?" he asked.

Maggie sat back down. "Well, there was Lou . . . and another guy from our nucleus."

"Yeah, you mentioned him. What was his name—Al . . . ?"

"Al Collins," she answered. "There are others as well, but from different nuclei."

Jack tossed the photo on the coffee table and took a sip of his tea. "What are their names?"

Maggie held her cup to her lips, but answered before she drank. "I would have to do some asking." She paused, then met his gaze and asked, "By the way, what did you mean the other day when you said you can tie the thugs from the textile mill to the FBI?"

Jack thought there was something peculiar about the way she asked him. Her tone had changed, and he got the impression that she had been waiting for the right moment to ask him this. "Just that," he answered. "The thugs down there know the feds who were in the ballpark."

She lowered her cup. "How do you know that?"

"I went down there," he said. "I checked it out myself. And when I say thugs, I mean thugs." The thought of Cromwell made Jack feel sick, not only at the memory of being assaulted, but because he found the man's arrogance repulsive.

Maggie quickly put the cup down on the table. "When did you do this?" she asked in surprise.

"A couple of days ago. Why are you surprised? I told you I was going."

"Did you go alone?"

"No. I went with Sue."

Maggie's face tensed. "Sue? I told you to stay away from her."

Jack frowned. "I don't remember you saying that. What's the problem? Just because she's leaving the party? That has nothing to do with me."

Maggie's face wrinkled in disgust. She shook her head. "Sue's a whore."

"What?" Jack blurted.

"She's a whore. You didn't know? She worked for years in a cathouse here in D.C. Serviced a lot of politicians, I can tell you that."

This did not fit in with his impression of Sue at all. *Maggie must be making this up.* "What does that have to do with anything?" he asked, his tone defensive.

Maggie lifted her brows and waved her hand. "I guess it doesn't . . . if it doesn't bother you." She crossed her legs and folded her arms. "Jack, I think you should drop this whole thing. I mean, you have to let the party conduct its own investigation. Isn't that what Petrov told you?"

"How did you know that?" asked Jack.

Maggie hiked her shoulders. "It's standard procedure," she answered. "They don't like others interfering. It'll just screw the whole thing up. The left hand has to know what the right hand is doing."

"I can't just sit back and wait," Jack retorted.

"Why not?"

"It's just not in my nature. Why do you think I'm still here in Washington?"

Maggie tilted her head. "So that's the only reason?"

Jack suddenly realized she wanted to know if he had feelings for her. He did not, but he also did not want to upset her. "Well . . . let's just say it's one of the reasons."

Maggie shook her head. "Let it go."

"Why? Would it make things more difficult for the party?"

"It might," she said.

"What about Lou?" he asked.

"Lou did his . . . he did his job. It won't be forgotten. The party will do its own investigation. The murderer will be identified and recorded for future reference."

Jack felt his face flush. "That ain't justice, where I come from," he growled.

"There will be no justice until the revolution," she said, as if it was something he should understand. "Don't you see that?"

"Is this coming from you?" asked Jack. "Or from the party?"

Maggie shrugged. "What difference does it make? I'm telling you, I know what's best."

Jack's fingers started to tremble. He set his cup down. "Best for who? The party?"

Maggie inhaled deeply. "You still don't understand us, do you? The goals of the party have priority over everything. This includes personal happiness, wealth, and health and even the very lives of those that serve it. That is the oath we take and that's what makes us who were are."

"So Lou's life didn't matter?" Jack snapped.

"You're looking at it the wrong way," she answered. "Lou took that oath. By taking the oath, he agreed that the goals of the party were more important than his own life. Lou was a link in the chain, that's all."

"I thought you loved him," said Jack.

Maggie snickered cynically. "You just don't get it." She reached toward a straw basket on the table and retrieved Jack's pack of cigarettes. "Of course I loved him. But that doesn't change the reality of the situation." She struck a match and looked at Jack as she lit the Lucky Strike. "You sound a lot like Lou, you know that?"

"What do you mean?"

"When you talk about justice."

"It's just common sense," he said.

"It's not a question of whether there should be justice;

it's a question of what is justice. Lou's problem was that he had the typical mentality of a socialist, not a communist."

"Socialist, communist . . . what's the difference?" Jack shot back.

She smiled. "I can give you a hundred."

"Give me one," said Jack. "One that matters in Lou's case."

"Moral strength," she blurted. "A socialist has the same vision as a communist, but he doesn't have the moral strength to carry out what is necessary."

"Like what?"

"Like the elimination of the parasites, the bourgeois. Look at the purges in Russia. The Soviets show guts. That's exactly what we need here."

Jack had not seen this side of her. *This is one cold fish*, he thought. "You call it guts," he grated, "I call it murder."

"Would you be justified in killing a parasite that infested your belly?" she asked. "Of course you would."

Jack lifted his cup and mechanically sipped the tea but paid no attention to the taste. "So, Lou was against this 'victory at any cost'?"

"Who knows?" she asked, and shrugged. "Lou thought too much."

"So you've had this argument with Lou before?"

Maggie snickered. "Sure, a lot of times. Usually after midnight with a bottle of Jack Daniels on this very table."

Jack placed the teacup on the table and folded his arms. "I just can't understand the way you think."

Maggie flopped back on the sofa and sighed. "I guess you'll never understand. I just told you how I feel. I have nothing more to add. But listen to me; you have to let Lou's murder go."

Jack looked into her eyes. "Not on your life, sister."

Maggie put her head down and sighed again. "Jack, you either give this up or I'm gonna ask you to get out of here."

Jack chuckled. "You serious?"

"We walk a very tight rope," she said. "We know how to react to these things. If you run around here playing amateur detective, you're just going to screw everything up for all of us."

Jack rose. "I see. Well, I wouldn't want to interfere with the goals of your party." He lifted his arms in a helpless shrug and continued, his voice heavy with sarcasm. "I mean, you guys have the weight of the whole world on your shoulders. You mustn't risk all that over a two-bit bum like Lou."

He collected his jacket and hat off the sofa and left the apartment.

* * *

A bell jingled as Jack opened the door to the office of the Chesapeake Security Agency. He put his hands in his pockets and approached a thin young woman sitting behind a plain wooden desk. She pretended not to notice him, intently turning the pages of a calendar book. As he waited, the memory of the day the fat man pounded him in the belly made his heart beat faster, and he cleared his throat angrily.

The receptionist reluctantly looked up, patting at her platinum-blonde hair. "Can I help you?"

"I want to see the fat man."

Her eyes widened. She was wearing too much mascara, he noted absently. "What?"

"You heard me. I want to see Cromwell."

"And who are you?" she demanded.

Jack thought for a second. Cromwell would never agree to see him. "Tell him Mullen's here."

She stared at Jack in disapproval and pushed a button on her intercom. "Mr. Cromwell, a Mr. Mullen wants to see you."

There was no answer. She looked at Jack and shrugged.

Jack poked his chin at the intercom and tried to appear in control. "You sure you know how to work that thing?"

She let out a short laugh as if to say "who do you think you are?" Then she said, "He's not in, Mr. Mullen. And I don't remember you making an appointment to see him."

"I don't need an appointment. Find the fat man and tell him Mullen is here." Jack sat down in a chair in front of her desk and folded his arms. He stared at her.

A man's voice came over the intercom. "You call me, Lydia?"

The woman leaped at a button on the intercom. "Yes, Mr. Cromwell. A Mr. Mullen is here to see you."

There was silence at the other end. "Mullen?" Jack finally heard over the speaker.

"Yes," she answered. "A Mr. Mullen."

"Send him in."

She pointed to a door behind her and returned to her calendar.

When Jack opened the door, he saw Cromwell sitting behind a large mahogany desk, signing papers. The office itself was impressive. Original oil paintings hung on wood paneled walls and a large oriental rug covered the hardwood floor.

Cromwell looked up, and his eyes widened. "Who the hell are you?"

Jack squinted and pulled his head back in feigned offense. "What?" he exclaimed. "You don't remember me?"

"Should I?" asked Cromwell.

"Come on," he said as he helped himself to a chair in front of Cromwell's desk. "You gotta remember. Gullane Textiles. You gave me a tour."

Cromwell sighed and sat back in his leather chair. "Yeah, yeah. So what's this all about?"

Jack felt his face turn red. "What's it about?" he replied. "It's about the shit hitting the fan." He pulled out a pack of Lucky Strikes and slapped the bottom of the pack against Cromwell's desk until a cigarette sprang up. "Mullen's getting heat and the way it looks now, you're the one who's gonna pay through the nose."

Cromwell kept his eyes on Jack's cigarettes. "What the hell are you talking about? Heat for what?"

"That red murdered at the ball park."

"The red?" Cromwell looked at him. "What red?"

"The red murdered at Griffith Stadium."

"Who gives a shit about a red?"

"Somebody's got to take the hit, and it might as well be you," Jack said. "I hear Mullen's gonna put the finger on you any day now."

"I thought you said you were working for Mullen."

Jack placed the cigarette in his mouth and lit it. "I lied. I'm a newspaper guy— *Washington Chronicle.*

Cromwell folded his arms. "So, you're a reporter? I

might have known." He reached for a wooden box at the edge of his desk and pulled out a cigar. "Mullen's getting heat? Don't make me laugh." He pointed at the door. "Now, get the hell out of here."

"The feds and industry are joining forces to knock off reds?" Jack said. "That's a hell of a story, and the *Chronicle's* willing to run it."

Cromwell bit the tip off his cigar, spat it into a wastebasket beside the desk, and reached for his paperwork. "You're on a wild goose chase, kid," he muttered. "Now, get out!"

Jack sensed that Cromwell was attempting to minimize the situation. He rose, drawing on his cigarette, and turned to leave.

"Wait!" Cromwell yelled. "What is it you wanted from me?"

Jack turned around and exhaled a cloud of smoke. "My sources tell me you weren't in on the killing. If you tell me what you know about the feds, it would set the story straight from the start. You know what happens, once a story breaks. It doesn't matter if it's true. It's what everyone remembers."

Cromwell clasped his hands on his desk. "Your sources?" His double chin quivered as he chuckled. "You got balls, I'll give you that. But I ain't some two-bit chiseler. I ain't afraid of the feds or the press. You know how many attorneys I got?"

Jack thrust his chin out. "How many?"

"Tell your editor to run what he wants," Cromwell said. "Sooner or later, he'll have to deal with me." Cromwell paused to scratch his nose. "How did you get involved in this?"

"I do what they tell me to," Jack replied.

"Sounds like reds are running the *Chronicle*," said Cromwell. He chuckled again. "I might have known." He swung his arms up and clasped his hands behind his head, staring at Jack. "Now, you get the hell out of my office, kid, and tell your editors what I just said."

* * *

Jack lay in bed the next morning, wondering what had made him storm into Cromwell's office and make a fool of himself. He snorted. What he was thinking, the day he told Cromwell that he was with the Washington Senators and wanted to know why Cromwell was killing their fans? Instead of handing the situation tactfully, he had blown a potential lead, just as he had done with Mullen.

He swung his legs to the floor and looked out the window beside the bed. A gray morning, with heavy cloud cover. He stretched, wondering again what made him act so impulsively. Anger had not gotten the better of him before—not like this, at least. He had always managed to keep his cool when on a story, and only bluffed when he was at a dead end.

He shaved, dressed in his speckled gray double-breasted suit, and walked to the Waverly Cafeteria on 3rd Street. Sue was clearing dishes off tables when he found her. He pulled the torn photograph from his pants pocket and asked her to sit down.

"You know this guy?" he asked.

Sue glanced at the photo. "Where did you get this?" she asked, taking the photo.

"I think Lou took it. You know this guy?"

She looked up. "Yeah, I know him. It's Vitovski."

"Who is he?"

"He's a big shot," she answered.

"What kind of big shot?"

Sue looked down and slightly shook her head. She placed the photo on the table. "I'm not supposed to talk about him," she said.

Jack placed his hands on his thighs and looked straight at her. "Sue, I'm not after the party. I'm after the people who killed Lou."

"I know, but—"

"You told me the party is dumping you out anyway. What difference does it make?" She seemed to waver. He glanced toward the kitchen. "Do you have to go back to work?"

"No, it's okay," she said. "It's time for my break." She drew a deep breath, then exhaled. "Ben Vitovski's an *apparatchik*," she whispered.

"A what?"

"The party has an underground. It's called the Apparatus. The members are called *apparatchiks*. Ben's an underground chief."

"Did Lou know him?"

"Yeah." She nodded. "Vitovski was fond of Lou."

"Why would Lou take his picture?" asked Jack.

Sue frowned. "I don't know."

"You think it's possible that this guy Vitovski was ratting out party members? For the FBI, maybe?"

Sue picked up the photo again and stared at it. "I guess it's possible. But an underground chief? That's a stretch."

"Who exactly is he?" asked Jack.

"I don't know. None of us know. The *apparatchiks* all have code names. 'Ben' isn't his real name. The only one who knows the real names is the underground chief."

"So Vitovski knows everyone's true identity, but no one knows his?" asked Jack.

"That's right."

"Why all this secrecy?" he asked.

"It's after the Soviet model. That's how they did it in Russia, and it worked. We follow their model."

Jack pulled out his pack of Lucky Strikes. "If this Vitovski ratted out Lou, then he ratted out the other guy from your nucleus who was killed. What was his name?"

"He's not dead," Sue moaned.

"What? Who?"

"Albert Collins. He ain't dead. He was shot, but he didn't die. He's paralyzed. He's in a sanitarium."

Jack sat back and tried to think this through. Lou's nucleus said Collins was dead—why the lie? He leaned forward and offered Sue a cigarette, but she declined. "But, they all said he was dead."

"They were just covering," she said.

"Why?"

"They say they have to for security reasons."

"So, where is he?" asked Jack. "Where's this sanitarium?"

Sue shook her head. "I don't know. I don't think anyone in the nucleus knows, either. I wanted to visit him at the sanitarium, like I did when he was in the hospital. But the nucleus never found out where he was sent. I remember them trying."

Jack sat in thought. "That's strange," he finally said.

Sue shrugged. "That's the way it works."

"That's a fine *how do ya do*," Jack muttered.

She smiled and changed the subject with, "Change

your mind about the monuments? I can show you around."

Her smile was infectious. He smiled himself. "I'd love for you to show me around. But maybe we can do something else. I don't want to see some dumb monuments."

Sue put her elbows on the table and rested her chin in her palms. She smiled like a schoolgirl. "Now, what kind of patriot are you?" she asked. "You call our national monuments dumb?"

Jack stared at Sue, thinking about what Maggie had said. Could this sweet girl have worked as a prostitute? He wasn't sure he could buy it. At any rate, he had the distinct feeling he had won her over.

"There must be something I can show you in this town." She touched the back of his hand. "I know—I'll take you to Jimmy Mack's."

"What's that?"

"A nightclub."

Jack tried to picture Sue sitting at a nightclub bar, waiting for a client. "I didn't think you were the type to hang around in nightclubs," he said.

"This one's different."

Jack shifted. "I haven't been in a fancy nightclub in a while."

"This one's not fancy, but it's good."

Jack chuckled. "As good as that chicken shack?"

Sue waved her hand. "Better."

* * *

"Judy?" Jack jiggled the hook on the phone. "Judy? It's me, Jack. Can you hear me?"

Another bad connection to St. Louis. He thought

he heard her voice for a second, but then it disappeared behind a wall of static.

"Yeah, I hear ya," he finally heard a woman's voice say. "But I ain't got no news for ya."

"Come on, Judy. You said you'd be able to go through the obituaries in forty-eight hours. I told you this is important."

"I didn't say I didn't check. I went through all we got on Washington. But we stopped collecting out of town obituaries two years ago. We ain't got nothing."

"The paper stopped collecting them? Why?"

"It's Foster, that cheap son of a bitch. He didn't want to pay for the storage space. We only collect the front sections of all out of town papers."

"You sure you went through everything?" asked Jack.

"You think I'm giving you the screw? It took me a whole morning to go through all those files. I went through them month by month."

Jack sat back. *Now what?* "Thanks anyway, Judy."

"You still owe me," she reminded him.

"Yeah, sure," he answered. "I'll see you soon."

"Wait!" she yelled. "One more thing. Has Ryan been taking about me?"

Jack frowned. "Ryan? No, why?"

"You tell that fathead, if he doesn't stop blabbing around like some old windbag who's got nothing better to do, then . . . then . . . he's gonna hear it from me!"

"I don't know anything about it, Judy," said Jack. "You'll have to tell him yourself. Thanks again. Goodbye."

Jack threw down the receiver, walked out of the

booth, and stopped to look at the gray-haired clerk. "So, what you think, Pops?"

"What's that?" the man asked, eyes on his paper.

"A paper too cheap to keep important records," said Jack.

The clerk turned to a new page in his newspaper. "Don't know. I don't listen in on people," he answered. "It's against the law, ya know."

Jack chuckled. "Yeah, sure."

He left the post office, wondering what to do next as he stepped onto Pennsylvania Avenue. *I'll have to go to a local library and check the obituaries myself,* he concluded. This Vitovski fellow bothered him. How did he fit into the picture? *Focus,* he told himself. *The next logical step is to find out if Mullen has a relationship with Vitovski.* He'd need a press ID. He studied the store signs as he started walking, looking for a pawnshop.

A man on the other side of the street caught his attention. Leaning against the wall of a stone building at the corner of 10th Street, the man kept his head down as Jack passed, his black fedora obscuring his face as he took a drag on his cigarette.

You're getting paranoid, Jack told himself. But as he approached 11th Street, something told him to turn left. Quickening his steps, he stayed on the left side of the street and made another quick left onto Independence Avenue.

Jack looked around for an obstruction and spotted a cluster of tin garbage cans under an awning. He darted over to the building, stood behind the garbage cans, and waited.

The man who had been standing at the corner of 10th Street appeared at the intersection of Independence

Avenue and 11th Street. Jack felt his throat tighten. Eyes glued to the man, he went down on one knee behind the cans. The man looked both ways down Independence Avenue and then took several steps down 11th Street. He stopped and deliberately tapped the top of his fedora twice. Within seconds, another man appeared, wearing a dark suit and a white boater. The one with the dark fedora pointed down 11th Street and then down Independence Avenue, in the direction opposite Jack.

Jack slowly became aware of the stench emanating from the garbage can. He looked up at the lettering painted on the awning above him: *Pennyland Shooting Gallery*. "Smells like they're shooting live targets," he muttered, then turned his attention back to the two men. They were trotting down the two streets running away from him. He hesitated; should he wait for them to disappear, or take off in the opposite direction?

The door of the shooting gallery flew open. An obese man stood at the doorway. "You coming in, or what?" he asked Jack.

Jack jumped forward without thinking, and stopped in the middle of the sidewalk. Deciding his next step had been decided for him, Jack turned down Independence Avenue in the direction opposite that of the men. He crossed 10th Street and turned around; the one in the white boater was now walking down Independence Avenue in Jack's direction. Seeing Jack looking at him, the man suddenly kicked into a run, heading full-speed toward Jack.

Jack whirled and ran. Zigzagging between cars, he crossed the avenue and turned right on 9th Street. Arms pumping, he pushed forward between pedestrians and turned left at the next intersection. Grabbing at a stitch in his right side, he spun for a look back; the man was right behind him, and gaining.

Before he could turn back, Jack slammed into something; he fell to the sidewalk and rolled, glimpsing an overturned ice cream stand. Beside it, a man in a white apron started yelling at him. Jack scrambled to his feet and pounded down the street, turning down the first alley he saw. His footsteps echoed along the narrow space between two brick row houses as he ran.

Just steps away from the street at the other end, someone tackled his legs from behind, and he tipped forward, hitting the ground hard with his right shoulder. He heard the *snick* as a switchblade opened and struggled to rise, but the man was now on his back. Jack heaved upward with all his strength. The man flew against the building, moaning as his back hit the brick wall. Jack rolled to his right and broke free. Scrambling to his feet, Jack turned and pinned the man's shoulders against the wall.

"Who are you?" Jack yelled. The man stared at him, panting. "Who do you work for?" Jack demanded, also breathing heavily.

The man did not answer. Jack heard footsteps and turned his head. The man's partner was running down the alley toward them. Jack threw the man to the ground and took off in the opposite direction, toward the open street. He managed to make it to the avenue and turned left, onto East Capital Street.

The sidewalk was filled with people, no doubt just getting out of work. He stopped running and put his right hand on this belly, rubbing the cramp as he tried to blend into the crowd. After a few minutes, the cramp became worse. When he was unable to go on, he stopped in the front passage of a bookstore, watching the throng pass in waves as he recovered.

When he saw no sign of the two men who had followed him, he entered the crowd, turning right on 6th Street and then left onto Massachusetts Avenue. Still short of breath, he stopped in front of Topps Drugstore Luncheonette and looked around; they were not in sight. He entered the drugstore and walked toward the rear, looking for the soda fountain.

"You got a men's room here?" Jack asked the soda jerk standing behind a shiny white counter.

The man pointed to a sign on the wall. "Sorry, pal. Customers only."

"I'll take a doughnut and a cup of coffee," said Jack. "Now where's the men's room?"

"To your left, all the way in the corner," the soda jerk answered.

Jack entered the men's room and turned the lock. Leaning against the door, he took slow, deep breaths and wiped the sweat off his forehead. He pulled off his jacket and leaned over the sink, turning on the faucet to splash his face with cold water. Shivers ran down his spine when he poured the water over his head. His breathing gradually slowed, and the cramp in his stomach melted away. He looked up into the mirror, removed the comb from his shirt pocket, and slowly combed his hair, wondering who the two thugs were.

When he felt his composure return, he left the men's room, paid for the coffee and doughnut, and left the drugstore. Turning onto Massachusetts Avenue, he stared at the stores lining the street, still thinking about the two men. They had to be from the same group that attacked him in the hotel. Both times, a knife had been pulled.

Jack doubted the FBI would kill a man in cold blood, but he could imagine factory thugs like Cromwell doing so.

Finally he made out a *Swap For More* sign in the block ahead—a pawnshop. Bells chimed as he opened the door and stepped into a small space stuffed with showcases. The air was stale and smelled of mothballs and cheap cigars. A short, bald man sat behind the counter with half a cigar in his mouth. He glanced up from his newspaper. "How are ya?" he asked.

"Couldn't be better," answered Jack. He walked up and stared at the items in the showcase where the man sat. "You do identification papers?" he asked without looking up.

The man pulled the cigar out of his mouth and took a long look at Jack. "Maybe."

"I lost my ID. I need a press identification paper for the *Washington Chronicle*."

The man placed the cigar in a tin ashtray. "A press ID? That sort of thing costs money."

"How much?" asked Jack.

The man examined Jack's clothes. "You're talking fifteen . . . maybe twenty dollars."

Jack pulled out his wallet. "Half now, half on delivery." He threw a ten-dollar bill on the counter.

The man grabbed the money. "You got the photo?"

"No," answered Jack. "You have a camera?"

The man grinned. "Sure, Mack. But that will be an extra buck."

Jack pulled his wallet back out and placed a dollar bill on the counter.

The man rose from his stool and walked to the main entrance. He locked the door and turned around. "Follow me."

Jack followed the man behind the counter, through a doorway covered by an old red curtain, and along the passage beyond. They entered a dimly lit back room that was cluttered with cardboard boxes.

"Have a seat," the man said, pointing into the right corner.

Jack turned; an old-fashioned box camera stood on a tripod several feet from a wooden stool. He combed his hair with his fingers and sat down.

The man tinkered with the camera. "Must be an interesting thing you got planned," he said matter-of-factly.

Jack fixed his jacket. "Not really. I'm just a delivery boy and I lost my ID."

The man snickered. "Poor kid." He lifted a flash lamp. "Hold still. On three."

The flash burned Jack's eyes.

"One more," the man said. The flash went off again. The man put down the lamp. "We're all done. Give me a couple of days."

Jack rose. "One more thing," he said. "I need a gun."

* * *

"Two names," said Jack. "I'll give you two names just so you believe that I have it."

Mullen folded his arms. "You're in no position to argue. I want the whole damn list."

They sat in the same small, cluttered office that Mullen had brought Jack to, the last time he was at FBI headquarters. Although there was no name on the door, Jack assumed it was Mullen's personal office. "Well, I ain't giving it to you, buddy," said Jack. "Not yet, anyway.

Have me arrested right now if you want. Arrest me for delivering alcohol, which is now legal, by the way."

Mullen shrugged. "I don't care about the repeal. The statute of limitations hasn't passed. I convict bootleggers all the time."

Jack chuckled. "Find a jury that will convict me."

"Don't believe me?" Mullen challenged.

"And don't forget to tell your superiors the whole story," Jack continued. "The only reason you caught me was because I came looking for my brother's murderer; a murder you can't solve. You'd be the laughing stock of the department."

Mullen sat back in his office chair. "So, what are the names?"

"You think I came in here for you to threaten me?" Jack retorted. "Maybe you didn't hear me. I said, you give me what you have on Cromwell, and I'll give you two names. Otherwise I walk."

Mullen sat in thought. "I'll tell you. But you'll be disappointed. Cromwell had nothing to do with your brother's death."

"Then who did?" asked Jack.

"I don't know," said Mullen. "Now give me the names."

Jack gave him an incredulous look. "You think I'm gonna buy that? Are you joking? That's not worth two names. When I said give me what you have, I meant show me the files on Cromwell and my brother."

Mullen leaned forward and spoke slowly. "That's impossible. No civilian goes into an FBI file. It's even tough for a congressman to get that privilege."

Jack sighed and sat back, thinking of what he should do next.

"The names," Mullen repeated.

"How do you know Cromwell isn't involved?" Jack pressed.

"I got my sources," answered Mullen.

"How come a hoodlum like Cromwell knows you? And how come he just happens to be the same thug in charge of security for that factory?"

Mullen looked away and did not answer.

Jack's heart started to beat hard. "And how come I can place you at the scene?"

Mullen remained silent.

"Answer me that!" yelled Jack.

Mullen tilted his head. His unconcerned expression looked forced. "I gotta admit, you bring up some valid questions," he said. "But I have to find out if I can trust you."

"You, trust me?" Jack shouted. "How the hell am I supposed to know if I can trust *you*?"

"Give me the two names, and I'll check them out."

Jack stared at the FBI agent. Could he trust Mullen? Should he? If Mullen was on the level, Jack would help the investigation by giving the FBI the names. On the other hand, if Mullen was crooked, the FBI agent could just be determining how dangerous Jack was. In that case, revealing the names could be Jack's death sentence.

"Well?" Mullen snapped.

Jack stared silently at the other man. *Does he have the list? Is he playing me for a fool?* Mullen's proposal the last time they met suddenly hit Jack. Mullen was willing to destroy Jack's record if he turned over the list. It could have been a trap, but if Mullen was a thug and had the list already, he would have taken no chances; he would have taken care of Jack right away.

Mullen shook his head. "I got things to do, you know," he muttered. "You're wasting my time."

Jack shifted his gaze to the photographs of J. Edgar Hoover and the middle-aged woman on the wall behind Mullen. "Is that J. Edgar Hoover?" he asked.

"Which one?" Mullen turned to the wall.

"What do you mean, which one?" asked Jack.

Mullen turned back to Jack and chuckled. "Never mind. What are the names?"

Jack recited from memory, "James Fredricks, Department of Justice. Timothy Keens, Department of Labor. That's all you get."

Mullen reached for a pen on his desk and quickly jotted down the names.

Jack watched him, thinking, *Why would Mullen jump at the names if the feds were involved in the murders?* Despite that reassuring thought, Jack got the feeling that, even though Mullen didn't have the names, he knew a ton of things he was not telling Jack. But did he know Vitovski? Jack wondered if he should simply ask Mullen or pull a bluff. Instead, he decided to save that for another day.

"You want more names, I got 'em," he said. "But you have to tell me more."

Mullen clasped his hands behind his head and sighed. He stared thoughtfully at a point above Jack's head and said, "You stay put in that hotel. We'll get back to ya."

* * *

Jack opened the door to the morgue at City Hospital and peeked inside. The three metal autopsy tables were empty and the morgue was scrubbed clean. Nevertheless, as he slowly walked in, Jack detected that strange odor in the air that he remembered from covering autopsies in St. Louis—a sickening mixture of rotting flesh and disinfectant. The smell, like the morgue itself, was something Jack could never get used to. Even a hardened cop could have trouble bearing the smells and sights of the morgue.

Jack would never forget his first experience in a morgue, at County Hospital in St. Louis. He had just been hired by the *St. Louis Herald* and, eager to make a good first impression, he had followed a police lieutenant to the hospital to get the scoop on a fresh murder case. When the lieutenant made his way down to a basement corridor and then pushed through a double door, Jack had rushed in behind him without looking at the sign on the door. As he searched for the lieutenant, his eyes fell instead on bloody coils of bowel, pulled up into the air. He stopped and stared; the body of a fat, middle-aged man lay on a metal table with its belly cut wide open. Blood streaked the sides of the body. Jack had quickly turned away from the horrifying scene; behind him, a bearded man in a bloodied white apron continued to cut the base of the intestine away from the body, muttering complaints about not getting Friday off. Jack felt his stomach tighten. He bent over, expecting to vomit.

The lieutenant he had been chasing walked up to him. "First time?" he asked. Jack nodded and waited, but the vomit did not come. "Have a smoke," said the lieutenant. "It helps."

Jack walked out of the morgue. He lit a cigarette in the corridor and sat down on a bench. The lieutenant was right; smoking helped. That day, Jack learned—the hard way—never to take the morgue lightly.

"Anyone here?" Jack now yelled. There was no answer. He walked around, relieved that the tables were free of bodies. He decided to wait for someone to make an appearance. The posters on the walls caught his attention. They'd been drawn by a talented hand. Some dictated dissection techniques for different parts of the body, while others showed the trajectory of gunshot wounds.

The door behind him opened. "Can I help you?" someone asked.

Jack turned his head. The morgue attendant with the crew cut stood inside the door, holding a brown paper bag in his left hand.

"Hey, pal. I was here before, remember me?" asked Jack. "My brother was the one killed in the ballpark."

The attendant squinted at Jack. "Oh, yeah. I remember. Griffith Stadium. So, what's up?" he asked, walking to a counter against the wall to throw the down the brown bag.

"I want to thank you for the scoop you gave me . . . it was helpful."

The attendant pulled a sandwich wrapped in wax paper from the bag and looked at Jack as if he knew there was more to Jack's visit than a simple thank you. "You want to find out more?"

Jack shook his head. "No, no."

"Sorry, pal, I told you all I know," said the attendant, ignoring Jack's answer. He pulled up a chair, sat down, and focused on unwrapping the sandwich.

"No, I need something else. You know the ambulance drivers here at the hospital?"

"Why?" the attendant asked, and took a bite of the sandwich.

Jack stared at the thick slices of rye bread in the man's hands. "You eat that in here?"

The man wiped his lips. "Where else am I gonna eat it?"

Jack tried to focus. "I need to know where a patient was taken from here. He was in this hospital for a gunshot wound. Then they took him to a sanitarium. The drivers must keep records of where they take the patients. I need to know where this guy went."

The man shrugged. "Sure, I know some drivers," he said around a mouthful of food. He set the sandwich down on the wax paper and reached into the brown bag. "But if I ask them that, the first thing they'll ask me is, 'Who wants to know, and why?'"

This caught Jack off guard. He was about tell the attendant that it was important to his investigation, but quickly realized the drivers would not want to get caught up in a murder case. "Let's just say I'm looking for a relative."

The man pulled a pickle from the bag and took a bite. "A relative, huh?" He licked his lips. "You doing a story?"

"What do you mean?" asked Jack.

"I remember you saying you're a newspaper guy. Is this for a story?"

Jack shook his head. "No, nothing like that. I don't even work here in D.C. I'm from St. Louis."

"Maybe they'll sing," said the attendant, "but they won't sing for free."

Jack reached for his wallet and pulled out a ten-dollar bill. He slammed it on the counter next to the brown bag.

The attendant's eyebrows rose but he quickly looked away. He reached for his sandwich. "So, did they ever find your brother's killer?" he asked.

"No," answered Jack. "But they're working on it."

The attendant swallowed with difficulty and reached for his pickle. "That's kind of curious that they can't solve it. With all those feds here that day."

"You're telling me," said Jack. "So . . . we got a deal?"

"I'll see what I can do," was the answer.

"The guy's name is Albert Collins," said Jack. "He came here in July." He pushed the ten-dollar bill toward the man. "You divide that with the drivers any way you want."

"What was it? Albert Collins?" the attendant asked.

"That's right."

The attendant crushed the brown paper bag with both hands. "Okay, give me some time."

★ ★ ★

The signs on the club's exterior announced dancing, 7-Up, beer, and steaks. Jack had put on his expensive suit, a midnight blue, six-button, double-breasted suit featuring sleeves tapering from shoulder to wrist, and high pockets. The new look, known as the "London cut," had just come to St. Louis from New York.

Sue was right, thought Jack as he and Sue entered Jimmy Mack's Nightclub on 9th Street just after nine p.m., *this place is different.* Instead of glittering silver and glass, the club had red brick walls and only a few cheap light fixtures. Most of the light came from candles in bottles on the old wooden tables. The main hall was only half full and, unlike most nightclubs in Washington, there were almost no soldiers present. And unlike the other clubs, there was no sign of cigarette or camera girls.

They also were not greeted at the door; Sue and Jack sat themselves down at a corner table.

"Well?" asked Sue. "What do you think?"

Jack nodded as he scanned the lounge. At the far end, six man brass band played a tune that Jack recognized as "Sent for You Yesterday" by Count Basie. "Well, you were right. It is different," he replied.

Sue laughed. "It's better than those clip joints filled with mobsters."

"Doesn't this place have a bar?" he asked.

"It's downstairs," she said. "And the gambling's in the back."

"They always play jazz here?" asked Jack.

"Sure, it's a pure jazz club."

"It's a lot different from the jazz clubs in St. Louis," he said.

A waitress approached. Instead of wearing the standard low-cut blouse and short skirt, she wore a sweater over a long dress. Jack ordered two Bohemian beers and glanced over Sue's shoulder at the front entrance. Watchfulness was becoming habit, he noted wryly, and turned his attention back to Sue. "You got a story?" he asked.

Sue stared the candle on the table. "Everyone has a story," she said softly.

"So, what's yours?"

She shrugged. "It's like I told you. My family lost everything during the Depression."

"Where are they now?" he asked.

"I only have a sister left," she answered. "She took off for the west coast years ago. Last I heard, she was living in southern California."

The beers arrived along with tall, tapered glasses. Jack

watched the waitress pour his beer, then took several long gulps; the brew was bitter, but cold and refreshing.

"And your parents?" he continued. "What happened to them?"

Sue tilted the beer bottle back and forth with her forefingers. "My father died of a heart attack after the Crash. Then my mother got sick. The doctors said it was heart failure." He voice grew flat. "I did what I could. I got doctors and the medications she needed."

Jack glanced at the door as two men walked into the club. They stopped and scanned the hall. Pretending not to notice them, Jack returned his attention to Sue.

Sue stared at the beer bottle in her hands. "Jack, if someone does a bad thing but they were forced into the situation—I mean, can you really blame them?"

"What do you mean?"

She still didn't look at him. "If someone had no choice but to do things for money, money that they needed to pay for their mother to get better, can you blame them?"

"I guess it depends what you did," he answered, though he already suspected what it was. It appeared that Maggie had been telling the truth. Sue had worked as a prostitute.

Sue looked up. "What's that supposed to mean?" she snapped.

Jack was not sure how to respond. After a moment he said, "I mean, if someone killed for money, it's not justified just because the money was used for good."

Sue looked back down at the bottle and grabbed the chain around her neck. She slid her fingers along the chain until they touched the gold heart locket. "I didn't kill anybody," she muttered.

Jack did not want to press the issue. If she wanted to

tell him she'd worked as a prostitute, she would do so. "Sue," he said, "the Depression was rough on everyone. You did what you could to survive." As the words left his mouth, Jack wondered if what he had said was true. Had he taken in Lou, things would have been rough, but they would have survived. In reality, Jack now realized, it hadn't been so much about survival for him as it was his own selfishness.

"I know, I know," Sue said. "It's just . . . I mean, it's not guilt; it's more like shame."

"Don't be so hard on yourself," said Jack. "You know what I did when things got rough?"

"What?"

"I went to Michigan hoping to get a job on an assembly line. But, damn it, not once could I make it through the crowd to even get to the gate. So I ended up working for the Mob."

Sue giggled. "You? With the Mob?"

Jack noticed a tear on her cheek. Sue saw the point of his focus and wiped off the tear. "I should have taken you to a clip joint where the mobsters show off their dough."

"The night is young," Jack quipped. He looked back at the front entrance. The two men had walked over to the opposite side of the lounge and stood against the wall.

"So, what did you in the Mob?" she asked. "Did you rub out the opposition?"

Jack chuckled. "Yeah, right! I was the hit man. So don't ever cross me, sister," he said in a nasal voice in imitation of Edward G. Robinson. "Or you'll get yours."

Sue laughed. "No, really, what did you do?"

"I delivered booze to speakeasies."

They looked at each other for a moment, then both laughed.

"Jack the bootlegger!" yelled Sue as she reached for her Bohemian beer. She took a sip and looked at him. "Is that why you changed your last name? Because of the Mob?"

"Yeah, the FBI was after me," he answered. He wondered if he should tell her that they might have been followed into the club.

"Good thing you told me," she said with a soft smile. "Now I know I gotta watch my step. I mean, you being a mobster."

"So, we're even. You're part of the red menace. I got to watch my step with you, too."

"I guess maybe you're right," she said. "I mean—everybody did something to get by."

"Sue, a couple of guys just walked in here," said Jack. "I don't like the way they look. I think we better leave."

Her eyes widened. "Now?"

"Let's wait a minute."

The Count Basie song ended to scattered applause. Sue looked as if she wanted to turn around but was resisting the temptation. "Are they the same guys who were after you?"

Jack did not respond; he watched the two men. One walked up to a piano and rested one hand on it as he looked around. "No," Jack finally answered. "That's the scary part. There are a lot of these guys."

Sue lift her brows in puzzlement. "So you think someone is still after you?"

"You bet," he answered.

"Who?"

"I don't know. But it would be good to find out."

Jack tried not to look at the two figures, but he followed their movements from the corner of his eye. The one by the piano proceeded to pull a plastic cover off the piano frame, then sat down on the piano stool. The other joined him and lifted a trumpet. Jack sighed in relief. "Forget it," he said. "They're musicians."

"Well, at least you'll survive the night," she said with a smile.

"We'll see. Like I said, the night is young."

"Any luck finding Al Collins?" asked Sue.

"Not yet. I'm working on it." He reached into his coat pocket and pulled out his Lucky Strikes.

He offered her a cigarette but she shook her head. "I'm trying to quit. Find anything else out about Cromwell or Mullen?"

"Not really. Mullen tells me Cromwell's not involved, whatever that's worth." He glanced again at the door as he lit his cigarette. "Someone got near me again."

"Again?"

"I was followed on the street," he said. "That's twice now; three's a charm."

"And you still don't know who," she added as if that said it all.

He shook his head. "They offered me a free shave, but I got away."

"What do you mean, a free shave? Did they try to kill you?" She leaned across the table. "Jack, it's just a matter of time until they get you. You've got to get out of D.C."

"I've got to pursue the list," Jack countered. "And I have to look into each death and find the common thread."

Sue shook her head in resignation and took a sip of her beer. "But what will you do if you find something out?" she asked. "Who will you go to?"

Jack looked down at the table. "I don't know,' he replied. "I'll worry about that later."

"Jack, this whole thing smells to high heaven. You have an FBI agent at the murder scene and this agent just happens to know the chief of security of a textile mill where Lou was trying to organize a strike."

Jack nodded. "I know, I know."

"And you have no one to go to," she continued. "No one to back you up. You're a sitting duck for these people, whoever they are."

Jack dragged on his cigarette. He knew she was right. He was out of his league. Instead of conducting a scientific investigation, he had been trying to advance it by bullshitting his way through. That was the only way he knew how to do it, as a newspaperman. But what he had done so far was even a bad job for an investigative reporter, let alone a detective. Instead of making contacts, he had confronted the leads, blowing any chance of learning more. New York might be his last chance to make some sort of headway, he thought. "So, what do you want me to do?" he asked. "Go back to St. Louis and forget the whole thing?"

"Why not?" she asked. "Sooner or later, they'll get you if you stay here. You know that."

Her response was predictable, but it showed she cared. He put out the cigarette.

"I'm serious, Jack. Go back to St. Louis."

"I'm leaving," he said, "but I'm not going to St. Louis. I'm going to New York."

Sue frowned. "New York? What for?"

"There's a guy I want to talk to there. He tried organizing a union in a machine plant. I got a feeling Lou was involved."

"What makes you think that?"

"It's a hunch."

"You're going all the way to New York on a hunch?" she asked.

Jack chuckled. "That's how we work in the newspaper game. If we didn't go on hunches, we wouldn't ever come up with anything."

Sue sat thinking. "Are you coming back here?" she finally asked.

Jack smiled and reached for her hand. "Are you kidding? I'll be back here as soon as I'm done." Her question made him even more confident that he had won her over.

As she leaned forward, the candlelight made her locket glow gold, catching his attention. "Where did you get that?" he asked.

"The necklace?" She touched it. "My mother gave it to me. Why?"

Jack stared at the necklace, thinking of prostitutes. Not once had he ever met one who was sentimental. "No reason," he answered. "Want to leave?"

"Sure," she answered.

When they arrived at her apartment, Jack leaned against the wall, finishing his cigarette as she searched for her keys. He longed to kiss her and hold her. The time for that, he thought, had finally arrived. When the keys finally came out, she looked up and appeared confused when she saw him watching her.

"So, can I come in?" he asked.

"I . . . I have to get up early," she muttered, ducking her head and sliding the key into the lock.

Her reaction surprised him, but he was not going to give up that easily. He reached out to touch her cheek, but she backed away.

"What's wrong?" he asked.

"Nothing."

"Come on, Sue. There's something wrong. I can tell. Let's go inside and talk it over." He leaned over to kiss her, but she pulled away.

"Why can't you kiss me?" he asked.

"I just can't, that's all."

"Why not?"

She let out an exaggerated sigh as if to let him know that he just didn't get it.

"Sue," he said gently, "I know something is bothering you. But I'm not a mind reader. Let's go inside and talk about it."

She looked as if she was going to say something, but instead she leaned forward and buried her head in his chest. "Please forgive me, Jack."

"For what? That you don't want me to come in?"

"Not that," she mumbled, her voice muffled against his coat.

"Then what?" He brought his hands up and held her arms.

"Just say you forgive me."

"Okay, I forgive you." He wondered if this had anything to do with her past. "But it's more important for you to forgive yourself."

"But you don't even know what I did."

Should he tell her what Maggie had said? No. "But I know how you feel," he said instead. "Something bad happened to you and you felt trapped. You were forced to do something you now regret. That's how I felt when I decided to leave Lou. Like I was being trapped into something."

"What does Lou have to do with this?" she asked.

"I know how you must feel because of him. Whatever it is you did, you've got to forgive yourself."

"You mean that?"

"Of course," Jack answered. "Now, let's go inside."

Sue lifted her head off of Jack's chest but continued to look down. She slowly shook her head. "No," she muttered.

Enough. Jack kissed her on the top of her head. "Good night, Sue."

✳ ✳ ✳

Jack stood in his hotel room rereading two newspaper clippings from the *Washington Chronicle*. The first was the article he had read in front of the FBI headquarters that described trouble at the tool and die plant in New York. The second, larger article had been printed several days later and gave a blow-by-blow description of riots at the plant after the attempt to hold a vote was crushed. Both articles quoted the man Jack was hoping to interview in New York: Peter Morgan, a worker at the plant leading the effort to unionize.

Jack folded the articles and placed them in the envelope holding the train ticket that would grant him passage from Union Station in Washington to Grand Central Station in New York City. He had decided to go the following Monday, early enough in the week to give himself several days to locate Morgan. Setting the envelope on the desk, he bent and picked up his black leather shoes, then moved over to the bed to put them on.

The soles of his shoes were badly worn, he noticed as he lifted one foot to tie the shoelaces. He did a lot of footwork as an investigative reporter, and had become accustomed to replacing his shoes frequently. But he had worn this pair out faster than any before; only a thin layer of hide remained where the ball of his foot rested.

He put on the other shoe while studying the map of Washington spread out on the bed beside him, searching for Connecticut Avenue. He had thought of going to the public library to look up old obituaries from the *Washington Chronicle*, but the reporter in him had taken over and he'd decided to approach each governmental agency individually; there was nothing like a firsthand interview.

As he folded the map, someone knocked on the door. He froze—more thugs? Dropping the map, he reached under his pillow and pulled out his gun, the loaded Iver Johnson Revolver that he had bought in the pawnshop. Holding the gun loosely in his right hand, he took several steps toward the door. "Who's there?" he yelled.

No answer.

He raised his arm and pointed the gun at the door. "Who's there?" he yelled once again.

"It's me, Maggie," he finally heard.

He let out a sigh of relief. "Hold on!" he yelled, and walked back to the bed to slip the gun back under the pillow.

As he swung the door open, he saw Maggie quickly put on a smile. She brushed her hair back behind her right ear. "Well? Can I come in?"

"Sure," Jack answered, wondering what she wanted. He stepped back to allow her entry.

Maggie walked in and glanced around the room. Not bad," she said. "But it must get to you after a while—I mean, it's so small. You getting cabin fever?"

Jack forced a chuckle and closed the door. "I've had

worse." He dragged a wooden chair away from the wall. "Have a seat," he said and flopped down on the bed himself.

Maggie forced another smile and smoothed her skirt as she sat down.

"What can I do for you?" he asked.

She hiked her shoulders, then let them drop. "I just feel so bad," she said. "I mean, the way I acted the other day."

Jack was not moved. "Hear anything from Petrov?"

"No, but don't worry about that. They don't hold your hand and give you updates every step of the way. Once they're ready, you'll hear from them. I guarantee you."

Jack shrugged. Neither spoke. Jack reached for his map to finish folding it.

"Jack, you should know I get carried away sometimes. I end up saying things I don't mean."

Jack continued folding the map. "Everybody's entitled to their opinion."

"Things that I regret," she added.

"Like what?"

She tilted her head and smiled. "You know what I mean . . . that you don't get it . . . and that Lou didn't have guts."

Jack threw the map back on the bed. "Don't worry about it."

Maggie rose and sauntered over to put her hands on his shoulders. "Will you forgive me?" she asked as she caressed the back of his neck.

Her touch felt good, but Jack did not want to give in. Nothing repulsed him more than insincerity. "Yeah, sure," he mumbled.

She settled on the bed beside him and slid both arms around his chest.

"Maggie, I gotta go," he said. "I got things to do."

She kept her face buried in his chest. "Just a few minutes . . . please."

Jack wanted to stand up but resisted the temptation. Although he thought she was being insincere, he did not want to seem cold-hearted.

"Where is it you have to go?" she asked.

That's it, he thought. *She's prying for information.* "I just have some stuff I have to take care of," he answered. He patted her head and very slowly rose, giving her a chance to pull back and not feel insulted. "I'd love to sit and chat, Maggie, but I've got to go. I'm late."

Maggie stood with a sigh and looked at him, running her fingers through her hair. "Okay . . . I don't want to keep you."

Jack reached for his jacket, draped over the chair, and put it on. "We can talk some other time," he said.

Maggie smiled and asked quickly, "When?"

Something about her smile . . . it seemed genuine, but inappropriate. *Is this girl insincere, or simply unstable?* he wondered, eyeing her as he fixed his tie. "I don't know. I'll stop by sometime."

She shook her head. "You don't believe me, do you."

"About what?"

"That I loved Lou."

Jack shrugged. "Actually, it's none of my business."

The smile vanished. "Just because you love someone doesn't mean you always have to agree with them."

Jack wondered how he was going to get her to leave. "Yeah, sure. I understand." He pointed to the door. "Now, Maggie, I've got to—"

Maggie let out a howl, then lowered her head and started to cry.

This is all I need, thought Jack.

Sagging down onto the bed, she covered her face with both hands as she sobbed. Jack sighed and leaned against the door. He folded his arms and looked out the window. *Now what?*

Maggie occasionally uttered a few muffled words as she cried, but Jack could not make out what she was saying. He sat down on the bed next to her and stared at the hardwood floor. "Maggie, it's obvious you loved Lou," he said. "If it means something to you that I understand that . . . well, then, I do. I'm sure you guys fought; all couples do. But he's gone. You're just going to have to live with it."

Maggie wiped her eyes. "I know," she muttered. "It's just that . . . "

"What?"

"My feelings shouldn't count," she said.

What on earth is she talking about? he thought. "I don't follow you, Maggie."

"My feelings. Who cares about my feelings?" she asked.

"It's important that you care," he answered.

She looked at him with tear-filled eyes. "I don't even care about my own feelings. Do you believe that?"

Jack was not sure what that meant or how to react. He *was* sure that she was on an emotional roller coaster. And, more importantly, if he sat here much longer, he wouldn't make it to the Department of Labor before everybody there went on their lunch break.

"Now Maggie, I have to leave," Jack tried. "I'll stay

here until you feel better, but after that, I have to go, and so do you."

Maggie extended her arms and hugged Jack tightly. "Kiss me," she whispered.

He gently took both her hands in his. "No, Maggie," he said softly. "Just take a nice, deep breath and relax."

She dropped her arms and put her head down to stare at the floor. He wasn't sure, but he thought that maybe she was losing her mind. "You okay, Maggie?"

Maggie abruptly rose. Without turning around, she walked out of the hotel room and slammed the door.

Jack stared at the door for a perplexed moment. Then he let out a gusty sigh and rose himself. Tracking down a few obituaries had to be easier than this.

* * *

Jack turned onto Louisiana Avenue, still struggling to find Constitution Avenue on his crinkled map. When he finally located it, he put away the map, pulled out his pack of Lucky Strikes, and lit a cigarette as he turned down Florida Avenue.

Maggie had reminded him of Petrov. To this day, the son of a bitch had not gotten back to him; he'd decided the Russian never would. Whatever was going on in New York, it was obviously important to the party, and Petrov was not about to fill Jack in on the details. And that meant that Petrov had met Jack for only one reason—he wanted to know about the list.

Jack eventually saw the capital building, which meant Constitution Avenue was not far away. His thoughts shifted to the Wage and Hour Division. He pulled out a scrap of paper from his pants pocket to check the name:

Timothy Keens, Department of Labor. Wage and Hour Division.

Replacing the sheet of paper in his pocket, he went over his approach. He would first explain how he had been working with Timothy Keens before his death and how he wanted to continue his report. The employees there would most likely turn him down, and that would be fine with Jack. He would then feign interest in Keens' life on a personal level, and move into his list of questions.

He stopped before the Department of Labor building, a massive stone structure with imposing white columns, until he had run through the questions in his mind. Then he slowly climbed the steps, entered the lobby, and looked around for Reception. The vast space magnified each small sound; Jack made out distant voices as he approached the desk and asked for the Wage and Hour Division. The receptionist directed him to the third floor, accessible through a double glass door she indicated with one manicured hand.

He found the Wage and Hour sign, knocked on the door beside it, and entered. Inside, a wiry man with thinning red hair stood over a counter, going through a stack of papers. He glanced up at Jack. "The secretary's on her break," he said. "You'll have to wait."

Jack nodded but didn't sit down. He pulled out his new *Washington Chronicle* ID. "Maybe you can help me. Jack Haynes of the *Washington Chronicle*. I was doing a story with Timothy Keens about the minimum wage before he died. I want to find out who took over for him and whether they're willing to finish the story with me."

The man's eyes widened. He slowly placed his handful of papers on the counter. "Who?"

"Timothy Keens," repeated Jack.

"I'm Tim Keens," the man protested. "Who told you I was dead?"

Jack took a step back; his mouth opened, but he was unable to utter a word. He slowly backed toward the door, staring at the man's puzzled face.

"Minimum wage?" the man repeated. "I never talked to you about the minimum wage. I've never even seen you before. You sure you got the right name?"

"You're Timothy Keens?" Jack heard himself ask.

"I should know my own name," the man said. "What on earth is this all about?"

Jack could not think. "Well . . . I . . . it's possible I got the name wrong," he managed to say. "Let me check my notes." He pulled out his notepad and went through the pages while he wondered what to do next. A man Jack thought was dead was standing right in front of him!

"Why did you think I was dead?" Keens asked.

Jack pretended to read his notes as he scrambled for something to say.

Keens folded his arms and shook his head. "No one in this office would talk to the press. That would be a function of the Secretary of the Department." He reached into his shirt pocket and pulled out a pair of wire-framed glasses. Sliding them onto his nose, he studied Jack intensely. "Who the hell are you?"

Jack turned around and left the office without answering.

* * *

Monday morning, Jack sat on the bed in his hotel room, tossing playing cards into his hat. The train to New York was leaving in two hours; the envelope containing his ticket rested on the bed beside him. He glanced at the envelope and thought of a man known as Pops, a cigar smoking, gray-haired man who had worked for the *Herald* for over thirty years. Jack hadn't known Pops very long; the old hand had retired the same month Jack joined the paper. During that short period, Pops usually sat at his desk, smoking his cigar and throwing unsolicited advice Jack's way.

One afternoon, old man Pops said something Jack would never forget. The seasoned reporter had been cleaning out his file cabinet, occasionally stopping to examine the contents of a folder. The file folders held his triumphs and his failures—cases he had worked on through the years. He would curse at one folder and chuckle at another. He laughed out loud when he came to one folder in particular. After examining its contents for half an hour, he turned to Jack. "Son," he said, "let me give you some advice. Let's say you're on a case and you've got a theory. And then something comes along that goes against your theory. This is what you do: don't fight it. That's the key. Drop your theory like a hot potato and follow the new lead."

Now, Jack opened the envelope and removed the newspaper clippings he'd tucked inside the week before. He placed them on the desk, then pulled out the train ticket. He stared at it for a second, then tore it in half and threw it in the wastepaper basket.

A dull hum grew into a racket as Jack made his way down the hotel stairs. As he entered the lobby, he identified the source of the noise—a group of tourists filled the lobby around the reception area. As Jack pushed through the crowd, he thought he heard heard his name called.

Turning, he saw the porter's head bobbing above the crowd.

"Mr. Haynes!" the porter called. "I have a message for you!"

Jack fought his way back through the crowd, pushing toward the front desk, where the porter was holding up a piece of white paper. "Thanks, Bub," he muttered as he grabbed the scrap. He turned and made his way toward the door without looking at the message. As he approached the exit, however, he glanced down at the paper and read: *Albert Collins went to a state sanitarium on July 12. Redwood Center in Bowie, Maryland.*

Perplexed, Jack stared at the note as he walked out the front door. As he turned down Larch Street, he realized that the morgue attendant at City Hospital must have sent the message. With that mystery solved, the scrap of paper went into his pants pocket and he pulled a small white pad from his coat pocket and squinted at it, trying to make out his own writing: *James Fredricks, Department of Justice, Special Assistant to the Attorney General of the United States.*

As he put away the list, he recalled the look on Tim Keens' face when he'd been informed of his own death. Jack must have looked just as astonished that he was alive. He chuckled. *Who knows what the guy thought?*

But what does it all mean? he wondered as he climbed the seemingly countless stairs of the Department of Justice building. He was breathing hard from the exertion as he entered the lobby and approached the porter. "I'm looking for James Fredricks," he said, and pulled out his press ID. "Jack Haynes, *Washington Chronicle.*" He waited, wondering where this would lead, as the porter put down a half-eaten apple and opened his logbook.

The porter raised his head, picking at his teeth with a forefinger. "You're in luck. He's in. Fourth floor, third door on your right."

"Thanks," Jack mumbled.

Still winded, Jack took his time going up the stairs, pulling himself up along the handrail. Again his mind turned to the list. *What could it possibly mean, if they're not dead?* There were two possibilities, he decided: either Maggie and the others had lied when they said the list contained the names of murdered communists, or he had simply come across a different list.

He stopped at the top of the stairs and planned his questions for Fredricks. Then, drawing a deep breath, he knocked on the glass pane bearing Fredricks' name and entered.

Inside, a short, bald man in a black suit stood next to a seated secretary. He stared at Jack. "Yes?"

"Hi, Jack Haynes. *Washington Chronicle.* I'm looking for Mr. James Fredricks."

The man nodded. "Yes, that's me."

"Can I have a word with you, Mr. Fredricks?"

The man reached up and adjusted the knot in his black tie. "Is this about the Rensler case?"

"Rensler case? No, nothing like that," answered Jack. "Can we talk in private?"

Fredricks stood thinking. "Sure, why not?" he mumbled.

Jack followed Fredricks into his office. The man indicated a chair, but Jack ignored the invitation. Fredricks closed the door and moved to sit behind his desk.

Jack pulled out his pad. "I was wondering if you would be willing to comment on your affiliation with the CPUSA."

"The what?" asked Fredricks, looking blank.

"The American Communist Party."

Fredericks stared at him. "Are you joking?"

"Written references to you have been found among the belongings of a guy named Harris."

"Who?"

"Harris—a member of the CPUSA. He was recently murdered."

Fredricks put his left elbow on the desk and rested his chin on his hand. "Oh dear."

Fredricks knows something, Jack thought. "Would you care to comment?" Jack repeated, keeping his tone noncommittal.

Fredricks' mouth opened but nothing came out.

"I've got a piece my editor wants out by tomorrow," Jack continued. "The police found notes at Harris' place. He refers to you as a member of the CPUSA. The *Chronicle* is going to run a story tying you to Harris and the CPUSA. Do you want to comment?"

Fredricks sat back and rubbed his forehead. He slowly folded his arms and looked up at Jack. "I don't know this Lou Harris. And I don't know anything about the communist party."

"How did you know his first name was Lou?" asked Jack. "I only called him Harris." Jack looked down and pretended to scribble notes on his pad.

Fredricks stared at Jack's pad of paper. He put both palms on the top of his desk and whispered, "You have to understand . . . I had nothing to do with this. Nothing."

Jack looked up, then slid his pen behind his right ear. "I'm not accusing you of anything, Mr. Fredricks. I'm just asking about your relationship with the communist party."

Fredricks shook his head. "There is none. I have nothing to do with the communists."

Jack shrugged. "Suit yourself. But I gotta run the story tomorrow. I ain't got no choice. If you want to clear your name, you're better off telling me what you know."

Fredricks' expression suddenly hardened in anger. He leaned forward. "And who do you think you are?" he growled. "You realize you're in the Attorney General's office?"

"Hell, I don't care what you say. Ain't no skin off my nose. I'm just doing my job. You got anything at all you want to tell me?"

Fredricks slowly shook his head. "No," he murmured.

Jack shrugged. "Suit yourself." He turned toward the door, opened it, then turned back to Fredricks. "I wish they'd give me a more interesting assignment," he said. "I'm getting sick of the mundane."

✱ ✱ ✱

Jack folded the wax paper over his cheese sandwich and set it down on the park bench beside him. He pulled out his list and ran his finger down to the next name: *Rex Hart, Legal Staff, National Labor Relations Board*. If Rex Hart was alive, he decided, there was no point in checking on the others.

He gulped down the last of his Coca Cola and tossed the bottle and the remainder of the sandwich into the trashcan beside the bench. Then he crossed Pennsylvania Avenue and entered the large white building housing the Labor Relations Board.

"Where to?" he heard as he entered. Looking in the

direction of the voice, Jack saw an elderly man seated behind a window, just inside the door.

"I'm here to see Rex Hart," Jack said.

The man picked up a phone. "Hold on."

Jack looked away, his eyes wandering down a wide, marble-floored hall to the staircase at its end.

"What's your name again?" the man asked.

"Jack Haynes, *Washington Chronicle*." Jack waited for the reaction.

"Do you have an appointment?"

"No," he answered. "But he'll see me when he hears what this is about. In fact, every reporter in town is gonna be up here in half an hour."

The man scowled and put the receiver to his ear. As he mumbled into the phone, Jack returned to his examination of the staircase. The curved banisters impressed him.

"Mr. Hart will see you," the man said. "Second floor. First office on your left."

Jack nodded and walked down the hall; as he slowly made his way up the staircase, he again rehearsed what he would say.

When he knocked on the door, a middle-aged little man swung it open. The man reminded Jack of a monkey; his shoulders drooped and his arms dangled at his sides as he stood in the doorway to his office and stared at his visitor, clearly curious. "Yes?"

"Mr. Hart?"

"Yes. Who are you?"

Jack pulled out his phony press ID. "Jack Haynes. *Washington Chronicle*. Can I have a word with you?"

"What on earth about?" the man asked.

Jack jerked his chin toward the office. "Can you just give me a minute? In your office?"

The man straightened. "I suppose so."

He stepped back to admit Jack to his office, then closed the door. Jack looked around. The office was small, lit by a dim overhead light. It smelled of mothballs and old, moldering books.

"The *Washington Chronicle*," the man repeated as he sat behind his desk. He pointed at a wooden chair in front of the desk. "Have a seat. What would the *Washington Chronicle* want with me?"

Jack cleared his throat and sat down. "Well, sir . . . are you willing to discuss your relationship with the CPUSA?"

The man raised his chin and stared at Jack. "What do you mean? The what?"

"The CPUSA," Jack repeated.

The man narrowed his eyes in confusion. "What's that?"

Jack looked down and shook his head. "Come on, Mr. Hart. Let's not play games. The American Communist Party."

The man hiked both shoulders in a shrug. "I have no relationship with the communist party."

Jack tried to appear bored. He sighed. "Boy, this is a long day. I'm an investigative reporter, Mr. Hart. That's my job. Written references to you have been found among the belongings of Lou Harris."

Hart tipped his head. "Who?"

"Lou Harris, a member of the CPUSA. He was recently murdered."

Hart sat there stone-faced.

"D.C. police found a ton of notes at Harris' place," continued Jack. "They didn't do much with them. Then Naval Intelligence came in. Word is, they found evidence of you cooperating with the CPUSA. Would you care to comment?"

Hart took a deep breath and exhaled. "I'm afraid you're going to have to leave, Mr. . . . ?"

"Haynes, Jack Haynes. I'm not trying to blackmail you, Mr. Hart. What I'm saying is about to become public record. Am I the first reporter here?"

"I don't know who sent you here or why," said Hart, "but this is complete nonsense." He swept his left hand through his hair. "I must ask you to leave."

Jack stared at Hart and Hart stared back. If there was nothing to what Jack said, he felt certain Hart would have asked more questions. He would have tried to figure out where Jack went wrong. But he just wanted Jack to leave.

A mole on Hart's cheek suddenly caught Jack's attention. He had seen it before; he was almost positive he had seen it in one of Lou's photographs. Jack rose. "If you've been threatened by the FBI or someone else, I'm the one who can make them back off. Don't underestimate the power of the press."

The man shook his head. "Please leave."

* * *

Jack tapped his folded newspaper on the reception desk in an attempt to annoy the nurse, a small, thin woman whose black hair curled out from under her white bonnet. Twice he'd politely tried to get her attention by saying, "Excuse me," and then by clearing his throat, but she continued to scribble in a book without looking up. Just as he'd started to wonder if she was hard of hearing, she slammed the book closed and looked first at Jack's newspaper and then at Jack.

Jack forced a smile. "Hello, there. I want to see Albert Collins."

"Hold on," she said.

Unable to sleep the night before, Jack had spent most of it walking the streets of D.C., thinking about what he had discovered. The people on Lou's list were alive. At least one of them was a subject in one of Lou's photographs; it was logical to assume that they all were. For some reason, Vitovski had approached all of these people, and Lou had found out. But what did Vitovski want from them? Was he trying to get information out of them? Jack didn't know, but now he had a new piece to add to the puzzle: Albert Collins.

He'd caught an early morning bus to Bowie, Maryland, and walked almost two miles to the Redwood Sanitarium, a run-down, two-story wooden building with white paint peeling off its façade.

"You family?" the nurse asked.

"Yeah," said Jack. "I'm his nephew."

"You're a little late, you know. Visiting hours are over in twenty minutes."

"Well, I want to see him, just the same," answered Jack.

The nurse ran her finger down a list. "Ward D, room 32."

Jack swung the door open to room 32. Only four of the six beds in the white-washed room beyond were occupied, all by white-haired men. The air was redolent of disinfectant. Jack slowly walked along the row of beds, examining the names on the bedposts. He found the name *Collins* scratched on a clipboard and approached the sleeping man.

Jack tapped his shoulder. "Mr. Collins?"

The man did not respond. His mouth sagged open and he did not appear to be breathing. *Is he dead?* wondered Jack in a moment of panic. He shook the man's shoulder. "Mr. Collins?"

The man's eyes slowly opened. The man tilted his head and stared at Jack. "What do you want?" he rasped.

"I want to talk to you, Mr. Collins. Can I have a minute of your time?"

The man's eyes widened. He tried to pull himself up with one arm. "Nurse!" he yelled. "Nurse!"

Jack stepped back in confusion. "It's okay!" Jack exclaimed. "I just want to talk to you."

"Who are you?" Collins demanded.

"My name is Jack Haynes."

"Nurse!"

"I'm Lou Harris' brother. You know Lou Harris?" asked Jack.

The man sat back and looked at Jack. "You're his bother?"

A nurse swung the door open and looked around. It was the same nurse Jack had seen at reception. She looked toward Collins. "What's the matter?" she asked.

Collins stared at Jack. "Where's Lou from?" he asked.

"Baltimore."

"What's this all about?" asked the nurse. She looked at Jack. "Who are you?"

"How did your mother die?" Collins asked Jack.

Jack jerked his head back. "What?"

"How did your mother die?" the man repeated.

The nurse walked over to Collins' bed.

Jack stared at Collins and shrugged. "It's none of your business."

"If you want me to believe you are who you say you are, tell me how your mother died."

"Who are you?" the nurse demanded of Jack.

Jack stared at Collins. "She died in a soup line."

Collins wiped his forehead with his left arm and looked at the nurse. "It's okay, nurse. I didn't recognize him at first . . . I wasn't awake yet. This is a friend of mine. It's okay."

The nurse frowned. "You know," she muttered as she turned away, "I was about to eat my dinner. And now it's getting cold."

Collins lifted his left arm in resignation. "I'm sorry. It's like I said, I was waking up."

As the nurse left, Jack pulled over a wooden stool and sat down next to Collins' bed. "Why did you ask me that?" he asked.

Collins grabbed the bed rail with his left hand. "Help me up, will you?"

Jack rose and raised Collins with an arm behind the man's back. "Why did you ask about my mother?" he asked as he placed a pillow behind the man's back. Until then, he hadn't noticed that Collins' right arm was lame. The right wrist was flexed tightly and the fingers were contracted.

Collins exhaled slowly. "Because Lou told me. I wanted to make sure you are who you say."

"How long did you know Lou?" Jack asked as he sat down on the stool again.

"I met him a few years ago."

Looking at Collins more closely, Jack noticed that the

right corner of his mouth sagged. "When you were in the same nucleus, you mean?" he asked.

"Why did you come here?" Collins asked sharply.

"I want to find out what happened to Lou," answered Jack.

Collins stared at the ceiling. "Well, you know he was murdered, right?"

"I know that. I want to know who did it."

Collins shook his head.

"I've come here all the way from St. Louis," Jack pressed.

Collins turned to Jack. "You smoke, Mr. Harris?"

"Yeah, why?"

"You can't get cigarettes here. Would you mind if . . . ?"

Jack pulled out his pack of Lucky Strikes, removed two cigarettes and placed them in his shirt pocket, and set the remainder of the pack on the commode next to the bed.

"Thank you," muttered Collins. "I don't know who killed Lou. I can't help you with that. I still don't know who shot me."

"I'm a reporter, Mr. Collins. I cover this sort of stuff all the time. It would make sense that the same person or group targeted you both. I know you've got to have some idea who pumped you."

"Company goons, feds—who knows?" Collins replied. "No one is looking into it, I can tell you that. The police don't care and neither does the . . . "

"The party?" Jack supplied.

"So you know Lou was a party member?"

Jack nodded. "That was the first thing I learned when I got to Washington."

"So how did you know I was here?" asked Collins.

"Like I said, I'm an investigative reporter. And I had some help."

"From who?" asked Collins.

"A woman."

"What woman?" Collins seemed overly concerned that others might know his whereabouts.

"A woman in D.C., Sue Pinkerton," Jack answered. "But don't worry, I'm the only one who figured out your location."

Collins nodded. "Let's keep it that way." He picked up the Lucy Strikes, placed them against his nose, and inhaled the smell of the tobacco. "Sue's a good woman," he said. "Not afraid to speak her mind. How did you meet her?"

"Through Maggie."

"Maggie Thorton? Oh yeah, Lou's girlfriend."

"You're right about Sue," said Jack. "She says the party is kicking her out."

Collins snickered. "I'm not surprised. I understand her. You probably don't know this, but I left the party."

"Really? Why?"

"I can't tell you exactly why I broke away. It just suddenly hit me that something terrible was happening."

"Then maybe the party targeted you," said Jack. "Did Lou get in trouble with them?"

Collins shook his head. "It wasn't the party. That's not how they work. If they don't like you, they give you the boot. They don't kill you. Unless . . . unless you're in deep shit."

"What do you mean?"

Collins pursed his lips in thought. "Any . . . any international political organization will do away with someone if he or she is detrimental to their cause. But that wasn't Lou."

"So why did you leave the party?" asked Jack.

Collins smiled weakly. "It's a long story."

"I got time."

"If you must know, it was the Soviets," Collins said. "They did things I could not condone."

"Like what?"

Collins grimaced. "That's a long story, Mr. Harris. It won't help you with your investigation."

"I got time," Jack said again. "The bus back to Washington doesn't leave for hours. And you don't look like you're going anywhere."

Collins almost chuckled. "If you insist." He put his head back on the pillow and stared at the ceiling. "We were naïve," he said. "It was the Depression. We were looking for justice. It looked like that's just what the Soviets were offering. Can you imagine a situation, Mr. Harris, where your convictions turn about to be totally wrong, so erroneous that you refuse to accept reality?"

Jack did not know what to say. He wondered if the question was rhetorical.

"Well, that was me," said Collins. "To say the Soviets are wolves in sheep's clothing would be an understatement. They are complete barbarians."

"How so?" asked Jack.

Collins took one last whiff of the cigarettes and placed them on the commode. "They found a loophole that seemed to be socially noble and it satisfied their desires. The loophole was communism. When the evidence of their barbaric acts came in, we ignored it. If the Soviets were not the answer, there was no hope for us."

"So, what did the Soviets do that you couldn't get over?" asked Jack.

"Things like the deliberate mass starvations."

"What starvations?" asked Jack.

Collins stared at him. "What starvations? Have you been living in a cave? The Soviet government deliberately starved millions of peasants to death, particularly in the Ukraine."

Jack had heard of the deaths, but he never paid much attention to international affairs, and his memory of the events was vague. "Oh yeah," he muttered. "I heard about that. I don't have time to follow that kind of stuff. I have my own job."

Collins grunted. He shifted onto his side to look at Jack. "What do you do?"

"I'm a reporter."

"For who?"

"*St. Louis Herald.*"

Collins' brows went up. "And you haven't taken an interest in the Purges? The Purges have been on the front pages of every major paper for years. How can you not realize it is a historical event?"

Jack was too focused to feel embarrassed. "So that was it?" he asked. "You left because the Soviets were starving the Ukrainians?"

"That's not all. The Soviets refused to cooperate with the Social Democrats in Germany against Hitler. They betrayed the Spanish Republicans. The list just goes on and on. But the Purges, the Purges were something I could not forgive. Stalin murdered millions, including the best minds in the country."

"What did Lou think of all this?" asked Jack.

Collins ignored the question. "The American Communist Party will tell you the Purges were necessary. That it was an act of high patriotism, how Stalin got rid of the traitors who wanted to negotiate with the Nazis. But he was just consolidating his own power. Do you know what the horror is? It's that communism allows him this. He can kill anybody and claim it was necessary for the cause of communism."

"So when did you leave?" asked Jack.

"About half a year ago. That's the ironic part. I left, but whoever it was who tried to kill me didn't know that."

"Did Lou try to leave the party?"

Not that I know of." Collins' earlier indignation had left him sputtering. Calmer now, he wiped saliva off his chin. "You know, every time I spoke up against the Purges, I was silenced. I remember bringing up the Purges and condemning them at a party meeting once. There were some Russians at the meeting, and one of them stood up, all red-faced, and asked, 'How many people died in the World War? And for what? Nothing! How can you blame the motherland for killing a much smaller number for the most promising social experiment in history?'"

Collins stared at the ceiling for a long moment. "It suddenly occurred to me that I was part of something horrific," he eventually said. "For the first time since my childhood, I began to pray to God. I now sought the God they told me was dead."

The nurse returned and lifted a clipboard hanging from the foot of Collins' bed. Collins looked at her. "So how was dinner?" he asked.

The nurse chuckled cynically as she scribbled on the clipboard. "Best I ever had. Like at the Ritz. I love cold dinners." She placed the clipboard back on his bedpost. "Visiting time is almost over."

Collins put his left arm behind his head. "Like the Ritz? And what am I having? Meatloaf again? I think you nurses are hoarding the food."

The nurse snickered and walked to the next bed. Collins turned to Jack. "Let me ask you this; are you familiar with the old method of how an Oriental king constructs a treasure vault?"

Jack slowly shook his head.

"This is how the old Oriental system works," said Collins. "A group of slaves is ordered to construct a treasure vault. After the slaves move the treasure in, they're taken away, and a second group of slaves is ordered to massacre the first group. This is to make sure the first group of slaves never reveals the location of the treasure. And just to make sure, a third group of slaves then massacres the second group."

Collins pulled himself up with his left arm. "This was exactly what Stalin did. In the first wave of the Purge, Stalinists had the secret police massacre their opponents in the party. Next, Stalin took care of the secret police; he had the leader Yagoda killed and replaced him with Yezhov. At the same time, he sent his own secret police to the gulag. In the third wave, he accused Yezhov of treason and had him killed. This gave Stalin complete control of the government."

Jack nodded, then remembered the photograph and pulled it out of his pocket; he handed it to Collins. "You know this man?"

Collins took the photo and extended his left arm to bring the photograph into focus. "It's Ben Vitovski."

"Who is he?"

"He's an underground leader."

"Did he know Lou?"

"Of course. They were friends. Vitovski was the one who pulled Lou into the underground."

Jack sat up. "What exactly does it mean to be in the underground?"

Collins waved his left hand. "It's totally different from being a party member. First of all, almost nobody knows who you really are. You go by a pseudonym. Take Vitovski—that's not his real name. None of us in the nucleus knew who he really was. The only one who knows the real identity of the underground's members is the chief of each nucleus. It's no picnic being in the underground. You can go months without any contact. Once they contact you, you have to jump into action. And if you're late for that meeting, it's considered a cardinal sin."

Jack took back the photo. "I believe Lou took this photo," he said. "Why would he photograph Vitovski?"

Collins peered at the photo Jack held. "Why's the photo torn?"

Jack shrugged. "Any idea why he'd photograph the chief of his nucleus?"

Collins shook his head. "No, I don't. But it does raise some questions."

"Like what?"

"If Lou took Vitovski's photo, he must have been looking for proof of something."

"Like Vitovski squealing to the feds?" asked Jack.

"Maybe . . . or maybe it's something else. In the underground, meeting places are memorized. No records are allowed—no notes, no maps—it must all be kept in memory. The points of meeting in the underground Apparatus are fixed."

"So, Lou could have been documenting where the underground met?"

"It's possible," answered Collins. "I don't want to imply anything, but if that's the case, it does raise the question of whether it was your brother who was working with the feds."

Jack thought of Wayne Mullen, the FBI agent. "You know anything about Lou having a list?"

"What kind of list?" asked Collins.

"Lou made some sort of list. People are looking for it."

Collins frowned. "I don't know anything about that."

"Did Maggie know Vitovski?" Jack asked.

"Maggie? Of course. It was Maggie who introduced me to Vitovski."

Maggie lied! Jack pounded his fist against his hand, then tapped Collins' bed stand. "Thank you, sir. I have to go."

"Sonny, do me a favor on your way out," said Collins. "Tell the nurse I want to go out on the balcony. I'm finally gonna have a smoke."

Jack smiled. "Sure."

"And remember," Collins added. "You couldn't find me, no matter who asks."

❋ ❋ ❋

Jack pulled one hand out of his coat pocket and knocked on the door, then lifted it to rub his tired eyes. Finally he heard footsteps approaching on the other side of the door.

"Who is it?" Maggie called through the door.

"It's Jack. I came to apologize."

The tumblers in the lock snapped. As the door slowly swung open, he kicked it wide open with his foot. Maggie fell back. He entered, grabbed her by her arms, and kicked the door closed. He covered her mouth with one hand when she opened her mouth to scream, keeping a grip on her arm with the other. He dragged her into the parlor. "Sit down!" he yelled as he threw her onto the sofa.

"Are you crazy?" she yelled. "What's wrong with you?"

"So you don't know Vitovski?"

"What?" she shouted.

"You don't know Vitovski? Why did you lie to me?"

Maggie covered her face with both hands.

"Why did you lie?" demanded Jack.

She gave no answer.

"Collins told me that you introduced him to Vitovski! Vitovski with the underground!"

Maggie sniveled and looked up at him. "Collins? You met Collins?"

Jack ignored her. "I ain't leaving here until you tell me what this is all about. I ain't leaving, and neither are you."

She put her head back down, rubbed her face, and started to cry.

"You told me all the people on Jack's list were murdered. Well, I found out they're all alive, sister. Why did you lie about that?" he yelled.

Maggie still did not answer.

"And why wasn't your place ransacked?" asked Jack.

She looked up. "What?"

"Why didn't they go through your place like they did with me in the hotel?"

"I don't know!" she yelled.

"Tell me what you know about Vitovski," he demanded.

Maggie jumped off the sofa and scrambled toward the door. Jack tackled her to the floor and pulled her arms behind her. "Forget it, sister," he yelled. "You're not going anywhere." She struggled as he lifted her to her feet and pulled her back to the sofa.

"Tell me about Vitovski!" he repeated.

She wiped her eyes. "I don't know anything about him. Like you said, he's an *apparatchik*. I don't deal with them."

"Bullshit," said Jack. "You even introduced Collins to Vitovski."

"Maybe I did. But I only met him a few times."

"Enough lies. Tell me what you know."

Still teary-eyed, she snickered. "What I know? It's impossible for someone like you to understand. I learned that the other day. I thought Lou understood, but I was wrong."

"Who killed Lou?" Jack demanded.

She turned stone-faced. "It is a faith," she said with conviction. "A vision of mankind. I thought Lou had it. You obviously don't."

"What vision?" Jack blurted. "What the hell are you talking about?"

Maggie glared at him, her teeth clenched in anger. "It's like I tried telling you the other day, but it went in one ear and out the other. Once you become dedicated to the revolution, there are no countries."

"Cut the bullshit."

Maggie ignored him. "There is no religion," she said.

"There is no community. The allegiance is only to the party. Nothing else matters. Lou broke that code."

"With his list?" he asked.

"Yes!" she yelled. "He betrayed the party."

"How?" Jack lunged forward and grabbed her by the arms. He shook her to make sure she understood. "Who killed Lou?"

Maggie tried to pull away by scratching Jack's arms, but he held firm. "Who killed Lou?" he repeated.

She stopped scratching. She put her head down and the tears came back. He stared at her as she sobbed. "What the hell is this whole thing about?" he shouted.

Suddenly, Jack lost all sense of his surroundings; he thought only of Lou and his list of federal governmental employees, of Lou putting together the list soon after joining the underground. He imagined Soviet and Nazi spies running amuck in Washington, and remembered what Collins had said about realizing he was part of something horrific. He thought of the saying *chickens are counted in the fall.* He released Maggie's arms.

"Soviet spies," he whispered to himself. "This whole thing is about Soviet espionage, isn't it? All the people on that list are working for the Soviets, aren't they? They're all Soviet spies. And Lou found out."

"It's not true!" she protested.

He looked at her. "Lou thought it was treason and he wouldn't put up with it, would he."

Maggie tried to catch her breath. "Lou couldn't see the wider picture."

"So they did away with Lou," Jack yelled. "They did away with him because he wouldn't betray his country."

Maggie tried to brush her hair back with her fingers

but it did little good. "I just told you. There are no nations. It doesn't matter if they're Soviets or Eskimos."

"And that's why you called me in St. Louis," Jack added. "You wanted to draw me in to see if he sent me the list."

Maggie was not listening. "This is for all mankind," she protested. "The only thing that matters is the revolution."

Jack grabbed her by the arms once more. "Who killed him?" he asked. "Who put the knife in him?"

Maggie shook her head and sniveled. "I don't know."

"And who gave the order? Was it Vitovski?"

"I'm telling you, I don't know!" she cried.

Jack let go of her arms. "Listen to me, bitch. You contact your commie friends and you tell them I have the list. I have the whole damn list. I know the names of fifteen high-placed people in the government who are working for the Soviets. And I got the photos Lou took. The photos are the key, aren't they?"

Maggie stared at the floor. "What is it you want?" she asked.

"I want to meet with Vitovski. We'll discuss the terms for me handing over the list and the negatives."

Maggie shook her head. "I don't know how to contact Vitovski."

"Well then, you lose, sister," said Jack. "And so does the party. Because in that case, I'm handing them over to the feds."

Maggie raised her head. Strands of hair obscured her red face. "You're crazy," she whispered. "You're out of your damn head."

"I'll meet Vitovski tomorrow morning at ten in that cafeteria where I met your cronies. The one on 3rd Street.

And if he shows up with anyone else, the whole thing is off."

Maggie tried to fix her hair with both hands. "You don't know what you're up against."

"Neither do you," he answered, and left the apartment.

* * *

The secretary with cat's-eye glasses cleared her throat and said, "Agent Mullen will see you now."

She was the same secretary who had tried to dismiss Jack the last time he'd come to FBI headquarters. He thought of sticking it to her, but decided to save his breath. He rose. "Where do I go?"

She tilted her pen upward without looking up. "Up the stairs, second door on your right."

As he climbed the stairs, Jack felt for the key to the locker in his right pants pocket. He had just checked into a new hotel and had changed clothes to throw off any watchers. Satisfied the key was there, he knocked on the door.

Mullen was rising from his chair as Jack entered. He paused and stared curiously at Jack.

"Good news for you, pal," said Jack. He pulled the key out of his pocket and held it up.

"What's that?" asked Mullen

"It's to a locker at the bus terminal. It's everything you want: the list and the negatives."

Mullen tilted his head. "Is that so?" His tone was skeptical.

"I'm not bullshitting you," said Jack. "I give you this, and you destroy my file. Is it a deal?"

Mullen grinned as he slowly sat down. "If it turns out to be the real thing . . . I'll agree."

"It's the real thing," said Jack, tossing him the key. "I just got a couple of questions for you."

"Shoot."

"Did you know it was the Soviets all along?"

Mullen regarded him for a moment. "Sit down."

Jack reached for a chair.

"What makes you think it was the Soviets?" asked Mullen.

It occurred to Jack that Mullen played his cards closer to his chest than anyone he had ever met. "Lou's girlfriend cracked. She's a commie. So, did you know it was them?"

"Yeah, I knew," answered Mullen. He wiped a hand across his forehead and leaned back. "So, what did Lou find out?"

Jack sighed. "He found out about the traitors."

Mullen reached into the pocket of his jacket but his hand came back empty. "What traitors?"

"Our own people in the government," answered Jack, "working for the Soviets."

Mullen rocked his chair back. "You know, it was Lou who came to me."

"Okay," said Jack. "So what did Cromwell have to do with all this?"

"Like I told you the other day—Cromwell had nothing to do with it."

"Then how come he knows you?"

"We paid him a visit during the investigation," answered Mullen. "We talked to the same people you did. You know, I gotta admit you're not bad at investigation."

Jack felt this was Mullen's attempt to sidetrack him. "Why did Lou come to you?" he asked.

"You ever hear of SMERSH?" asked Mullen.

"No."

"It stands for *Smert Shpionam*—Death to Spies," answered Mullen.

"What the hell is that?"

"The assassination division of the NKVD. They killed your brother."

"The Soviet secret police? So why the hell don't you do something?" Jack asked.

Mullen raised his arms in a helpless gesture. "What do you want me to do? These guys aren't like two-bit mobsters from St. Louis. They leave no evidence; they're highly trained and proficient. And they can vanish like the wind after the job is done."

"Why didn't you tell me this before?" asked Jack.

Mullen reached into another coat pocket but his hand still came back empty. "How the hell was I supposed to know if I could trust you?" He stared at the key in his hand, then pointed it at Jack. "This is your last chance. Is this thing for real?"

Jack nodded. "It's for real. Now, you were with Lou that day at Griffith Stadium, weren't you?"

Mullen nodded. "I was there. But I didn't stay with him. I laid low, stayed in the background."

"Why?" asked Jack. What was going on—what was the plan?"

"Your brother told me the whole story. It all started with the Russians making a pact with the Nazis. You see, your brother had recently been sent to the communist underground. That's when he started working with a guy named Vitovski. They call them *apparatchiks*. But they didn't tell Lou everything that was going on; they only told him what they thought he needed to know."

Mullen opened the top drawer of his desk and pulled out a pouch of Beechnut tobacco. "How the hell did this get in here?" he muttered, staring at the pouch. He shook his head and turned back to Jack. "These American reds are like sheep for the Soviets. If they don't do what they're told, their loyalty to the cause is questioned. So these little sheep obey. But that changed with the Nazi-Soviet pact. It pissed some of the reds off. Some were so pissed, they left the party. And one of them spilled the beans to Lou."

"Who told Lou?" asked Jack.

"I'm not sure who it was, but someone told him that Vitovski had recruited a number of Americans in the government to work for the Soviets." Mullen paused to open the tobacco pouch. He put a wad in his mouth. "Lou wasn't sure if it was true, so he checked it out himself. He followed Vitovski after underground meetings and took pictures of him meeting with people: in the train station, at department stores, cafeterias, movie theaters, and Griffith Stadium. Then he followed the people meeting with Vitovski so he could identify them. When he was convinced, he came to me. In the end, your brother was a patriot."

"So what happened that day?" asked Jack. "The day he was murdered."

Mullen sighed. "I thought I had enough to arrest Vitovski, but we had to find him. Lou still had no idea where Vitovski lived or worked. So Lou had the idea of drawing Vitovski into one of his meetings with the workers."

Mullen reached for a white paper cup on his desk and spat into it. "We waited until Lou had a real meeting with a worker, in case the party checked it out. Some textile worker from Virginia finally wanted to meet with Lou. So Lou told Maggie he needed Vitovski there for credibility. Lou, Vitovski, and the worker from Virginia all agreed to meet at Griffith Stadium."

"So how did you guys screw up?" asked Jack, his voice tinged with bitterness.

"We thought Vitovski took the bait, but it backfired. They must have already decided to dispose of Lou. Vitovski showed up, all right, but so did *Smert Shpionam*. They took care of Lou."

"You couldn't do anything about this? Didn't you have backup?"

Mullen lowered his head. "I couldn't get the manpower. If it was a Nazi ring, they would have given it to me. But not for the Soviets."

"So this is how the magnificent FBI works," Jack sneered.

Mullen looked up. "Look, pal, Hoover started cracking down on spy rings a couple of years ago. But by the direct order of Roosevelt, the Nazi rings have priority. Besides, why do you think I'm letting you go?"

Jack tried to let the whole thing sink in. There were so many things going on at the same time. "Thanks for the honesty," he said. He rose, walked over to the single window, and stared down at the parking lot. He put his fingers through his hair and tried to figure this whole thing out. When it came down to it, he thought, the trigger for Lou's murder was the outbreak of war in Europe. "So what about these Soviet killers? he asked. "Did you spot any of them?"

"I saw the guy who knifed him," answered Mullen. "I saw him follow Lou into the men's room."

"Do you have a name?"

Mullen shook his head. "No. I went through hundreds of mug shots. We don't have a file on this guy."

Jack turned to Mullen. "What did he look like?"

"He was stout. Wore a brown suit and kept looking over his shoulder. For a pro, he looked kind of nervous."

"Meaning what?" asked Jack.

"He had a tic," answered Mullen. "Kept jerking his head and his shoulder."

Tic? thought Jack. *Tic?* That sounded familiar. He moved absently back to his chair and sat down.

"God damn Nazis," grumbled Mullen. "Not only do they take up all our time, but we're not making any progress."

Jack barely heard. *Tic . . . the killer had a nervous tic.*

"These bastards penetrate everything: government offices, military bases, you name it."

It suddenly hit Jack; Maggie had described the chess player's habit of moving his jaw and then his shoulders up and down when he was nervous. *What the hell was his name?* Jack rose. "Thanks for the scoop."

Mullen looked at him in surprise. "Where you going?"

"I've got some business to take care of," said Jack. "And then I'm going back home—to St. Louis."

"What business?"

"Let's leave it at that," Jack said.

"I told you once before," Mullen warned him, "you're not calling the shots. Just remember I haven't destroyed your file yet."

Jack did not want to hear any more of this. He folded his arms. "So, what are you gonna do? Arrest me?"

Mullen narrowed his eyes. "What are you planning?"

Jack just looked at him. Mullen spat tobacco juice into his cup, then glared at Jack. "If you think you've found the killer and you want to go after him yourself, you'll get no support from me. You kill this guy, you're a murderer. And don't forget you got a record."

"I thought we had a deal," said Jack.

Mullen placed the cup on his desk and shook his head. "Not if you break the law.

You get into trouble, your file from Michigan will magically reappear. Even if the list is for real."

Jack was about to answer when the name of the chess player hit him—Reznov. *The chess player's name is Reznov. Reznov is with Smert Shpionam.* He turned his attention back to Mullen. "Okay, let's say I don't break the law. What if this whole thing was exposed to the public? That's what Lou deserves."

"You mean, in the press?"

"Yeah."

"Forget it," said Mullen. "No one will print it. Not in this town."

"Why not?"

"It's a can of worms."

Jack just looked at him, unsure what to say.

"It's pretty simple," Mullen continued. "You tell me where he is, and we'll pick him up."

"You got enough to convict him?" Jack asked, and sighed when Mullen did not answer. "You saw this guy go into the men's room," he said. "Did you see him kill Lou?"

"No," Mullen muttered.

"How long after that did you find out Lou had been stabbed?"

"About ten minutes," answered Mullen.

Jack held his eyes. "Are you absolutely sure this guy was the only one in the head when Lou was there?"

Mullen shrugged. "You know there's no way I could know that."

Jack threw up his hands. "So the guy went into the men's room. So what? So did every guy in the joint who had a beer. You got nothing."

"You don't know that," countered Mullen. "You've never seen us conduct an investigation."

Jack raised his arms in a grand shrug. "So what you gonna tell a D.A.? Or a jury?" he asked.

Mullen slowly exhaled. "The truth is, if they were Nazis, I could get enough men on the case. Maybe we could prove it. But the Russians, that's another matter. Like I said, they give Nazi investigations priority. Still, it's worth a try."

"Forget it," said Jack. "I'm doing this on my own."

Mullen reached for the cup and spat into it. "I'll pretend I never heard that."

Jack made a half-turn toward the door but then turned back to Mullen. "What's with the Soviets, anyway? Why are they recruiting our people?"

Mullen made a face. "The Nazis . . . the Nazis are an arrogant bunch of bastards. They have their spies here to learn about their enemy. But the Soviets, that's a different story."

"Meaning what?"

Mullen looked into his cup full of spit. "The Soviets are cleverer, much cleverer. They're trying to secretly control American foreign policy. They know there are a lot of communist sympathizers here in the States, particularly in the federal government." He looked at Jack. "And you didn't hear that from me."

"What're you gonna do with the list?" asked Jack.

"If it's real, it's going straight to the top."

"Meaning what?"

"It'll go straight to a security officer with the State Department. A guy named Nelson. We're not going to screw around. He'll take it the top."

"Meaning who?"

"Roosevelt himself. Like I said—if your stuff's for real."

Jack turned to the door. "It's very real. You'll see."

"One more thing," said Mullen. "Where did you find the list?"

"In my brother's old baseball glove," Jack answered without turning back to Mullen.

"Where was it?"

Jack stared at the door. "In Thorton's apartment."

Mullen snickered. "And the photos?"

"They were in the glove, too." Jack looked over his shoulder. "Why didn't you guys go through his stuff?"

"We did," said Mullen. "The girl doesn't know it, but we sent two guys to her place. They went through all her stuff when she was at work. The fatheads must have missed it."

Jack chuckled, opened the door, and left Mullen's office.

* * *

Jack had spent the entire evening planning the best way to approach the Soviets. He wanted to take Reznov back to Griffith Stadium to meet his fate, but he didn't want the Soviets to get suspicious—they had to recognize a motive on his part. So he decided to play the greedy brother wanting to make a buck on this whole ordeal.

Now, as he stood on 3rd Street, he sent nervous fingers inside his trench coat to follow the shoulder harness down to the holster where his revolver rested. It was still there. *Of course it's still there,* he admonished himself as he looked up and down the street. He saw nothing unusual in the morning crowd. Likewise, the steps leading down to the cafeteria. Taking a deep breath, he removed his hand from his coat and approached the eatery to meet Vitovski.

The aroma of fresh-brewed coffee hit him as he entered the cafeteria. It was 10:00 a.m. and the restaurant was not busy; the locals had already gone off to work and only the tourists remained. He scanned the hall; seated against the wall on his right was the white-haired man from the photographs: Vitovski.

Jack looked over his shoulder one last time and approached the man. Vitovski was of medium build and, as the photographs had indicated, well-groomed. He wore an expensive looking single-breasted black jacket over a white shirt and a silver tie.

Vitovski saw Jack approaching and motioned with his hand for Jack to sit down. Jack dragged over a wooden chair, hiked up the bottom of his trench coat, and sat. Vitovski lifted a steaming cup from the table before him and sipped from it before saying, "Why don't you take off your coat, Mr. Haynes?"

The remark did not sound hospitable. Jack suspected Vitovski wanted to dominate the exchange. "I'm fine," he said.

"So, you wanted to meet me," said Vitovski. "What is it you want?"

Vitovski spoke elegantly, in a tone that seemed almost pretentious. Jack could not quite place his accent; it sounded French, but Jack was not sure. He held Vitovski's eyes and asked, "How did you know it was me? We've never met."

Vitovski chuckled. "I have been in this business a long time, Mr. Haynes."

"And what business is that?" asked Jack.

Vitovski ignored the question and looked away as if to convey he had been insulted.

"You look older in your photographs, Mr. Vitovski," Jack observed. Vitovski took another sip from his cup without reacting. Jack stared at the cup. "You don't drink your tea out of a glass? I thought all Russians drank tea out of glasses."

"I don't want to play games, Mr. Haynes," said Vitovski. "What is it you want?"

"Then I'll get right to the point," snapped Jack. "I've got the list and the negatives. They're for sale. One thousand dollars—in cash. I don't care who buys them. You or the feds, it makes no difference to me."

Vitovski put down his cup, frowning. "Come now, Mr. Haynes, you and I both know the FBI does not pay for evidence."

Jack leaned forward and tried to sound deliberate. "Oh yeah? You sure about that?"

"Why don't you go straight to them?" asked Vitovski. "Why do you give me first chance on your offer?"

"Because of Lou," answered Jack. "You worked with him. I guess I owe him that much, even though your cause means nothing to me."

"But Maggie tells me you now suspect us of killing him," said Vitovski.

"I suspect everyone," Jack replied. "What good does it do me? How will I ever know what really happened? But I know one thing. I have the list and it's worth money. Besides, the FBI would like to have it, but you need it, don't you?"

Vitovski hiked one shoulder.

Jack forced a chuckle. "Actually, the list isn't worth that much—anybody can put together a list. It's the photographs, right? That's where the proof is. Now, you want it or not?"

Vitovski reached for his cup but did not raise it. Instead, he wiped a drop of tea off the cup's side. "You are quite correct," he finally said. "The list and the photographs are of use to us, just as they are to your federal agents. But how do I know you have not made multiple prints from the negatives?"

Jack thought Vitovski was playing it too cool, as if trying to hide his anxiety. "I heard how efficient your boys are," said Jack. What do you call them, SMERSH?"

Vitovski did not respond. He slowly turned over his palm, as if to say he did not know what Jack was talking about.

"I'm not dumb enough to try to screw you," Jack said. "Certainly it's worth a thousand dollars, probably a lot more. But I just want to finish this thing."

Still Vitovski stared at his cup, running his finger over the rim. Jack rapped his knuckles several times against the table. "Well?"

"We have the same attitude on this matter, Mr. Haynes. I also want this issue over as quickly as possible."

"So let's do it," said Jack.

Vitovski raised his cup and took a sip. "When can we have them?" he calmly asked.

"I only want one person there," said Jack, "or the whole thing is off. Somewhere public, like a movie theater."

"We could do that," said Vitovski.

"I got a better idea," Jack quickly added. "How about Griffith Stadium?"

"Why Griffith Stadium?"

"The Senators are playing the St. Louis Browns tomorrow," Jack replied. "I was gonna go to the game anyway."

Vitovski nodded. "That's right—you're from St. Louis. That can be arranged."

"I want to meet with someone I can trust. Someone I've met before."

"Like who? Maggie?"

"Maggie?" Jack chuckled. "Maggie's unstable. I want a quick exchange, not someone who may start an argument and then cry her eyes out. I want someone professional. How about . . . how about one of the guys I already met? Like Ray or . . . what was that guy's name? The chess player."

Vitovski raised his eyebrows. "You mean Reznov?"

"That's right, Reznov!" exclaimed Jack. "Someone like Reznov. Someone I've met before. Reznov would be fine."

"I guess I can arrange that," Vitovski muttered.

Jack rose. "Fine. I'll meet Reznov at the concession stands on the first base line half an hour after the game is over. If the next game is rained out, we'll meet at the following game."

"Why after the game?" asked Vitovski. "Why not during the game?"

"Less people. So, is it deal?" asked Jack.

Vitovski nodded. "The way I look at it, more people is better. But if that's what you want, I see no problem. He'll be there."

"And remember what I said," Jack added. "In cash."

* * *

Jack crushed out his cigarette and banged on the wooden door. After his meeting with Vitovski, Jack could think of nothing else but to see Sue. He wanted to tell her about the people on the list, about Collins, and about Vitovski. He wanted to hold her and tell her that he loved her.

"Who's there?" he heard from the other side.

Jack's heart skipped a beat at the sound of Sue's voice. "It's me, Jack."

The door swung open. Sue stood in the doorway wearing a blue robe. She smiled and pushed back her brown, curly hair. "My hair is a mess."

"I went to the cafeteria but they told me you have the day off," said Jack.

"I should have told you. I always have Wednesdays off. Come on in."

Jack looked around as he entered. He had not been in her apartment before. The furniture was old and looked as if it had come with the apartment. The room was only remarkable for several oil paintings of landscapes on the walls.

Behind him, Sue closed the door. "Have you had breakfast?" she asked.

He turned. "Sue, I found Lou's killer," he blurted, ignoring her question.

Sue raised her eyebrows and folded her arms. She slowly approached Jack. "Who is it?"

"It's a Russian," he said. "A Russian spy." He stared at Sue, wondering how she would react. She pushed her hair back, but did not speak. He turned around and flopped down on the couch. "Lou had a list, alright," he continued. "But the people on his list aren't victims, as Maggie's friends said. They're Americans working for the federal government and spying for the Soviets."

Sue slowly sat down herself. She appeared to be deep in thought. "The *apparatchiks,*" she whispered. "I bet you this whole thing happened because Lou joined the underground."

"That's exactly right," said Jack. "Lou went into the underground just when the Soviets made a pact with the Nazis. You weren't the only one pissed off."

She looked at him. "What do you mean?"

"Someone spilled the beans to Lou about the spies. Any idea who it could have been?"

Sue shook her head. "No way. The *apparatchiks* are a different breed. I don't know anything about them. But . . . but what are you gonna do? Are you going to the police?"

"This isn't a matter for some two-bit coppers," said Jack. "It's an FBI case, but they don't have enough evidence to convict the murderer."

"How do you know that?" she countered.

"The FBI told me so themselves."

Sue opened her mouth, then shut it, apparently at a loss for words. She appeared worried. Shaking her head, she urged him, "Let them do a proper investigation. They should find this list."

"They have the list. I gave it to them. They have photos

too, but they don't have Lou's killer. I've got to take care of that myself."

Sue put her head down. "Jack, don't try to play the hero. Give the FBI time. I know you loved your brother, but don't let emotions cloud your thinking."

"The FBI won't devote the manpower," he said. "It's like I said—they told me so themselves."

Sue rubbed her hand through her hair, leaving it a total mess. "If the FBI has the list," she said slowly, trying to think this through, "they have to pursue it to the end. If they're short on manpower, it'll just take a little longer, that's all."

"The killer's a Russian," said Jack. "He could be back in Moscow at the drop of a hat. He ain't gonna be waiting around for the FBI to pussyfoot around."

"Who is this Russian, anyway?" she asked.

"You ever hear of SMERSH?"

Sue looked up. "Yes."

"What did you hear?"

"Not much," she answered. "But I know some members were afraid of them."

"Why?"

"Rumors . . . rumors that the Soviet secret police would take care of someone if they got out of line."

"Well, Lou got out of line," said Jack. He folded his arms, his mind wandering to Griffith Stadium—its layout, the passageways, the exits.

Sue looked down at the floor. "Jack," she finally said. "They'll kill you."

Jack did not acknowledge her warning. He was deep in thought.

"Jack?" When he did not respond, Sue stood and walked over to him. "Jack? You okay?"

He finally turned to her and smiled. He reached for her hand and then gently pulled her down on the sofa beside him. He stroked her neck and inched up closer to her.

Sue pulled back. "Jack, why did you come here today?' she asked. "Did you come here for my support? Did you want me to tell you it's okay to kill someone? Did you want me to stop you?"

Jack's mind raced; the questions caught him off guard. He stared into her eyes. "I—I came to tell you that I care about you." He brushed back her hair. "You're hair *is* a mess," he added, and smiled.

Sue chuckled and reached for his hand. She held it to her cheek and then kissed it. "I love you, Jack," she whispered. "I don't want anything to happen to you."

Jack put his finger on her chin and lifted it. "I love you, too." He leaned over to kiss her, but she shook her head. "No. No, Jack . . . Jack go back to St. Louis."

Jack gently cupped her cheeks in his hands. "I'm going to St. Louis, and you're going with me. But I have to do this first."

She stared at him. "You want me to go to St. Louis with you?"

"Of course," he replied. "It would mean everything to me."

"And if I don't go?" she asked.

"Then I'll stay here."

She reached up and grabbed his hands, held them tightly. "Jack, I'll go with you if you leave now," she said, her voice urgent. "Come on—we'll take the train. We'll get updates from the FBI."

Jack shook his head. "Sue, the FBI won't get the job done. Don't you understand that?"

"They'll kill you, Jack. Let's go to St. Louis. We'll let the FBI do their business."

Jack tried to appear confident to ease her worry. He smiled. "You ever been to St. Louis?"

Sue shook her head. "No."

Jack's smile widened. "We got some pretty hot jazz there."

"Jazz is decadent," said Sue, sounding resigned.

"That's a funny thing to hear from someone who likes to go to Jimmy Mack's Nightclub. If you think jazz is decadent, wait till you listen to it with gin in your belly."

Sue shook her head and almost chuckled. "I don't drink gin."

Jack grabbed both of Sue's arms. "We'll go to St. Louis together," he said. "As soon as I take care of this."

Sue raised her right hand and finger-combed his hair. "You make it sound so simple," she said, forcing a smile.

They sat on the sofa without speaking. Jack's mind returned to Griffith Stadium, its entrance on Georgia Street. It led straight to the passageway down the first base side. He thought of approaching Reznov before he even made his way into the stadium, but he could not assume the Russian would use that entrance. He would have to stake out the first base side of the passage.

Sue touched Jack's cheek. "Your mind is miles away," she whispered. "I can tell."

Jack tried to refocus on Sue. Noticing an easel against the wall, he pointed to it. "What's that?"

Sue's hand left his cheek. "I paint sometimes," she answered. "I'm not very good."

Jack looked up at the walls. "Are those your paintings?"

"Yeah. Like I said, I'm not very good."

Jack did not know anything about art, but they looked like the kind of works you would see for sale in a store. "They look wonderful to me," he said.

"Oh, stop," she replied. "What I need is some art lessons from a professional."

"What's stopping ya?" he asked.

She shook her head and gave him a sardonic smile, as if Jack had asked a dumb question. "It's called money."

They both chuckled. Jack leaned forward to kiss her but she looked away. He reached for her hand and kissed its palm, then placed it back on his cheek and rubbed his face against it, enjoying the feel of her skin. "Sue," he whispered, "that thing that's bothering you. Have you forgiven yourself?"

She sighed. "Why do you want to bring that up?"

"Because I think it's important."

"Why?" she asked.

He looked into her eyes. "Because I know you have feelings for me, but . . . you can't show them."

Sue looked down. Her expression told him that he had hit the nail on the head. She tried to say something, but stopped and pulled her hand away from him to cover her face with both hands.

Jack hugged her and remained silent. After a moment she wiped tears from her eyes and looked up at him. "I do love you," she said.

"And I love you," he answered. "And if you love someone, there's nothing wrong in showing it."

He leaned forward again, and this time she did not back away. He pressed his lips to hers and she welcomed them, parting her own lips to let him explore her warm mouth. Her arms came up, languorously circled his neck, and she held him tightly, as if to tell him she wanted more. He became more aggressive and Sue responded with an urgency of her own, until he had to stop just so he could breathe. He lifted his mouth away and buried his face in her neck.

"Come with me," she whispered, her voice husky. She led Jack to the bedroom, a room very different from the rest of the apartment; here, the hand-carved mahogany bed and dresser gleamed softly with the polishing of a loving hand, and a large antique mirror dominated the long wall. Vases of fragrant flowers sat on tables on both sides of the bed.

When she started to unbutton her blouse, Jack buried his face in her hair and cupped her breasts in his hands, then started removing his own clothes. As she pulled him onto the bed, his fingers seemed to run of their own volition, exploring first the curve of her waist and then her thighs. She gasped when he caressed her back and forth; when they joined, he felt her heart pounding against his chest, a counterpoint to his own hammering heartbeat.

"Everything will be okay," he whispered when they lay trembling side by side afterward. He lifted a hand to wipe beads of sweat from his forehead, and she nestled closer to cuddle. Smiling, he settled her head onto his shoulder.

❊ ❊ ❊

Jack stared at the façade of Griffith Stadium as the usher tore his ticket in half. The game was well underway and the entrance was relatively quiet, as the hawkers had already made their way into the stands. He walked up to an empty wooden bench that stood just to the side of a restroom. Placing one foot on the bench, he retied his shoelace, using the opportunity to feel his sock to make sure the switchblade was still in place.

As he straightened, he felt for the gun in his jacket pocket. His heart skipped a beat when he felt the gun's barrel. Could he kill a man? Could he kill Reznov? He thought of Lou. *Yes.*

He walked toward the first base line, looking for a tunnel leading into the lower stands. A hawker approached him and lifted a stack of papers into the air. "Program, buddy?"

"No, thanks," said Jack. "Who's winning, you know?"

"Nobody's paying me to keep score," the man said, and walked away.

Jack continued along the concrete passage that ran behind the stands. He spotted a tunnel on his left and turned down it, suppressing a small thrill when he made out the green grass of the field at the end of the tunnel.

An usher appeared as he entered the stands. "Ticket, please," the man said. Jack produced his stub and examined the field while the usher checked it. "Section fifteen is to your right," said the usher. "Just before the next pole."

Jack looked for the scoreboard. "That's alright. I just want to check out the score." He found the scoreboard on the left field wall; the St. Louis Browns were winning 2–0 in the bottom of the seventh. Jack walked back into the tunnel, emerged into the passage behind the stands, and looked for the concessions. He saw three nearby: lemonade, peanuts, and hot dogs—no customers. The peanut guy appeared to be complaining to the hot dog vendor. Behind the concessions, a sloped concrete walkway led to the upper deck of the park.

Jack passed the concessions, scooted halfway up the walkway, and stopped. He pulled out his Lucky Strikes and looked back down to the passageway. It was unlikely that Reznov would be coming from the entrance off of right field; all the buses dropped off their passengers on the left field side. That meant Reznov was almost certain to come from the left or the center entrance.

Jack lit his cigarette and looked up. The passage he was on made a sharp turn and then led farther to the upper tier. A concrete support column ran from the stadium's foundation to the upper tier, dividing the walkway. His fingers trembled slightly as he inhaled on the Lucky Strike. The sloped walkway, he decided, was his best chance to surprise Reznov. Satisfied, he left the walkway and proceeded to his seat in the lower level.

Jack paid little attention to the players running back and forth across the field. He stared at the outfield grass, his mind blank, and only occasionally glanced up at the scoreboard to check the inning. The ninth inning finally came. The Senators were losing 4–0. As the Washington team came down to their last out, Jack rose, lit a cigarette, and headed for the passage behind the stands, filing behind others leaving the stadium.

As he entered the main passage circling the stands, he turned left and walked against the traffic. Keeping to the far right of the passage, he entered the walkway leading to the upper deck. As he made his way into the upper stands, the batter on the field below swung at a high fastball. The ball went flying into right field where the outfielder caught it; the game was over.

Jack sat down in the first empty seat he saw. The ground crew ran onto the field and began their various assignments. As the spectators passed by him, he thought of the Russian he was about to confront. *Is he a martial arts expert? Will he be alone?* He glanced at the clock adjacent to the scoreboard—3:55. The meeting with the Russian was scheduled for 4:25.

The stands finally emptied. Jack rose. His nervousness had passed; now he felt sleepy. He stretched his muscles and yawned. How he wished he could leave the stadium, go back to Sue's place, lie down, and hug Sue until they fell asleep. He reluctantly reentered the walkway leading to the lower level. Only one concession remained there, the peanut vendor. The man was shaking his head and talking to himself as he closed up his stand.

Jack walked up to the concrete support column and leaned against it. The wheels of the peanut cart squeaked as the vendor started leaving. Jack's hands trembled as he searched his suit for cigarettes. The trembling became more severe; he had to stab the match into the tip of the cigarette so it would light. He peered beyond the column at the passage below. The crowd had thinned considerably, but a few fans were still exiting the park. Still no sign of the Russian. Jack looked at his wristwatch; 4:20.

He inhaled deeply on the cigarette, then exhaled. When he saw the cloud of smoke he had created, he realized it would give away his position. He threw the cigarette to the ground and extinguished it.

A shout from below made him turn his head. Three men walked past together. The one nearest Jack laughed as the man in the middle forked over some bills to the others, no doubt from a bet on the game.

Jack looked to his right. There were no others in the passageway. He leaned over and felt for the knife in his sock. Still there. The knife, he decided, would be the best way to go. Although the passageway was empty, there were still others in the park who would hear a shot if it was fired.

A man eventually appeared in the passageway below. Jack squinted and leaned past the column, trying to remember what Reznov looked like. When he saw the figure twitch his neck and shoulders, he had little doubt that it was Reznov. Nausea surged in Jack's stomach. He bent over, thinking he might vomit, but the feeling passed and he managed to lift his head.

Reznov continued down the passage, glancing right and left as he walked. Jack moved back behind the column and waited. He removed his hat and tossed it gently to the ground. *This is it,* he thought, and wiped his forehead.

Leaning slightly to his left, Jack saw Reznov almost directly below him. He stepped onto the lower beam of the railing and pushed himself to the top of the rail.

Reznov passed below. Taking a deep breath, Jack jumped off the rail onto Reznov's back. They both slammed onto the concrete floor; even with Reznov beneath him, the air whooshed out of Jack's lungs at the impact. Recovering first, Jack grabbed Reznov's arms and pulled them back. "Remember me?" Jack gasped. "I'm Lou's brother."

Reznov struggled, but Jack managed to roll him over by thrusting his knee into Reznov's shoulder. As Reznov flopped onto his back, Jack pinned his shoulders to the ground. "You've been here before, right?" grunted Jack, glaring into Reznov's eyes. "The day you killed Lou."

Reznov gasped for air and shook his head. "Jack, Jack, not true, not true. I was here—I was here, but I try to protect Lou." His breath reeked of alcohol. "FBI, Jack, FBI. They kill Lou. You have to believe me."

Jack reached for the switchblade in his sock. "Bullshit!

You killed Lou, you son of a bitch!" he yelled. "And now you're gonna pay." His fingers found the knife tucked into his sock and pulled it out.

"Tiepier! Tiepier!" Reznov yelled.

Suddenly, an arm swooped under Jack's chin and jerked his head back. He was violently twisted backward off of Reznov. Jack lowered his right arm, blindly stabbing behind him. When he missed, Reznov grabbed the arm, twisting it forcefully.

Reznov grinned. "You think I come here alone, swine?"

Jack managed to plant his left foot on the concrete and quickly rotated to his right, facing his attacker. He stared at the big young man clenching his teeth beneath a thin black moustache; the face looked familiar.

All three now struggled for Jack's knife. Impulsively, Jack head-butted the big man square in the nose. The man's head snapped back and he dropped to the ground, giving Jack control of his knife. Jack turned back to Reznov.

The Russian had pulled out a knife himself. "So, what you think?" asked Reznov. "That we pay you? You will die like your swine brother."

Jack glanced at the other man. He was trying to rise. Jack bent, grabbed the man's hair, and slammed his face into the cement floor. Straightening, Jack pointed his knife at Reznov. The two stared at each other.

Reznov lunged forward, swiping at Jack with his knife. Jack jumped back; the Russian's blow missed. Sucking in air, Jack bounced on his feet, waving his knife slowly back and forth. He glanced at the other man; he was still down on his knees, but slowly rising. *What now?*

"Zdies! Zdies!" Reznov yelled to the other Russian.

Reznov suddenly lunged forward again. Jack bobbed to his right; again Reznov missed. But now the big man regained his feet. They had Jack sandwiched, with Reznov to his left and the other to his right. *There's two of them. How can I handle two?* Jack's first impulse was to run, but something told him to stand and fight.

Without thinking, he dove toward the right, tackling the other Russian and dragging him to the ground. Reznov lunged toward Jack's back with his knife; still gripping the other man tightly, Jack rotated to his side, swinging the big man into his place. The big man with the moustache moaned. Jack was not sure, but he thought Reznov's knife may have gotten him.

Reznov stabbed again, wildly, and missed. Jack tried to scramble to his feet and Reznov lunged forward again. Jack instinctively threw his left hand up. The knife slashed between his second and third fingers, leaving a burning trail of pain in its wake. Gasping, Jack managed to get to his feet and raised his right hand holding the knife into the air. His left hand dangled at his side, dripping blood.

Again Reznov lunged. Jack pushed Reznov's knife arm down with his bloody hand, knocking Reznov off balance. Seeing this, Jack swung his own knife forward. Its point touched Reznov's chest; Jack pushed with all his might. His hand shook as he tried to advance the knife. It felt as if he was trying to push it through a stone wall, then it suddenly penetrated deep into Reznov's chest. Reznov groaned. His surprised eyes stared into Jack's face.

Jack moved the knife back and forth until it came out. Panting, he turned to the other man. The Russian remained on the ground, but Jack saw him reaching into his pocket. Swooping forward, Jack stabbed at the arm.

He missed, but a gun tumbled out of the man's hand, clattering onto the cement. The man reached for the gun; Jack jabbed him in the side with his knife, then kicked the gun away as the man sank to the ground.

The Saratoga Hotel, Jack suddenly realized as he studied the man's face, twisted in pain. *This is one of the son of a bitches who beat me up at the Saratoga.*

Jack turned back to Reznov. The Russian lay unmoving. But through the corner of his eye, he saw the big man crawling toward his gun. Jack pulled out his own gun and was about to strike the man when he slipped on the blood-slick ground. Lunging forward, Jack managed to strike the crawling man on the head. He crawled over to the man's gun himself, picked it up, and threw it over the railing into the parking lot. "There goes your gun, SMERSH boy," said Jack, gasping for air. "You're done."

A sound behind him made Jack turn; Reznov was trying to rise from the ground. Staggering to his feet, Jack jumped Reznov, throwing the Russian back onto the concrete. Turning him over, Jack lay on Reznov's back and moved his right arm, knife in hand, over Reznov's back ribs. "So, is that how they train you SMERSH boys?" he panted. "To stick it between the seventh and eighth ribs?"

He pushed the knife into the left side of Reznov's back and the man moaned. Again Jack moved the knife back and forth and pulled it out. He lifted his head and tried to catch his breath.

A sharp pain shot through his right side.

As Jack hit the ground, he realized the big man had knifed him. The entire right side of his body burned as he squirmed on the ground. The man lunged at him again, but Jack managed to turn his body to his left just enough for the Russian to miss. He grabbed the hand holding the knife with his left hand and twisted the man's arm until both the knife and its wielder fell to the ground.

Jack and his attacker lay in a growing pool of blood, gasping and staring at each other until Jack lifted his left leg and kicked the man in the stomach. Jack reached out, grabbed the man's knife, and staggered to his feet holding a knife in each hand. He looked for the Russian, but his vision blurred. His head started to spin and his legs gave way. Jack dropped to the ground.

When his vision cleared, he made out the Russian staggering away, holding his right side. Jack sucked in air and tottered to his feet, clutching his own flank. He paused, thinking he was going to drop to the ground again, but the feeling passed and he managed to slowly walk after the man. "You guys at SMERSH always run away like this?" grunted Jack. "Come on back, Boris; the fun's just starting."

The man headed toward the tunnel leading to the field; Jack slowly followed. "Where you going, Smershy? Come on back here," Jack muttered. He entered the tunnel himself and saw the man making his way onto the field through an opening in the gate. The pain in his side worsened, forcing Jack to stop. He dropped the knife from his right hand and grabbed his side. His hand felt warm and slick as he pressed it against his body. He looked down at the blood. Taking a deep breath, he staggered forward again.

Jack found the opening in the gate, entered, and scanned the field. The Russian spy was crossing the pitcher's mound toward the third base dugout. Managing a slow trot, Jack headed for the third base dugout himself. He scanned the stands when he stopped on the pitcher's mound to catch his breath, but saw no one. Blood continued to drip from his left hand onto the mound. He pushed it under his right armpit to try to stop the bleeding. After several deep breaths, he looked toward the third base dugout.

The bastard's gonna get away, he thought as he saw the Russian hobbling down the steps into the dugout. He staggered forward. The pain stopped Jack from fully lifting his head. It hung from his shoulders like a melon in a sack as he crossed the grass.

When he saw the third base line beneath his feet, he managed to lift his head and peer into the dugout. The sun was setting behind home plate and shadows obscured the inside of the dugout. Panting, Jack staggered forward. "Come on out, Boris," he managed to yell. "You can't hide forever."

Jack looked down and saw the first step into the dugout. He looked back up, searching for the Russian, but saw only shadows against the back wall. "Come on, Smershy!" he groaned. As he lowered his right foot to the dugout's first step, muscle spasms in his side made him wince. He bent over slightly and changed the knife to his bloody left hand. "Let's go, Boris!"

The left side of the dugout was a dead end; the right side appeared to lead to the clubhouse. His head started spinning again, but he managed to lower himself into the dugout. He swung his head left; it was clear. Turning to the right, he saw only shadows. He lifted the knife to his hip and staggered forward.

"Hey, you!" someone yelled. The voice came from behind him, and sounded distant. "You! What the hell are you doing in there?" a man yelled again. Jack grabbed a rail for support and turned his head. A man stood in the outfield. He held a cigar in one hand and a water hose in the other.

Jack was thinking how to react when he was jumped from behind. The concrete burned his palms as he hit the ground. A hand tried to pull his knife away. Jack fought back, and the knife went flying to the left side of the dugout.

As the Russian climbed off of Jack and crawled toward the knife, Jack's eyes fell on a baseball bat lying on the ground to his left. He reached for it and, using it for support, managed to get to his feet. The Russian reached for the knife. Jack swung the bat and struck him in the back of the head, driving the man to the ground. Drawing a deep breath, Jack struck the man's head again. "You son of a bitch!" he grunted. He pounded over and over again, until he realized he'd lost control.

He threw down the bat and leaned over with his hands on his knees, gasping for air. The man lying on the ground stared upward with lifeless eyes. The skin over the man's forehead was split open, and thick globs of blood oozed down his face.

"Game's over, Smershy," grunted Jack as he stared at the man. "You lose."

✻ ✻ ✻

Jack grimaced as he lugged his suitcase out of the hotel lobby, holding his side with his free arm. The wound in his side was still oozing pink fluid and he'd had to change the dressing twice since waking up.

As he exited the hotel, a bellhop ran up. "Taxi, sir?" he asked.

Jack nodded and dropped the bag on the pavement. "What time you got, buddy?"

The bellhop glanced at his watch. "Eleven on the dot."

The train was leaving Union Station at half past noon. This gave him Jack over an hour to pick up Sue and have their bags checked onto the train.

The bellhop looked left and right but saw nothing. "Won't be a minute," he said, his eyes still searching.

Jack patted his coat for his cigarettes but could not find his pack of Lucky Strikes. As he searched through his pant pockets, he saw a figure approaching from the corner of his eye. He looked up; saw a gray-haired man in a black overcoat. The man stopped several feet away. He stared at Jack with his hands in his pockets. Jack stared back.

The man lifted his prominent chin. "I am glad to see you are alive, Mr. Haynes." He had an accent, but Jack did not think it was eastern European.

When Jack did not react, the man casually looked up and scanned the sky. "We are not sure what went wrong. But it is clear that you are a man of great resolve."

Jack continued the search for his cigarettes and wondered if SMERSH had the nerve to kill him right in front of a hotel in broad daylight. "Yeah, well, tell Petrov that Lou's murder has been solved."

The man chuckled. "I won't have a chance. You see, Mr. Petrov has been called back to the motherland."

"That's too bad," said Jack. "You know Vitovski? Tell Vitovski the deal's off."

The man continued to smile. "I cannot. He too has been sent home, but under different circumstances. His incompetence will land him in Siberia."

Jack finally found the pack in the inside left coat

pocket and pulled it out. "That's too bad." He looked behind the man and to his left and right to see if the man had backup. He did not see anything unusual. Jack thought of looking behind him, but he didn't want to appear weak.

The man nodded. "Yes, it is a shame. But this unfortunate event should not interfere with our agreement."

Jack jerked his head back. "Our agreement?"

"Certainly you have not forgotten, Mr. Haynes. You agreed to turn over your records to us for a cash payment."

Jack pulled a Lucky Strike from his pack and lit it without offering one to the gray-haired man. "I'm afraid it's too late, Pops."

"What do you mean?"

"After your guys showed up drunk at the ballpark and started yelling at me how much they hate Americans, I made new plans."

The man's salt and pepper eyebrows lifted. "Drunk?"

"That's what I said. They were stewed. Singing in some foreign language. I was just supposed to meet one guy, Reznov. Oh, he showed up alright. But he was plastered, and the guy with him was drunk too. I high-tailed out of there as fast as I could."

The man appeared to be at a loss for words. "We . . . we are still unsure of what happened. But this state of intoxication is news to me."

About to draw on the cigarette, Jack instead pulled it back. "It was a pathetic sight."

"So, what are these new plans?" the man asked.

Jack exhaled a cloud of smoke and looked right at

the Soviet agent. "They tried to kill me. Did you know that?"

The man shook his head and stared at Jack's bandaged left hand. "It is scandalous. My apologies, Mr. Haynes."

"I thought I was meeting with a professional," Jack added.

"How has this changed your plans?"

"How?" asked Jack. "I'll tell you how. The list and the negatives are now in the possession of a friend of mine. He's a lawyer. Don't bother looking for him. He's not in Washington or St. Louis. And if anything happens to me or to Sue, he mails them to the FBI. Got that?"

The man removed his brown derby and wiped his forehead. "There was no need to think of such things. We can still make a deal that is beneficial to both of us."

"Not on your life, Pops. I'm through with you guys. You're better off staying away from me."

A cab finally pulled up to the curb and the bellhop opened the taxi door. Jack put a quarter into the bellhop's hand and threw his cigarette to the ground. He took a deep breath and held it. He had learned that this little maneuver minimized the pain in his abdomen whenever he bent over. He entered the car's back seat and exhaled.

The Soviet agent leaned in as Jack was about to close the door. "Mr. Haynes," he said. "Do not forget, you will always be one breath away from us."

"Where to?" asked the driver.

Jack ignored the driver. "What do you mean, a breath away?"

"Simply that," the man answered. "You will not leave our attention no matter where you are. We will always be there."

Jack was not intimidated. The Russian sounded like a

mop-up guy attempting to intimidate him one last time before Jack totally disappeared from the picture. "That's fine with me," he answered. "Drop in anytime."

Jack slammed the door closed and the taxi took off.

*＊＊

The wind blew through the train's window and made a mess of Sue's hair. She brushed it back and smiled at Jack. "Where are we?" she asked. "You know?"

Jack lowered his head and peered out the window of the B&O train. The land was flat and barren; the corn had already been harvested. Only an isolated tree occasionally dotted the terrain. "Looks like we're in Indiana," he answered. "It won't be long now."

They were standing in the train's corridor. The train was only half full and they had a second-class compartment to themselves. Sue seemed a little unsure that she had done the right thing. After resigning from her job, she had given up her apartment and put her furniture in storage, reducing her possessions to three suitcases. Jack sensed her apprehension.

She grabbed the chain around her neck. "I hear it gets really hot in St. Louis," she said.

Jack shrugged. "That's in July and August. It's hot everywhere in the summer. I don't think it's any worse than Washington. And the autumns are beautiful—you'll see."

Sue stared out the window; she appeared to be deep in thought. Jack stared at the fields and tried to think of something to say to comfort her. Nothing came to mind.

Sue reached for Jack's left arm. "How's the wound?"

Jack shook his head. "No problem." He turned his gaze to the sky above the fields.

Sue felt for the dressing beneath his shirt and traced its outline. "The first thing I'm gonna do when we get there is go to a drugstore and get you some fresh liniment," she said. "I don't like that stuff I bought in D.C. It smells cheap. God knows what they put in there."

"It smells like iodine to me, and it sure burns like it," said Jack.

Sue rested her head on Jack's shoulder. "Does your boss know you're coming back?"

Jack chuckled. "I hope so. He seemed sober when I talked to him. Besides, I'm not even sure I want to go back to the paper."

"No?"

"I'm sick of working as a snoop. There must be something else I could do."

Still holding her necklace, she smiled as she looked out the window. "I'm sure you can do a lot of things," she said. "What did that Russian spy say to you? That you have great resolve?"

"Maybe I could write for a magazine," Jack mused.

"I'm sure you could," she said. Her tone was mechanical. It was not so much that her words sounded insincere, but more a reflection of her uncertain frame of mind.

Jack raised his good arm and rubbed her back. "Sue, everything's gonna be fine."

She smiled at Jack but did not answer.

"I'll tell you what," he continued. "I'll keep my job at the paper until I find something better. Don't worry about money." Jack thought. "And you'll take lessons. You'll take art lessons, just like you wanted."

Sue smiled. "And we'll live happily ever after."

Jack was not sure if she was being cynical or if her mood was finally improving. They both stared out the window.

"I hope St. Louis jazz is just as good as you say," she said.

Jack raised his chin. "Jazz? There's no jazz in St. Louis. What made you think we had jazz?"

She lifted her head. "But you said—"

"Oh, yeah," Jack slowly answered. He made a face, as if he had something to confess. "To tell you the truth, I made that up just so you would get on the train with me."

Sue laughed. "You're incorrigible."

Jack smiled back. "You're quite naïve, you know that?"

"I should have known better than to get mixed up with a newspaper guy."

Jack started to laugh himself, but a muscle spasm in his abdomen stopped him. "Well, look at me," he said. "I'm involved with a commie."

Sue looked as if she wanted to poke Jack in the chest, but thought better of it. "That's right," she said. "A filthy red."

They both looked out the window in silence. Jack liked the way she responded to his smart-aleck remarks. He had not expressed much of his sense of humor since coming to Washington. It was comforting to know that it clicked with Sue.

Sue rhythmically slapped the top of the window with both hands, as if playing the drums. "You never did see the monuments, did you?"

Jack shrugged. "No. Maybe I'll catch 'em next time."

For some reason, when Sue mentioned the monuments, his thoughts shifted to Griffith Stadium. He could still feel the slickness of the blood covering his arms and staining his clothes. The thought of his knife entering Reznov's chest made him feel nauseous. *The priest at the orphanage was right,* he thought. *Revenge does not heal wounds, but fills them with pus.* Now there was little hope that the calm he'd experienced that day after confession would ever return.

"What're you thinking about?" asked Sue.

"The Soviets," he whispered. "I never want to see those bastards again as long as I live."

* * *

Agent Wayne Mullen stepped off the city bus in front of FBI headquarters and turned the collar of his overcoat up against the chill air. It was a late September morning and the temperature had dropped considerably in the last few days. In his briefcase he carried all his papers on Lou and Jack Harris.

Mullen had given Haynes' list to his boss, Carl Duggan, who in turn gave it to Harry Nelson, a security officer with the State Department. Because a number of governmental officials from several agencies were potentially involved, the FBI had chosen to bypass the usual channels; Nelson would be delivering the information straight to President Roosevelt himself.

The night before, Mullen had studied the Harris brothers' files to make sure he had all his ducks in a row. He knew there would eventually be a detailed inquiry, maybe even congressional hearings, and he realized he would be in the center of it all. This was the last thing an FBI agent like Mullen wanted. Federal agents focused on proving guilt and arresting criminals, not answering countless stupid questions from politicians.

He entered the main building, made his way up the stairs and was about to enter his office when he saw Duggan walking toward him. Mullen paused at his door, reaching for the tobacco pouch in his jacket pocket while he waited for his boss to approach.

Duggan stopped at the door to his own office. He didn't look at Mullen.

"Well?" asked Mullen. "Did Roosevelt get the list?"

Duggan removed a ring of keys from his pocket and searched through them. "Yeah, he got it," said Duggan. "Nelson told him all about it."

"So what's gonna happen?" asked Mullen. "Are we on the case?"

Duggan did not answer. He found the key to his office and placed it in the lock. "No, we're not," he finally said.

"Why not?" asked Mullen.

"Nelson said he told Roosevelt the entire story and handed him the list," Duggan said. "Roosevelt looked at it for a second, handed it back to Nelson, and told Nelson to go fuck himself."

Duggan walked into his office and slammed the door closed. Mullen stood staring down the hallway long after the echo had died.

=END=

Further Reading and Sources

Chambers, Whittaker. *Witness*. Washington, D.C.: Regnery Publishers, 1980.

Evelyn, Douglas E., and Paul Dickson. *On This Spot: Pinpointing the Past in Washington, D.C.* Washington, D.C.: Farragut Publishing Company, 1992.

Goralski, Robert. *World War II Almanac, 1931–1945: A Political and Military Record.* New York: Bonanza Books, 1981.

Klehr, Harvey; John Earl Haynes; Fridrikh Igorevich Firsov. *The Secret World of American Communism*. New Haven, Connecticut: Yale University Press, 1995.

http://www.ibiblio.org/hyperwar/ETO/Dip/

http://www.fsmitha.com/h2/ch22.htm

http://www.ihr.org/jhr/v17/v17n4p30_Michaels.html

http://home.comcast.net/~furrylogic/fbi.html

http://www.baseball-almanac.com/teamstats/roster.php?y=1939&t=ws1

http://kclibrary.nhmccd.edu/decade30.html

http://www.ballparksofbaseball.com/past/GriffithStadium.htm

http://www.fas.org/irp/ops/ci/docs/ci1/ch4d.htm

http://www.fbi.gov/libref/historic/history/worldwar.htm

http://www.ballparks.com/baseball/american/griffi.htm

http://www.baseball-almanac.com

http://www.wharf.com/ariel/1930s_men.htm

http://www.loc.gov/loc/lcib/0102/red_ink.html

http://www.dss.mil/seclib/govsec/appa4.htm

http://college.hmco.com/history/readerscomp/rcah/html/
ah_051202_iistrikes.htm

http://www.vahistory.org/intro.html

http://bonus-expeditionary-force.biography.ms/

http://www.lyricsdepot.com

http://mlb.mlb.com/NASApp/mlb/mlb/history/postseason/
mlb_ws_recaps.jsp?feature=1924

http://info.detnews.com/history/story/index.cfm?id=
115&category=business

http://xroads.virginia.edu/~UG00/3on1/radioshow/
1920radio.htm

Note from the Author

I will not attempt to summarize the influence of the Soviet Union on American foreign policy during the 1930s and 1940s in this brief note. Nor will I try to review the infiltration of the American government by Soviet spies during this time period. For anyone interested, there are many sources on this subject. A few are listed in this work's bibliography. This note is only to address a specific point I have been asked about by readers of this book concerning the book's ending, where Roosevelt ignores a list of Americans suspected of being Soviet spies. This fictional scene is based on the testimony of Whittaker Chambers, who left the American Communist Party and testified on the degree that the Soviets had penetrated the American federal government. In his book, *Witness* (Regnery Publishers, Washington D.C., 1980), Chambers writes on page 470*:*

> *. . . I went about my work at Time. Then, one day, I am no longer certain just when, I met a dejected Levine. Adolf Berle, said Levine, had taken my information to the President at once. The President had laughed. When Berle was insistent, he had been told in the words which it is necessary to paraphrase, to "go jump in a lake."*